MARCIE'S MOUNTAINS

A Christian Romance

By

Ruth Kyser

Cover Design by SelfPubbookCovers.com/andrewgraphics

ISBN: 9781097855490

In memory of those hardy men and women
who settled the wilderness of America.
Many of them came with nothing
but their hopes and dreams,
and built a country and a culture
with their hands and their hearts—
one log at a time.

"He is like a man which built an house,
and digged deep,
and laid the foundation on a rock:
and when the flood arose,
the stream beat vehemently upon that house,
and could not shake it:
for it was founded upon a rock."
--Luke 6:48

AUTHOR'S NOTES

I'm often asked where I get the ideas for my books. Most of my ideas come from daily life— the lyrics of a song that touch my heart, something I see happening around me, or a dream I might have (or even a nightmare.)

The idea for this story came about because of an old book I found which explained how to build a log cabin. It was so interesting and as I learned about the work entailed in cutting down the trees, shaping the logs, notching the logs so they'd fit just so, and hauling them to be stacked, I realized exactly how much work our ancestors had to do to provide themselves and their family a warm place to live. And no cabin was built in exactly the same way. Each pioneer left his mark on his cabin just in the way he put it all together.

Many years ago, my parents and I visited family friends in Pennsylvania who lived in a house that had a log cabin attached to it—the original dwelling of the family. They had preserved the cabin and using it as a family room—and I immediately fell in love with the space.

So when I read about how the cabins were built, it made me wonder how much of the history surrounding those cabins had already been lost.

If you drive the backcountries of America—especially in the southern mountain states of Appalachia and the Smoky Mountains—you can still see remnants of those old structures. Some of them have been taken care of and are often still being used. But way too many of them are vacant and falling to ruin.

And as Dean McRae so clearly states in *Marcie's Mountains*, if we don't do something to save them, soon it will be too late, and they'll be gone.

I admire those entrepreneurs who have developed a business to take down and reuse the old cabins and barns of our past. There's something to be said for doing things the old way, and I'm glad those past creative talents haven't been totally lost. This book honors those who are saving the old structures as much as the ones who built them.

Once again, I've placed this story in Eastern Tennessee. If you've read any of my past books—particularly *The Healing Hills*, or *A Place Called Hart's Desire,* you already know how much I love the mountains. If you haven't already, I pray that someday you will have the opportunity to see and experience them yourselves. If not, I hope that my words will convey to you at least a little of the beauty and majesty of these sacred hills.

God bless.

Ruth Kyser

Marcie's Mountains

1

Over and over, the same two thoughts raced through Marcie Starr's brain.

I can't believe I'm actually doing this. This is crazy.

As she slowly drove the twisting narrow roads through the mountains of her childhood, she continued to repeat those phrases. This was *not* where she wanted to be. At all. But when your boss sends you on a project, you go. Even if it's the last place in the world you want to go.

Marcie knew she should feel honored that her boss Bob Avery, the managing editor of *Architecture: Yesterday and Today* magazine, believed she was capable of covering and writing this article on her own. And honestly, under normal circumstances, Marcie would have been thrilled to be sent on the road for a two-week on-site assignment to collect information and photos for an upcoming article in the magazine—an article that was slated to be a prime piece. So, when Bob had first approached her with the mission, Marcie had been eager to accept.

That is—until he had told her the location.

Marcie had known right away that she didn't dare turn down this chance to prove herself, though. If she refused this job, she knew the opportunity likely wouldn't happen again anytime soon; there were plenty of other staff more than willing to pick up any jobs Marcie didn't want. So she'd pasted on a big smile and taken the assignment with enthusiasm, well aware that it would be one of the most challenging things she'd ever done.

Tilting her head, Marcie peered out the windshield at the rocky cliffs rising on the right side of the car and the sloping roadside to her left which fell to a deep valley. Rhododendron and Mountain Laurel bushes grew at the tops of the hillsides and ridges that Marcie knew fell to deep ravines. In many spots tall trees growing on the hills cast their deep shadows over the road. These mountains were rugged places and still possessed an ancient feeling of wilderness about them, and many who had lived in the city for as long as she had would have felt lost on these roads. But Marcie knew these hills like the back of her hand—as she should. She had been born and raised in these very mountains.

Another mile or two down the road the voice on her GPS informed Marcie she was nearing her destination, so she slowed even more and started to watch for the sign that would announce the end of her trip. Another sharp curve appeared in the road, and she cautiously drove her small four-wheeled-drive SUV around it, and finally saw what she'd been looking for.

McRae's Recycled Logs and Materials

She couldn't help but smile, remembering what the company's website used as a portion of their mission statement:

We're preserving our nation's history—one log at a time.

Bob Avery had heard of *McRae's* salvage and restoration operation through a friend of his who had heard about them from another friend. *McRae's* was quickly gaining a reputation in the south for their work at reusing and restoring old log cabins and frame barns all over the area. Which was precisely why Marcie was here and was going to write a story about them. It sounded like it would be an interesting article to write, and she couldn't wait to get started.

Even though a part of her still thought she was crazy to have come.

Just the other side of the sign, Marcie turned the car onto the dirt road that was plainly the entrance. The narrow lane led back through thick woods and deeper into the hills, and after traveling almost a mile on the narrow trail, she was beginning to wonder if she had made a wrong turn. Then the drive suddenly ended, and the woods opened up into a large clearing.

When she got her first good look at the sizeable authentic-looking cabin sitting at the end of the driveway, Marcie released a quiet whistle of admiration. The log house sat in an open area on a gentle rise of land—an ideal spot for a home in these woods. Even though stately tall trees surrounded the structure, the trees were far enough away that if one fell in one of the many storms Marcie knew often swept through these mountains, the house would be safe.

The cabin was one-story in the front, rising to a two-story structure behind. A covered porch ran across the front, and ample large windows looked like they'd allow plenty of light into the house. The structure probably wasn't that old, but the dark green steel roofing made the place look as if it had been a part of the woods forever.

Off to the left side of the house sat a sizeable hip-roof barn. Instead of being painted a bright red as so many were, this one had a weathered look as the gray barn siding had been left unpainted. The most amazing part of the barn—and the real charm of the building as far as Marcie was concerned— were the three tall stained-glass windows filling the upper portion of the end facing the house. It didn't look like any barn Marcie had ever seen before.

Perhaps this assignment was going to be a good one after all.

Marcie parked her vehicle and turned off the engine, then took a deep breath and opened the car door. Being situated out in the hills, Marcie half-expected a passel of hound dogs to come running around the corner of the house to greet her. So, she was surprised when she shut the car door and stood next to it a moment and heard nothing but the sounds of birds singing in the trees. She gave a quick glance around and noted several trucks and a newer-looking SUV parked in the yard, so she knew someone was there. And supposedly, Mr. McRae was expecting her.

With that in mind, Marcie walked up the three wooden steps leading to the house's entrance. The enormous wooden front door of the house was itself a work of art. The more she studied it, the more Marcie was sure it had been crafted from reclaimed wood. Six large glass panes filled the majority of the door which also boasted a big authentic-looking iron latch. Marcie loved the look of the door, so quickly pulled out her cell phone and shot a couple of photos. If this door was any indication of *McCrae's* work, this assignment was going to be a treat.

She had just slipped the phone back into her pocket when the big door swung open, and Marcie raised her eyes to gaze into the face of one of the most handsome men she'd ever met. The first thing she noticed—in addition to the part about him being so good-looking—was how tall he was. The man was barefoot, but he still stood a good six inches taller than Marcie's five-foot-ten frame. The blue jeans he wore, along with the white t-shirt stretched across his broad shoulders, looked good on him. The man's ruddy face was covered with a day's worth of whiskers, which only added to his rustic appearance. The second thing she noticed was the man's thick richly colored red hair and the sparkling green eyes staring at her as if he was as surprised by her appearance as she was with his. Too bad the website hadn't had a photo of the owner on it, because if this was the owner, it was going to be an interesting couple of weeks. Then the man spoke, and Marcie finally had the where-with-all to close her mouth, which she was sure was still hanging open.

"You must be Marcie Starr from the architectural magazine." His deep voice held that eastern Tennessee mountain drawl that Marcie knew so well—the words sounding like sourwood honey dripping from his lips. Just hearing his voice made her want to sigh in contentment, like a cat with a full belly.

She finally croaked out what sounded to her ears like a weak-sounding, "Yes."

The man reached out to shake Marcie's hand, and she automatically took hold of his, feeling the warmth and strength in the callous-covered palm.

"I'm Dean McCrae. Welcome to *McRae's*."

He continued to stare at her a few more seconds, then released her hand and stepped back from the doorway, motioning for her to follow him into the house. Marcie stepped across the threshold and as she got her first look at the inside of the house, released a little gasp.

"This is beautiful, Mr. McRae."

Unlike what she had expected from seeing the outside, the inside of Dean McRae's house wasn't your typical modern-day log cabin interior. Comfortable looking sofas and chairs filled what was obviously used as a living room, but that wasn't what had Marcie's attention as she raised her eyes to take it all in. Someone had spent a lot of time and effort to add rustic charm to it, making it look more like an authentic old cabin than most did. The house had open ceilings showcasing the huge log trusses running from one side of the house to the other. Every wall was filled with six-paned windows, and the floor was made of what looked like reused barn flooring—wide oak boards polished to a lustrous shine. A few round braided rugs were spread across the floor, but the original patina of the flooring was being allowed to show off, and Marcie was glad. It would have been a crying shame to cover up those boards with carpeting.

"Come on back to the kitchen. I just took the steaks off the grill, so your timin' is perfect. The boys and I were just sittin' down to Sunday night supper."

Still feeling tongue-tied, Marcie dutifully followed Dean through the open room and stepped through a wide arched doorway into a large kitchen. Here too, the ceiling was high and open, which only added to the ambiance of the room. Even though the kitchen was filled with modern-day stainless steel appliances and what looked like granite countertops, the cupboards appeared to be made of recycled cherry wood and sported black iron hinges and knobs. Marcie would have like to have looked around even more, but Dean McRae was pulling her attention toward the end of the room where a table was located.

Seated around the pine trestle table were seven people. Marcie quickly noted that one of them was a woman, and spread amongst the men sat three boys, the oldest two looked to be in their teens. As soon as the men caught sight of Marcie, all of them—including the eldest of the boys—stood from their seats to greet her. Marcie barely resisted the temptation to grin—instantly recognizing the Southern manners of her childhood. That kind of old-fashioned chivalry was something you rarely saw in the city.

"Folks, this here is Miz Marcie Starr from the magazine. She's the one I told y'all about, come to stay and shadow us for a spell so she can see what we do here at *McRae's*."

She felt Dean's hand on the small of her back, prompting her to step further into the room. As he led her closer to the table and introduced her, Marcie gave everyone what she hoped was a friendly smile.

Starting at the end of the table closest to where they stood, Dean made the introductions.

"This fellow here is Gordie, his wife Sally, and their three boys, Matt, Mark, and Luke."

Marcie gave them a smile, quickly noting the three boys' faces turning a shade of red at being introduced like they were three of the first four books of the Gospel. She also noted Gordie's round face sported a gray mustache, and that he was wearing what looked like a well-worn pair of bib overalls. She truly had returned to the mountains of her memory. His wife Sally, dressed in a dark blue cotton dress, gave Marcie a shy smile and a nod.

"Over here we've got Mac." Marcie nodded in the direction of a tall, muscular man with dark brown hair and a quick smile. Mac gave her a little nod, and a quick bow and Marcie had to restrain herself from giving an answering curtsey.

Lastly, Dean pointed toward a slim young man with short sandy colored hair and a beard to match. "And that character there is Dutch."

Dutch gave her a little nod and lifted his hand to give her a quick salute.

"It's nice to meet you all," Marcie said, giving them another smile and hoping they couldn't tell how nervous she was. She had thought she was prepared for this job but hadn't realized she was going to meet the entire crew right away.

Dean pointed to a couple of empty chairs near the head of the table.

"Pull up a chair, Miz Starr. We're just gettin' ready to bless the food and then we'll dig in."

Marcie hesitantly walked behind everyone and took the chair just to the right of the head of the table, feeling everyone's eyes following her every move. Dean trailed after her, and once he took his seat at the head of the table, reached out his right hand toward her. She lifted her head and looked around in confusion until she realized everyone was holding hands—more than likely for the blessing of the food. She nervously took hold of Dean's hand, trying not to notice how warm and sturdy his felt, and wishing hers wasn't so sweaty.

As Marcie listened to Dean's deep voice ask the Lord to bless their food, she felt a warmth sweep over her—especially when he added an additional thanks for her safe arrival. With his 'amen' Marcie raised her head, hearing more 'amens' echoing from the others at the table. How could she have forgotten what this was like—sitting around a table with a family and eating a big meal together? But then, it had been a long time since she'd been a part of a real family.

Once the prayer was finished, Marcie was kept busy passing the platters of food people kept handing her. Bowls of aluminum foil-wrapped baked potatoes, green beans with onions and little bits of bacon, a big bowl of tossed salad with what looked like blueberries and walnuts in it, and a basket of what smelled like freshly baked rolls. And, of course, the big pieces of grilled steak. She took a bit of everything, wondering how she would ever be able to eat it all. And she was sure the butter she accepted from the offered dish and spread over her mushed-open baked potato was the real thing. Marcie sighed; so much for keeping to her diet.

"So, Miz Starr, what do ya think of our mountains?" the man Marcie thought was named Dutch or something strange like that, asked her. He was probably about twenty-five—maybe even a few years younger, with a thin build. But by the look of the muscular arms poking out of the sleeves of his T-shirt, he wasn't a stranger to hard work.

"They're beautiful. I've forgotten how pretty the mountains are this time of year."

The woman gave a little nod and a smile at Marcie's answer. If she remembered correctly from Dean's introductions, Sally was married to the man Dean had introduced as Gordie.

"You should stick 'round until the end of the month when the leaves really start changin'. The colors 'cross the mountainsides makes it look like God himself has spread a vibrant quilt over the whole countryside."

Marcie took a bite of her salad and smiled at Sally's colorful description of what autumn looked like in the mountains. She couldn't have described it better herself—and she was supposed to be the writer.

While she ate, Marcie sat back and listened to the banter going on between the others seated around the table. It was easy to tell they looked upon each other with obvious affection, and she couldn't help but wonder if they were somehow related. The group talked and acted like they were an actual family.

"So, are you all related?" she finally asked.

Chuckles echoed around the room, and Dean just grinned as he shook his head.

"Nah, but we've worked together for so many years, it probably seems that way."

The man named Dutch spoke up then, "Can't say as I'd want to be related to all these characters. Although my stomach does 'pprecciate the favor of Gordie's wife's good-cookin.'"

That statement resulted in more laughter.

A few moments later, Marcie noticed Sally get up from her seat at the table, quickly returning with two sliced apple pies—one in each hand.

"And now, folks, it's time for dessert. I thought y'all might enjoy a little apple pie." She set the pies on the table top—one directly in front of Marcie—and then punched Dean McCrea in the shoulder playfully. "And yes, Dean, I *did* bring a gallon of vanilla ice cream so you can put a scoop or two on top."

Laughter rang out amongst those around the table and Marcie couldn't help but notice the redness seeping up Dean's neck and creeping into the tips of his ears as if he were embarrassed at having been singled out. He took the joking in good stride, however, and quickly thanked the woman.

"Sally Gordon, you are a jewel amongst jewels. I sure hope your ugly husband appreciates you."

More laughter, even from Gordie, Sally's husband.

"Dean, you have no *idea* what a jewel this little lady is. She's a keeper!"

Once Sally returned to her seat next to him, Gordie leaned over and gave his wife a quick kiss on her cheek, and Marcie smiled at the look of love that passed between the two of them. Evidently, there *was* such a thing as a happily married couple—or maybe the two of them were just good actors when there were others around.

Even though she felt as if her stomach might burst from all the good food, Marcie didn't want to hurt Sally's feelings, so she took a small slice of the apple pie and even allowed Dean to plop a small scoop of ice cream on top. The pie was delicious, with just the right amount of sugar and cinnamon to make the bites melt in her mouth. It had been a long time since she'd had homemade pie—of any flavor. But Apple had always been one of her favorites.

As the plates around the table were scraped clean, the conversation turned to the next day's work, and Marcie paid closer attention to the chatter between Dean and the men. They were discussing a cabin they planned to dismantle the next day. It sounded as if she'd arrived just in time to see the crew in action.

"I'm not sure we'll be able to get it all done in three days but hopefully, if we get an early enough start in the morning, we might," Dean stated.

"Well, folks. I reckon that's a sign." Sally stood and looked pointedly at her husband. "Time to get the dirty dishes cleaned up and head on home, Mister Gordon. The boys have school tomorrow, and I still have clothes I need to take off the clothesline. And it appears y'all need to get up early in the mornin' too."

With those words, it was clear the party was over. Everyone stood and started to clean the dishes off the table, and Marcie followed Sally as she carried dirty plates and silverware to the kitchen. She was surprised when even the young boys chipped in to help, albeit with a little grumbling on the side. It didn't take the gang long, and the leftovers were put away, and the dirty dishes were loaded into the dishwasher. Marcie helped what she could but mostly sat on a stool at the center counter, watching the others move around the kitchen and chatting as they worked. It was easy to tell, this wasn't the first meal they'd shared in this kitchen.

Then goodbyes were said, and Marcie found herself the surprising recipient of a firm hug from Sally.

"You make sure you wear your hard hat when you go out with these yahoos in the mornin'. And watch out for snakes."

Sally chuckled as she gave Marcie's arm a little pat. "I'm so glad to make your acquaintance, Miz Marcie. Hope to see you again real soon. We'll have to have you over for supper one night before y'all leave."

With that, the Gordon family left—thanking Dean for the meal. They were quickly followed out the door by Mac and Dutch. When the front door closed on the last person, Marcie and Dean suddenly found themselves standing alone, just inside the big wooden front door and watching Gordie's vehicle leave the yard.

"Well," Dean said, as he slipped his bare feet into a well-worn pair of leather moccasins sitting on a mat just inside the door. "Let's go get your luggage outa the car and get you settled in."

Marcie trailed after him down the front steps, noting the temperature outside was quickly dropping now that the setting sun had dropped behind the trees. She'd forgotten how cold it could get in the evenings in the mountains—even in late August.

She punched the key fob to unlock her car and grabbed her camera bag and laptop and watched as Dean took hold of her large suitcase as if it didn't weigh anything. She would have had to roll it across the yard and struggle to get it up the porch steps, but Dean carried it as if it were filled with feathers.

She followed him through the front door and back through the house. He glanced behind him once as if to make sure she was still following him, then Marcie slowed her steps as Dean led her through a door and into a room located just off the kitchen area.

"I hope you'll find this comfortable," Dean's voice was quiet and sounded shyly uncertain as he placed her suitcase on the floor next to the bed.

Marcie took a moment to gaze around the room. Unlike the rest of the house—which had high beamed ceilings, this room felt cozier.

"This is beautiful, Dean," she murmured. She looked from the multi-pane windows along the outside wall to the door leading into an attached bath, then Marcie stepped closer to the bed and ran her fingers lightly across the cotton patchwork quilt which looked hand-stitched.

"This room was built from a cabin, wasn't it?"

Dean shot her a quick grin as if pleased with her observation.

"Yup. Well, the logs are actually from several cabins. The boys and I added this room to the back of the house a couple of years ago, using parts and pieces from some old cabins we salvaged. Didn't turn out too bad, if I say so myself."

Marcie couldn't hold back her chuckle. "No, it didn't. It's a really nice room."

Then she turned serious as a sense of uncertainty swept through her. "Listen, Dean, I hope I'm not pushing you out of your bedroom. I can still drive back into town and get a room at the small hotel I saw."

He gave his head a firm shake. "No way. If you're gonna get a true taste for what we do, you need to be here on site."

Dean grinned. "Besides, at night you'll have the whole house to yourself." She noticed a little red tinge seeping up from his neck. "Wouldn't be right havin' me stay here in the house alone with a woman I'm not married to."

Marcie almost laughed, then realized the man was serious. She'd almost forgotten what it was like here in the hills—where doing the right thing and making sure appearances were kept meant everything.

"Well, then. Just where *are* you planning to sleep?"

Dean grinned and pointed out the window toward the large barn she'd noticed when she'd driven into the yard.

The barn?

"Oh, Dean! I don't want to drive you out of your house and make you sleep in some smelly old barn. That's not right."

The man's deep laughter bounced around the small room, and Marcie couldn't help but smile in response. She didn't know what he found so funny, though. She meant it. She didn't feel right about putting the man out of his own house. That hadn't been her plan at all. Her original plan had been to stay at a small hotel in the nearby town of Marysville, but when she'd talked to Dean on the phone a week earlier, he had talked her out of it. And he'd assured her there was plenty of room at his house.

Dean finally got his laughter under control, gave her what looked like a flirtatious wink, and reached out and put his hand on her lower back and turned her toward the door.

"Come with me, young lady. You need to see why it's no sacrifice for me to sleep in the barn a few nights."

Feeling the warmth of Dean's large hand on her back, Marcie almost stumbled as he turned her around and steered her out of the room. When he dropped his hand from her back and stepped ahead of her to lead the way, she released a breath she hadn't realized she was holding. What was there about this man that so unsettled her? Whatever it was, she needed to get over it as they were going to be spending the majority of the next two weeks together. All day. Every day.

Marcie tagged along after him as he crossed through the house to the kitchen. He paused at the back door long enough to look behind him as if to check if she was still following him.

"I'm coming."

She felt like giggling as Dean opened the wooden screen door and allowed her to step onto the covered back porch ahead of him. Here again, were the southern manners and charm she had all but forgotten.

Then she stepped onto the porch and was able to get a good look at the view from the back of the house and caught her breath at the sight before her. Spread out behind the house was a wide open field, and beyond that sat a huge red-sided pole barn. But it wasn't the barn nor the forests nor the mountains rising in the distance that caught her eye and took her breath away. It was the sight of several stacked log cabins near the pole barn that had her attention.

Dean gave her a grin, and it was all Marcie could to do not grin back at him. What she was looking at must be the heart of the operation, and she could hardly wait to see it all.

"Is that where we're headed?" she finally croaked out—hoping beyond hope that it was.

He shook his head. "Ah, the Wood Lot. Nope. But once I give you a tour of the barn, we'll walk back there and take a little look-see around if you'd like. We should still have time before it gets too dark. Although I guarantee, you'll get your fill of seein' it over the next few days."

Marcie followed Dean down the steps and across a grassy yard that sloped downhill toward the huge gray-sided hip-roofed barn. Soft light was pouring out from several of the lower story windows, and as Dean opened a heavy-looking wooden door, Marcie heard what sounded like a football game blaring on a television somewhere.

"Must be the boys are watchin' tonight's game. It's just a preseason game." He gave her an apologetic look. "I'll ask them to turn it down."

She quickly shook her head. "No need. Let them enjoy their leisure time."

Besides, Marcie was too busy looking around at the interior of the enormous barn to worry about the noise coming from the TV. What she had expected to be a neglected building had instead been remodeled and made into living quarters— exceptionally nice living quarters. A large great room was in front of them with a big-screened TV on the wall, and comfortable looking sofas and recliners placed in front of it. Dutch and Mac sat in the recliners, so involved in watching the game they hadn't even noticed her and Dean's entrance.

Then Marcie's gaze turned to the right side of the room where a kitchen area was located. What looked like oak cupboards were covered with granite-topped counters. A long wooden table with benches on either side sat just outside the kitchen— apparently the dining area. That side of the barn was a wall of windows that looked out over the wood lot and mountains, allowing in plenty of late afternoon light.

The place was gorgeous, and Marcie instantly wished she'd brought her camera with her. If this was an example of Dean McRae's work, the man was a genius.

"So, what do ya think?"

At the sound of Dean's deep voice, Marcie focused back on his face.

"It's…not at all what I expected," she finally admitted. "I mean, it looks like a regular barn from the outside. I never would have guessed this is what it looked like inside. This is gorgeous. Did you design this?"

Dean's face broke into what was becoming a familiar grin, and the same deep dimples she'd noticed earlier reappeared, along with a rosy color on Dean's cheeks. The man was actually embarrassed at her praise. It was quickly becoming apparent to Marcie that Dean McRae was a humble man.

"You like it?"

She nodded. "What's not to like?" And there *wasn't* a thing she didn't like about it. It was bright and roomy, yet somehow Dean had managed to make a barn into a warm and homey place.

"Dutch and Mac live here most of the time—other than during holidays when they usually go home to visit family. Or when they use their vacation time. They're both single, so this works out great for them to have someplace to crash during the work week." He chuckled. "I like to think of it as a modern-day bunkhouse of sorts."

Marcie walked over to the kitchen and ran her fingers lightly across the countertop and noted the nice appliances, including a dishwasher. She was surprised to see how clean and neat everything was. Evidently, 'the boys' were fairly good housekeepers.

"Hey guys," Dean hollered loud enough to get the attention of the two men lounging in front of the TV.

Dutch looked up in surprise and immediately grabbed the remote and turned down the volume of the game. Two sets of eyes looked from Dean to Marcie and back again.

"Whatya need, boss?"

"I'm going to show Miss Marcie the living quarters upstairs. Is there anything up there she shouldn't see?"

Marcie almost chuckled when Dutch—the one she thought was the younger of the two—dropped his eyes for a moment and then looked back up at Dean.

"I didn't make my bed today, boss. My room might be a tad bit messy. Maybe you can skip showin' her it?"

Dutch's face had turned beet red as he spoke, and Dean glanced over at her long enough to give her a cute little wink.

Mac spoke up then. "Yeah, Dean. Mine's not so neat either."

"I'll just show her the spare rooms nobody's using right now, how's that? By the way, I'll be bunking here during the duration of her visit, so be forewarned."

The other two men exchanged glances, then nodded at Dean as if willing to accept that sacrifice for the team.

Marcie chuckled as she gave Mac and Dutch a little wave and followed Dean toward a stairway built along the back wall. She could see the stairs had been made from logs cut in half. Even though the look was rustic, the staircase was beautiful, and Marcie thought it fit the décor of the rest of the barn perfectly.

Once they reached the top of the stairs, they turned down a well-lit hallway where an open area with a railing looked out over the great room below. Marcie paused for a moment to stand at the rail and gaze down on the room below. Dean had hung ceiling fans from the high ceilings, and they turned quietly in the open expanse.

Behind her, Marcie heard Dean tug open a door and turned around to find him motioning for her to enter the room. It was a comfortable looking bedroom, with a bed much like the one in the spare room she would be using. Another patchwork quilt covered the bed, and dark blue curtains hung over the small window that looked out into the woods. A small desk, chair, and dresser completed the furniture in the room. Marcie was surprised to see there was even an attached bathroom.

"Do all the rooms have their own bathrooms?"

He nodded. "I wanted the guys to be as comfortable as possible. They spend most of their time livin' here, so I wanted them to feel at home."

Marcie gave a little nod. "Well, it's nice. You did a good job."

"Thank you, ma'am," Dean answered, those dimples appearing again along with his smile.

"Now, there's one more room I want to show you. Then we'll take a quick walk out to the Wood Lot before it gets dark."

Dean pulled the bedroom door closed, then headed to the end of the hallway and opened another door—this one a tall rustic-looking wooden door on rollers. Marcie decided it must have been made from barn siding and she was so busy studying its construction, she didn't react to the room inside as quickly as she might have if she'd been paying attention. But when she finally did step into the room, Marcie couldn't hold back her gasp of surprise.

It was a huge room—although what probably made it seem so vast was the ceiling. Unlike the bedroom Dean had just shown her, the ceiling in this room was not lowered and ran all the way up to the original rafters of the barn. But what had caused her breathless intake of breath was the windows. These were the tall stained-glass windows she had noticed when she had first driven into the yard and saw the barn. The late afternoon sun was shining through the stained glass, casting a colorful glow over everything in the room—from the polished wide-plank floors to the top of the big wooden desk in the center of the room, to the architect's table sitting along one wall.

After gazing toward the windows a moment, Marcie's eyes turned to the bookshelves that filled the wall directly to the left of the doorway, then noted the rest of the walls were covered with framed photos. Marcie strolled across the floor so she could get a closer look at them. They were old black and white photos of cabins—some with people standing or sitting in front of the cabins when they were still being used as homes. Others were photos of tumbled down log cabins in disrepair, left to fall down due to neglect.

Before she even thought about it, Marcie pulled out her cell phone and quickly took a few shots of some of the more poignant pictures. Once she finished, she stuck her phone back in her pocket and turned around to find Dean watching her.

"Oh. I hope that's all right. I just thought I'd like to have photos of those—not that I'll use them in the article or anything—they'll be poor quality…."

Dean gave her a little smile, then stepped closer to her—close enough his elbow brushed her arm, and she felt goosebumps rush up her arm to her neck.

"This one here," Dean pointed to the first black and white photo that had caught her eye. It was of three men seated in wooden chairs in front of a cabin. They were dressed in rough work clothes, and all three of them wore scruffy-looking hats. The man on the left held what looked like a violin in his lap, and the one on the right held onto some sort of phonograph or Victrola on his. The man in the middle held a shotgun in his arms and Marcie couldn't help but smile at this perfect photo of Appalachian mountain history.

"This photo came from a job we did in West Virginia. We dismantled the little cabin, which surprisingly wasn't in too badda shape. We only had to replace two logs on the bottom row when we sold it."

Dean glanced over as if to make sure he still had her attention. Well, he did. Having him stand so close to her was setting off all kinds of alarms in her head, but Marcie forced herself to concentrate on the story he was telling and not on how good the man smelled.

"The current owner of the cabin was the granddaughter of this man right here," he pointed to the man in the middle. "His name was Moses Parker, and he lived in that cabin until the day he died." Dean sighed. "It was the first cabin we ever bought. Paid $1,000 for it and sold it for $4,000." He grinned. "You might think that was a lot of profit, but by the time you figure the cost of tearing it down, moving it, the labor to create the new logs, and rebuilding it for the new owners—well," he chuckled. "We made a little bit, but not much."

He smiled at her again, his green eyes gazing into hers until she felt almost under a spell as she listened to him recount the story. "It was a learnin' experience for all of us." He released a little sigh. "Each time we take a cabin down, we learn something new about how they were constructed. They're all jist a little different.

"Anyway, the granddaughter had two copies of this old picture, so she gave me this one to have as a keepsake."

Dean pointed to the others hanging on the wall in front of them. "I like lookin' at these every now and then. They remind me of what life used to be like, and the history of all the logs we move from one place to the other. The logs and the boards always have stories to tell, if you'll just listen."

She watched as Dean's large hand reached out and picked up a round piece of wood that had been sitting on a small table under the photos. He handed it to her, and she finally recognized what it was—a hand-carved wooden peg like those used in log cabins to help hold the top row of logs to the rest of the structure.

"That little gem came out of that first cabin. I decided to keep it so I would remember how much work it was to take it down. But more importantly, to remember how much *more* work it was for the man or men who originally built it. Can you imagine cutting down the trees to make the logs, hewing the logs, cutting the notches, lifting the logs into place, hand-drilling the holes for the pegs, and pounding them in—all without the benefit of modern tools we use now?"

Dean shook his head as if in awe, which Marcie totally understood. It really *was* unbelievable when you took the time to think about it.

Marcie handed the piece of wood back to him with a smile, feeling a little as if she were standing in a holy place. Hearing Dean tell his story about that first cabin made it seem as if she'd stepped back in time.

Even though they'd lived in a lovely frame house in town, Marcie well remembered riding in the car as a child down the country roads around her hometown. Back then there had been plenty of old cabins in the hills and the valleys that people had still lived in.

"You really love what you do, don't you?"

Dean glanced over at her, the look on his face turning wistful. "I surely do, Miss Marcie. I surely do. I don't think I'd ever want to do anything else."

The two of them continued to stare at each other for a few more seconds, then Dean raised his eyebrows.

"So, are y'all ready to see the Wood Lot?"

Marcie gave herself a mental shake as if to pull herself back into the room. She needed to stay on track. She was here to write an article about this man's business, not be attracted to the man himself. She needed to remember that.

"Sure. I can't wait to see it."

The two of them made their way back down the stairs, waving as they went through the main room at the two men still watching the football game, and left the barn.

While they walked through the yard in the deepening afternoon shade, Marcie continued to be surprised by the layers of Dean McCrae. He appeared to be a caring man—even taking the time to make sure his employees had someplace to live when they were working for him. And it was easy to tell from the looks of his house and the barn he'd just showed her that he was a talented architect and builder.

What more surprises did Dean have in store for her during the next two weeks?

2

Dean led the young woman at his side across the yard and down the grassy path back of the house that led toward the Wood Lot. The early evening shadows were just beginning to reach the far edges of the woods, so hopefully, he had time to show her around before it became too dark.

While he walked, Dean turned his head a bit to observe the woman beside him. Marcie Starr was nothing like he'd envisioned she would be when they'd talked on the phone a few weeks earlier. He'd expected a much older woman— perhaps in her forties or early fifties. But Dean didn't think this woman was even as old as his thirty years.

And she was a tall one. Dean hadn't known many women who came anywhere close to his six-foot-plus-several-inch frame. By the looks of her, Miss Starr must be at least five-foot-ten.

And, of course, there was the obvious. She was gorgeous.

Not gorgeous in the three-layers-of-makeup, and just-came-from-the-beauty-salon gorgeous, he'd seen when he'd lived in L.A. years earlier. But with Marcie's shiny black, straight long hair which hung half-way down her back and the deep pools of her dark brown eyes, it was difficult for Dean to keep his eyes off her. Something told him it was going to be a long two weeks.

"How long have you owned this property?"

Marcie's question pulled his brain back into focus. He needed to remember she was a reporter and she was here to write an article about his business. That was it.

"I bought this fifteen-acre plot five years ago—about a year after I moved back from L.A."

She glanced over at him as they walked, and Dean saw her right eyebrow raise as if a question had appeared in her mind. Dean felt reasonably certain he knew what was coming next.

"What did you do out in L.A.? Somehow, I don't see you as being the California type."

Dean chuckled. If she only knew.

"Yeah, well you'd be right. I was only there for about two years. I worked for an architectural firm specializing in designing large commercial buildings—all very modern. It didn't take me long to realize it wasn't where I wanted to be— and certainly not what I wanted to do with the rest of my life. So I came back home—to the mountains."

He felt a sense of contentment sweep over him as he allowed his eyes to gaze around at the surrounding woods and hills. When Dean recalled the concrete and steel of the city he'd left behind in California, it only depressed him. Here—in this green and open country, he'd found himself and his faith again. And he'd been able to heal.

"Best decision I ever made."

"So you grew up around here?"

As the two of them grew closer to the Wood Lot pole barn, Dean nodded.

"About an hour from here. My momma still has a place not far from where I grew up, just a few mountain ranges across the way. You'll get to meet her before you leave, I promise." He gave her a wink and felt a warm feeling in the area of his heart as he thought about his momma. "No one should go through life without meeting Miz LizBeth."

They'd reached the barn, and Dean pulled a key out of his pocket and unlocked one of the big overhead doors. As he pushed the heavy door up on its tracks, he gave a little grunt, then he and Marcie stepped into the building. Dean automatically reached to the left where he knew the electrical panel was and switched on the overhead lights. He took a deep breath of air as the smell of wood and sawdust greeted him. Dean didn't think there was a more beautiful aroma in the world. Well, other than maybe the light fragrance wafting from the woman standing at his side. She smelled pretty good too— kind of fresh and flowery.

"This place is awesome."

He watched the woman as she strolled around the building. She calmly checked out the stacks of salvaged windows along one wall, the old hardware they kept in wooden crates in a corner, and of course, all the tools of the trade. There were chainsaws, circular saws, table saws, and a drill press—tools were hanging everywhere. He and the boys had taken a great deal of time to organize and make this building into what they needed to do their jobs, and Dean was feeling grateful that at least right now, it looked orderly and neat. Some days it didn't.

Marcie stopped in front of several old wooden framed windows, and lightly touched one of the panes of glass.

"Dean, is this Crown glass?"

She turned and gave him a look of disbelief, her eyebrows raised. "Where did you manage to find some of these windows—with the panes still unbroken?"

He smiled as a warmth of appreciation swept over him. How many women he knew would recognize the glass in those old windows as antique wavy glass, let alone actually know what the glass was called? None he could think of. Perhaps Marcie Starr *did* know what she was doing when it came to historical architecture.

Dean walked over to stand next to her, again appreciating her height. It was an entirely different experience being able to talk to a woman without having to look down all the time.

"They came from an old house we tore down in Kentucky. Not a cabin, mind you. But nonetheless, it was old. We took it down for parts. I was so excited when we found this old glass intact in some of the windows. I couldn't believe it."

He watched as her long and gracefully tapered fingertips almost reverently traced the pattern running through the window glass.

"What a find!"

The two of them strolled around the barn a little longer, then left the building to check out the cabins stacked in the yard before it got any darker. Dean pulled down the door and locked it, then turned to follow Marcie as she strode around the perimeter of the closest cabin, her chin raised as she tilted her head back to see it all.

"You have it tagged, I see."

Dean nodded. "Yup. Before we start to dismantle a cabin, Mac and Gordie tag each and every log, so we know how to put it back together. And we draw a detailed diagram of the structure with each tag location noted, length of logs, etc."

He gave her a grin. "It's kinda like playing with Lincoln Logs. On a much larger scale, of course."

"Of course."

She laughed along with him, and the sound of her laughter made Dean's smile grow broader. He could get used to that sound. Marcie sounded like she was a happy, upbeat person, and he liked that about her.

He turned toward the west and noticed the sun had dropped behind the trees and hills. Darkness was quickly moving in, and he knew it was time they head back to the house. Dean didn't want to be out after dark—at least not without his shotgun. He was sure Miss Starr wouldn't appreciate having one of the many black bears in the area appear out of the darkness and approach her. For that matter, neither would he.

When they reached the back door of the main house, Dean held the door open for her, then followed her in, flipping on light switches as he went.

"I'll lock up when I leave," he said as he stopped at the foot of the stairs to head up to his bedroom. "I just need to grab a couple of things from upstairs, and I'll be out of your hair."

MARCIE stood alone in the kitchen and wondered what she should do next as she listened to the sound of Dean's heavy footsteps going up the stairs to the second floor. She still felt terrible that she was the cause for the man leaving his own bed. Now that she'd seen The Barn, though, it did make her feel a little better knowing he wouldn't be sleeping on a bed of straw on the barn floor.

Releasing a sigh of resignation, Marcie finally walked into the bedroom she'd been assigned and hefted her heavy suitcase up onto the bed. She might as well get settled if this was where she was going to be spending the next two weeks. Moments later, she turned at the sound of knuckles knocking on the room's door jam.

"Unless you need somethin' else, Marcie, I'm outa here."

She turned and gave Dean a smile. "Thanks again for letting me stay here."

His green eyes studied her a few seconds, then his lips lifted in a slow smile, making that little dimple appear again in his right cheek.

"No problem. Try and get some sleep. Breakfast is at seven." He chuckled. "Then we go to work. Dress in something warm and comfortable, and wear some sturdy shoes." He gave her another one of his little winks as he added, "I'll provide the required hard hat."

Marcie grinned as she leaned over and picked up the well-worn pair of work boots she'd just placed on the floor next to her bed. Mr. McCrae needed to learn this wasn't unfamiliar territory to her. She'd come prepared.

"Will these do?"

Dean's green eyes lit up in surprise when he saw what she was holding.

"I do believe they will."

Then his look softened. "Good night, Miz Starr. Sleep well. I'll lock up when I leave."

"Good night," Marcie replied as she watched Dean turn and walk away.

A few moments later, she saw the lights go out in the great room and heard the front door close.

She was alone. In a stranger's house. In the middle of the woods on the side of a mountain in the middle of nowhere Tennessee. A place she'd promised herself she'd never come back to.

Perhaps she'd been foolish to take this assignment, but she was here. Now Marcie just hoped and prayed she didn't make a complete mess of it all.

THE next morning, Marcie woke to the smell of coffee brewing. And was that bacon she smelled? She hadn't eaten bacon in years. Who was making bacon?

Stretching out in the cozy bed, she yawned and blinked her eyes open. She wasn't home in her own bed. This was the McCrae place, and she was staying in Dean McCrae's house while Dean was staying over in The Barn.

So who was cooking breakfast?

She quickly rolled out of bed and padded into the bathroom, took a quick shower, and dressed. Jeans and a lightweight T-shirt covered by a flannel shirt would be her uniform for the next few days. She also tucked a zippered hooded sweatshirt into her backpack in case it turned out to be a cooler day than predicted. Marcie remembered well how much colder it could be in the higher elevation of the mountains.

Today's jaunt was definitely going to be different than what she was used to back in D.C. While on assignment for the magazine over the past several years, Marcie had wandered through dozens of historic old buildings and homes, and none of them had required the work boots she was currently pulling on over her heavy cotton socks. While she tied the boot laces, Marcie stared at the toes of her boots for a moment, almost wishing they were steel-toed boots. But her toes should be safe. She wasn't going to be doing any of the heavy work, after all. She'd just be trying to stay out of the way and shooting photos and taking notes. Lots of notes.

Marcie pulled her long hair into a quick ponytail to keep it out of her way, and once she was satisfied with what she saw looking back at her in the mirror, she slowly opened her bedroom door and entered the kitchen. There she found Mac and Dutch seated around the small kitchen table, munching on toast and conversing with Dean, who was manning the stove.

Again, he was barefoot. This morning Dean looked like he was ready to work—wearing brown work pants and a white T-shirt, his muscular, tanned arms bare. The morning light coming through the kitchen window accentuated the reddish-blond hairs on those same arms. Marcie tried not to stare at him as she wished everyone 'good morning.'

Dean turned around long enough to give her a quick grin as he dished up what looked like a large farmer's omelet and handed it to her.

"Good-mornin', sunshine. Did you sleep okay over here by your lonesome?"

Marcie held back the temptation to stick her tongue out at him for his patronizing comment. Instead, she gave him her brightest smile. She wasn't exactly a morning person—at least until she'd had a cup or two of coffee.

"I slept very well, thank you. So well, in fact, I must not have heard my phone alarm."

She took the offered plate of food and sat down next to Dutch at the table who was finishing off his own omelet.

"I'm sorry I'm running late, Dean. I promise it won't happen again."

Dean gave her a steady look as he reached out and handed her a coffee mug filled to the brim with black coffee. Marcie immediately inhaled the aroma. Even without drinking a drop, she felt more awake.

"No worries," Dean answered as he plopped down in the chair across from her, his own plate filled with the twin to her omelet. "Just so long as we get out of here on time this mornin', I'm happy."

Marcie concentrated on eating the tasty omelet on her plate, amazed at how good a cook the man was who currently sat across the table from her. Had he minored in culinary arts or something? The omelet was one of the best she'd ever eaten, and she'd dined in some of the best restaurants in Washington, D.C.

"This is really good, Dean. Thank you, but I certainly don't expect you to cook breakfast for me every morning."

She heard Dutch's chuckle as he sat back down next to her after refilling his coffee cup. "One thing I can guarantee, Miz Marcie, is if you hang around with Dean McCrae long enough, ya'll discover the man *does* like to eat. Therefore, it seems only fittin' that he also knows how to cook."

"And I think I'm a pretty good cook if I do say so myself," Dean replied. He'd finished his omelet and was now leaning back in his chair and gazing across the table at her with a mischievous twinkle in his eyes.

"Oh," she held up her fork and swallowed another bite of the fluffy omelet. "You are *definitely* a good cook. I was just wondering where you learned it."

He released a chuckle that sounded like it rumbled deep in the man's chest.

"That would be my momma."

Mac spoke up then. "Miz LizBeth McRae is the best cook in the state. Wait until you've tasted her sausage gravy and biscuits!"

Dean gave her one of his winks, and Marcie hoped she wasn't blushing.

"Momma *is* a pretty good cook. If you're lucky, you may get to find out jist how good before you go home."

She took another sip of her coffee, surprised to find her plate empty and her stomach full. When the others stood and started to clear the table, she quickly gulped her last bit of coffee and took her plate to the sink.

"I can fill the dishwasher for you, Dean."

He stood in front of the sink, quickly rinsing off the plates and silverware and methodically placing them in the dishwasher. He gave his head a little shake.

"Won't take me long." He glanced over at her. "Why don't you go ahead and get whatever you'll need to take with you today. Soon as I'm done here, we're headin' out."

She gave a little nod, but before she turned to leave the room, added, "Thanks again for breakfast."

Leaving the kitchen and Dean McRae behind, Marcie went to her room and grabbed her backpack, checking first to make sure all her notebooks, pencils and pens, and a camera were inside. She also threw in a couple of energy bars she always carried with her, and an extra pair of socks. The socks might sound like an odd item to some people, but Marcie knew from past experience that if you spent a lot of time on your feet, having a fresh, clean pair of socks came in handy. Besides, if she was going to be tromping all over the mountains, she might step into a wet area, and as far as she was concerned, there was nothing worse than walking around all day with wet feet.

By the time Marcie made her way back to the great room, she found the house was empty. She stepped out onto the front porch just in time to see Dean heft a large cooler into the back bed of his pickup, then slam the tailgate shut.

He glanced up and saw her. "Guess we're ready." His eyes landed on the backpack she'd thrown over her shoulder. "You got everything y'all are gonna need?"

She gave him a smile and a nod and hurried down the steps, hoping her smile looked more convincing than she felt. After stashing her backpack behind the seat, Marcie climbed in the passenger side of Dean's pickup and fastened her seatbelt, noting the inside of the truck was a lot cleaner than she'd expected. And the pickup wasn't a beat-up older model like she'd half-thought Dean McRae would own. It wasn't brand new, however, and the mud splashed up the side of it told the story of how many country roads it had traveled.

Well, she'd been down a few of those roads in the past too.

Marcie turned toward Dean long enough to see his grin as he put the truck in gear and they followed Mac and Dutch just ahead of them in an older pickup. Dean's face held a look of excitement, and it was easy to tell he really loved what he did.

Then she realized who was missing in the equation.

"Hey! What about Gordie? Isn't he comin'?" She flinched as she realized how quickly she'd fallen back into the habit of speaking like the locals. Marcie had worked for years to rid herself of the 'hillbilly' lingo, and after not even twenty-four hours of being back in the mountains, it was as if she'd forgotten everything she'd learned.

Those dimples turned on her again before Dean turned his eyes back to the road. "He'll meet us when we get to the main road. He's bringin' the big flatbed with the hydraulic forklift."

She raised her eyebrows in question, and he just gave her another grin.

"Oh, it's gonna be a good day, Miz Marcie. You just wait for us to show you how we do things 'round here."

3

Dean glanced across the cab of his pickup toward Marcie Starr. He could almost hear the wheels of her brain working as she tried to figure out the purpose for the forklift. She didn't know it yet, but during the next two weeks, she was going to learn a lot about taking down and restoring old log cabins—more than she could ever imagine.

Marcie had surprised him this morning when she'd come out of her room dressed for work. He couldn't imagine Miss Starr had many occasions to wear denim and flannel back in D.C., but he had to admit they looked good on her. And with her black hair pulled back into a ponytail and with the baseball cap she'd popped on her head just before they'd left the house, she almost looked like a teenager. Definitely cute.

He'd also noticed she seemed to talk differently this morning—with hints of the local drawl creeping into her speech. He'd noticed it twice already, and he wondered if Marcie were even aware she was doing it. Dean felt it softened the woman somehow—hearing that slow, southern drawl coming from those lovely lips in her quiet musical voice.

Suddenly it felt as if it was getting warm in the cab of the truck, and Dean rolled down his window a bit, then cleared his throat and turned his concentration to the road. He needed to get used to seeing the woman sitting in the seat beside him since she'd be with them practically day and night the next two weeks. And since that was the case, he was going to have to concentrate on business—not on how good her long legs looked encased in a pair of jeans.

"So, how far is it to this cabin you're going to work on today?"

Marcie's question drew his mind back to what he should be thinking about. The job ahead of them.

"'Bout twenty miles. It's at the top of Hawk's Ridge. The road's a little rough, but we should be able to get up it okay."

"Is this a cabin you're planning to re-sell?"

Dean shook his head. "I doubt it. The owner's payin' us a little something to tear it down and haul it out. He plans to build a new house on the site and wants to get rid of the cabin before they start."

He glanced over at her briefly, noting her dark brown eyes were focused on him as he talked. It was a little disconcerting having someone hang onto your every word, but then she was here to get information for the article she was supposed to write, so Dean guessed he'd have to get used to it.

"The structure's not in the best shape, and someone covered it with wood siding years ago, so I don't know what we're gonna discover when we start tearing it down. It might be we only get a little bit of wood that's even salvageable. We've done jobs like this before where we start ripping off the siding only to find termites have gotten into the logs and there's not much good wood left. That's always disappointin', but I guess it comes with the territory.

"As for this cabin, we'll haul what we can use out of there and burn what we can't salvage—although Gordie takes a lot of stuff I'd just toss and makes furniture out of it. He's pretty talented. While you're here, maybe you'll have a chance to go over to his place and check out some of the creations he builds in his garage during his spare time."

She gave him a little nod and turned her head back to look out the passenger window at the passing scenery, which was okay with Dean. For the next few miles, Dean knew he needed to keep his eyes on the road in front of them and concentrate on his driving. They'd reached a portion of the road he wasn't all that familiar with, having only been there once before when he'd come to initially look at the cabin. It was a narrow dirt road and was in pretty rough shape, and he was sure the owner was going to have to do some significant work on the road before building his house. Dean just hoped and prayed Gordie could get the flatbed up the side of the mountain without any trouble. Thankfully, it hadn't rained recently, so at least they wouldn't have to deal with mud.

MARCIE held her breath as Dean maneuvered his truck around another sharp curve, noting how close the edge of the road appeared from where she was sitting. They were climbing steadily, and she turned around a little in her seat to look back, thankful to see Gordie and the big flatbed truck was still following them.

She'd been on a lot of roads like these as a child, but she'd been younger then and had looked on it more as a thrill. Now it was just plain scary. Thank goodness, she wasn't the one doing the driving.

Fortunately, just when Marcie was sure her nerves weren't going to hold out much longer, Dean drove up a little rise and came to a stop in a large clearing in a flat area. It was a wooded spot on top of a ridge, and Marcie stepped out of the truck with a sense of relief. She almost laughed at the feeling of exultation that swept through her. It had been a long time since she'd stood on top of a mountain. She'd forgotten how freeing it felt, and just barely caught herself from lifting her arms and releasing a shout of joy.

Instead of shouting, Marcie took a deep breath of the air, noting how crisp and clean it was. The aroma of lush green plant life tickled her nose, and the smell of the pine and oak trees standing at the edge of the forest wafted across the clearing. Standing there, Marcie could hear the sounds of the mountains all around her—birds singing in the tops of the trees and the breeze whispering through the pine branches, and somewhere down in the valley, the sound of a lonely train whistle. Hearing it brought a smile to her face, and she immediately closed her eyes and felt the stress of life seeping out her pores.

It smelled like home.

This. *This* was what she'd missed when she moved to the city. Until that very moment, Marcie hadn't realized how much she'd missed it.

The sound of truck doors slamming behind her brought her eyes open, and Marcie swung around to find Dean McCrae's green eyes studying her, a frown on his otherwise handsome face.

"You okay, Marcie?"

She'd noted whenever he spoke to her without the other guys around, he always dropped the Miss, which made her feel different somehow—like he wanted to be friends. Marcie swallowed hard and pasted a smile on her face as she stared back at him.

"I'm great. Just enjoying the view. It's absolutely gorgeous up here. I can understand why the owner wants to build a house in this location."

She frowned and added, "Although how he's planning to do that with the shape that road is in, is beyond me." She released a little shudder at the idea of having to go up that road daily.

The look on Dean's face relaxed, and he laughed. "Yeah. Well, thankfully, we don't have to worry about that. But I agree, he's gonna have to do some major work on that road before they haul much up."

Marcie stood and watched Dean push his truck seat forward and grab something from behind it. After closing his truck door, Dean walked over and handed her a yellow hard hat, then reached up and put on his own hat, covering his thick head of red hair. Marcie thought it was almost a shame that he had to cover up that gorgeous head of hair, but understood the need for safety.

"Gotta wear this if you're gonna be on the work site."

She accepted the hat and gave it a quick look, wondering if she should remove her ball cap first, but then decided to just plop it on her head. As it turned out, it was a good thing she'd left her other hat on as the hard hat was rather large. Even on top of the baseball cap, it almost covered her eyes, and she pushed it back up a bit so she could better see.

Dean gazed at her and chuckled. "Sorry about that. Guess they don't make them in small."

Although she was again tempted to stick her tongue out at the man, Marcie gave Dean what she hoped was a confident smile.

"Maybe it's because they know all guys who work in construction have big heads."

He chuckled and shook his head. Mac, who had just walked over and had obviously overheard the tail end of the conversation, turned toward Marcie with his hand over his heart and his head dropped to his chest almost theatrically.

"Miz Marcie, you crush my heart with your mean words."

She finished digging her backpack from behind the seat and slung it over her shoulders, then walked over to give Mac a playful nudge in the shoulder.

"I meant Dean, Mac. Not you."

Mac's head came up, and a bright smile swept over his face. "Oh! Well, the boss *does* have a big head. Gotta agree with ya there."

Dean gave a look toward Mac which she supposed was supposed to look fierce, but she could see the humor in his eyes. "Ain't you funny as all get out?"

Then he smiled and shook his head again. "Enough chit-chat, folks. Let's get to work."

Dean gave her one last grin before he turned and pointed toward the small structure sitting in the tall weeds at the edge of the woods.

"*That* is all we need to worry about."

Marcie walked next to Dean as they headed in the direction of the small one-story house. She was just going to have to trust him that it was a log cabin as it was difficult to tell by looking at the gray wood siding covering the outside of it. Chips of white paint were still on a portion of the siding, but the majority of the paint had long ago worn away, leaving only weathered wood. Dean had been right when he'd told her the place wasn't in very good shape. One end of the roof had fallen in, and as Marcie looked at the house with dismay, she couldn't help but wonder if there were really anything left of the place that was worth saving.

"It looks awful," she stated the obvious as she and Dean grew closer to the building.

His deep chuckle warmed Marcie and made her own lips automatically turn up in a smile.

"Ya think?"

He stepped just inside the gaping doorway and peered around the darkened interior, then motioned for her to come closer. She stepped next to him, suddenly aware of how close they were standing in the small space, then looked toward where he was pointing.

"You can see there was once a stone fireplace at that end of the cabin. Outside, there's still a little of the old stonework that's visible."

He cautiously stepped inside, testing the wooden floorboards one at a time with his booted feet as he went.

"Walk directly behind me, Marcie, and I'll show you what I mean. But be careful. Don't need you fallin' through the floor."

Marcie carefully stepped through the doorway, trying to shadow Dean's footsteps the best she could, visions of her falling through a rotten floorboard and breaking an ankle causing her to be extra cautious.

She gasped as he pulled a large piece of water stained wallboard off the end wall, and uncovered an opening. Surrounded by logs was what looked like the remainder of an old stone fireplace.

"Oh, my goodness. I wonder why they covered it up."

Dean shrugged his broad shoulders. "Who knows?"

He glanced around and then pointed to a hole through the wall in the back corner of the house. "Looks like they might have had a wood stove over there. They probably thought it would heat the place better, so just closed up the old fireplace."

As Dean went back out the door and stepped into the yard, she followed him. In front of the house, Dutch and Mac were lugging large-looking tools that looked like extra-long crowbars, and several ladders over from the trucks and dropping them in the tall grass.

"Where do ya want to start, boss?"

Knowing she needed to stay out of the way, Marcie pulled her backpack off and moved a distance away from the group of men. Pulling out her camera, she cautioned herself to focus on her mission. She had to remember why she was here, and that was to get not only the story of what *McCrae's* did on a job but to also get plenty of photos. She just hoped Dean was a patient man as she was going to ask a lot of questions. A lot.

She watched Dean grab a tool from Mac that looked like a giant crowbar and then motioned for the others to follow him. Marcie was just getting ready to tag along after them when she heard the sound of machinery coming up the hill behind her. It sounded like Gordie had gotten the forklift started and was on his way to join them.

The screeching sound of nails being pulled out of wood drifted across the yard to her, so she hurried around the end of the cabin so she could get some photos of the men working. Marcie snapped photo after photo, and even though she made sure to stay back out of the way, whenever she could, she zoomed in to get a better look at the action without actually getting closer.

After a while, though, Marcie quit taking photos and simply stood and watched the men work. They'd pulled off all the old wood siding on this end of the house, and the original log structure could now be seen clearly. The original chinking was still there although it disintegrated quickly and fell off when one of the guys touched it with their crowbar. The cabin itself looked pretty good to her untrained eyes though. Then Marcie noticed Dean was leaning in and looking closely at some of the lower logs with a frown on his face.

Gordie had reached the front of the house with the forklift and silence once again swept over the clearing as he turned off the engine. Marcie watched him jump off the machine and stride across the area toward the end of the house where they were all now congregated.

"Whatya find, boss?"

Marcie moved in a little closer so she could better see what had everyone's attention. Dean had stood back up and was now pulling more board siding off the higher logs as if he was looking for something. He glanced briefly at Gordie and Marcie as they walked over and stood one on each side of him.

"It's not in nearly as bad a shape as I thought it would be." He gave Marcie a quick dimple-filled grin and reached over and patted Gordie on the shoulder. "I was really concerned when I saw the roof had fallen in on one end. Fortunately, I think it only happened recently, so the logs haven't been damaged yet by the weather. Now, if the rest of the walls are in this gooda shape, the cabin might actually be something we can sell as a whole—not just take it down for parts."

He grinned at Marcie again. "It's gonna be a good day!"

It didn't take the four men long, and they had the entire cabin bared. Then Mac and Dutch cautiously went inside and started pulling off the rest of the wallboard that hadn't already fallen off on its own. A short time later, they came back outside to report that the one end of the house was pretty sketchy as that was where the roof had caved in.

Hearing that, Gordie went and got in the forklift and fired it up.

Marcie was so busy shooting photos of all the action, she didn't realize Dean was standing right next to her until he spoke.

"Now pay close attention, Marcie. You're about to see some magic."

She lowered the camera long enough to turn her head and found Dean smiling at her, his green eyes lit with excitement. At the sound of Gordie moving the forklift, she turned back to watch him position the forklift as close to the damaged end of the roof as he could. With a precision she wouldn't have believed possible, Gordie used the front tines of the fork to carefully tug the pieces of roofing off the top of the house and move them to the ground. Then he went back and ripped off the portion of the roof that hadn't caved in yet and slowly added it to the pile of wood off to the side of the cabin. All without doing any damage to the log structure itself.

Dean chuckled. "Gordie's one of the best I've ever seen with that thing. It's like watchin' someone peelin' the skin off an onion."

Marcie smiled at the analogy, but couldn't argue with the notion. Gordie appeared to know exactly how to do what he did. She was just thankful she'd thought to get some photos of him in action. Too bad she didn't have a video camera. That would have been even better but didn't translate well to printing in a magazine.

Once the dangerous roof was out of their way, the crew went to work removing all the extra wallboard and siding, getting right down to the bare flooring and logs. Marcie moved in closer so she could get more action photographs and found herself smiling as she listened to the four men banter back and forth while they worked. It was like watching and listening to a passel of boys playing around, but they seemed to get the job done. And had a good time while they were doing it.

Marcie couldn't hold back her laughter when she heard Gordie holler one time when he sent Dutch to the truck to get something they needed.

"Hurry up, Dutch. I'm tellin' ya, if you were movin' any faster, boy, you'd be goin' backwards."

After they'd worked for about ten minutes on tearing out the wide floorboards and hauling them outside, Dean strolled over and stood next to her, his arms crossed across his chest and a big grin on his face.

"I love it when we get good surprises. We've had so many times we thought we were getting a good cabin only to find out the termites had arrived before we had. So it's nice when it goes the other way for a change."

"That's gotta be disappointing," she murmured, noting the sheen of hard work on Dean's forehead. The sun had warmed up the mountaintop considerably from when they'd first arrived. Warm enough, she'd finally removed her flannel shirt and tied it around her waist by the sleeves.

"Not just disappointing. When it's a cabin you've already got sold, it can be a deal-breaker."

Dutch and the other guys came out of the cabin, and Dean walked over and clapped Dutch on the shoulder before turning and heading over to where he'd parked his pickup truck. He called out over his shoulder as he went.

"It's lunchtime, lady and gentlemen. Time to take a breather."

"I'll second that," Dutch mumbled, then grinned over at Mac as they both took off for the truck as if in a race. Marcie shared a chuckle with Gordie as they turned to follow the two young men at a more leisurely pace.

"So, what do ya think, Miz Marcie? Is it like you thought it would be?"

She glanced over to find the older man's eyes trained on her, studying her face carefully.

"I honestly don't know what I expected. Whatever it was, this is so much better. It's like…" Marcie struggled to come up with some way to describe what the experience felt like for her.

"I guess it's like watching someone unwrap a Christmas present that you didn't wrap. You have no idea what's inside, but you can't wait to see what it's gonna be."

The two of them had reached the rear of the pickup truck by that time, and it was apparent Dean had caught the tail end of what Marcie had said as he gave her a quick grin.

"That is *exactly* what it feels like, Miz Marcie. Every. Single. Time." His grin grew even wider as he took off his hard hat and threw it in the back of the truck and ran his hand through his thick hair as if trying to loosen it from being plastered down by the hat.

"And it doesn't matter how many times we unwrap that package, I love it. Every. Single. Time."

Marcie joined the rest of them as they congregated around the truck and reached out to accept a wrapped sandwich from Dean, along with a bottle of cold water. She couldn't believe how organized the man was. He'd even packed them each a lunch.

"Thank you, Dean," she said quietly.

His green eyes sparkled as he gave her a little nod. Then he looked around at the others, and they all stood quietly and removed their hats and dropped their heads while Dean offered a heartfelt thanks for the food and the good day they'd had so far. Marcie listened to the man's deep voice, talking so easily to God, and felt a certain amount of wonder in her heart at hearing him pray.

Had she ever felt that close to God where she could just talk to Him like that—like He was right there with her? Perhaps when she'd been younger.

Maybe...before the accident that had changed her life forever.

DEAN grabbed a bottle of orange juice from the cooler and carried it and his sandwich to an old tree stump he'd noticed earlier at the edge of the clearing. Once there, he wearily lowered himself to the stump and released a contented sigh of accomplishment. They'd gotten much more done this morning than he'd thought they would. If things continued to move along as they had, they were going to be ahead of schedule on this job—which was always a good thing. And rare. It usually went the other way and took them longer to get a cabin down than he'd estimate—usually due to bad weather.

Chewing a bite of his sandwich, Dean allowed his eyes to scan the area. The chilly morning had warmed up to be a beautiful day, and the noontime sun beating down into the clearing felt almost hot on his shoulders.

His allowed his eyes to drift over the mountains below and he released another sigh of contentment. It sure was a beautiful spot. No wonder Marcie had looked so happy when they'd arrived on the mountain that morning. It didn't matter to Dean how many times he came out to the hills and worked, their changing beauty never failed to amaze him.

Thank You, God, for bringing me back to these mountains. I praise You for their glorious beauty. You sure did a good job when You made them.

Then his eyes moved across the clearing to where Mac, Dutch, and Gordie sat on the tailgate of one of the trucks and ate. As usual, they were joking back and forth as they scarfed down their lunches. His three employees were good men, and he was so thankful for them. They were more like brothers to him than employees. They were all hard-working, honest men with integrity and grit, and Dean knew there was no way he'd be able to do what he loved to do without them. Those three were as much a part of *McRae's* as he was.

While Dean sat watching them, Gordie jumped off the tailgate and stretched, then gave his head a little shake at something one of the others must have said. Gordie then turned and gazed across the clearing toward the edge of the woods. Dean swiveled his own head in that direction to see what had caught Gordie's eye and saw Marcie Starr sitting cross-legged on the ground, munching on an apple she held in her left hand. Her right hand appeared to be writing or drawing on a pad of paper.

Dean was just thinking about heading in that direction to chat with the lady when he saw Gordie stroll toward her. Pausing to think about it, Dean decided that might be the better move. He should probably steer clear of the woman as much as he could. He had enough thoughts about how good Marcie smelled and how lovely she was without actually seeking out her company on purpose. Going down that road would only get him in trouble.

A kind of trouble he didn't need at this point in his life.

WITH a sandwich Dean had given her in her hand, Marcie had purposely chosen to take her lunch break in a spot well away from the group of men, hoping to have some time to herself. She'd walked around the clearing for a while and had finally found a spot with an opening in the trees that offered a clear view of the mountains below. With the sight of the mountain ridges spread under the sky before her, she was finally able to release a sigh of pleasure. Low lying clouds brushed the tops of the mountain ranges which stretched toward the distance. It was a sight Marcie had missed—more than she'd realized.

Untying her flannel shirt from around her waist, she placed it on the ground, then plopped down on it cross-legged and proceeded to scarf down her sandwich in record time. She couldn't believe how hungry she felt and wondered if it had anything to do with the mountain air—or perhaps it was the fact that breakfast—as delicious as it had been—had been a long time ago.

Once her sandwich was gone and she'd guzzled down half of her water, Marcie felt more refreshed and leaned back on her hands to look at the vista below her, and the worries and stress of life seemed to evaporate into the mountain air. It was nice to just enjoy the view for a while without having to think about doing her job.

Munching on an apple she'd brought with her, Marcie dug around in her backpack and pulled out a sketch pad and a small pencil box that held her sharpened sketching pencils. Her fingers almost itched in expectation at the opportunity to draw again.

A Bible verse that had always been one of her favorites came back to her—even though she hadn't picked up a Bible in years. It was funny how things you learned as a child never left you.

I will lift up mine unto the hills, from whence cometh my help. My help cometh from the Lord, which made heaven and earth.

It had been a long time since she'd thought about these mountains and how much they had once meant to her. How she had always felt so close to God in these hills—as if she were somehow closer to Him here. It had been a long time since she'd thought much about Him at all.

With the sound of a woodpecker in the distance, tapping away on what sounded like a hollow tree somewhere deep in the woods, Marcie lowered her head and focused on the blank piece of paper before her. Once the tip of her pencil touched the paper, it was as if the rest of the world disappeared.

Fifteen minutes later, a shadow fell across the page darkening it, and Marcie turned and glanced over her shoulder and up into the sunshine, not sure at first who was standing behind her. Then Gordie dropped down on the grass next to her.

"Purty spot. I can see why you'd wanta draw it."

Marcie looked up from the page and gave the older man a smile. Gordie seemed much quieter and reserved than the rest of Dean's crew, but Marcie figured that was because he was a family man and more mature than the rest of them. Or perhaps it was just who he was.

"I haven't had much time to do any sketching since I moved to D.C." She sighed in contentment. "I've missed it."

Gordie nodded, a wooden toothpick sticking out of the corner of his mouth.

"From what I can see, you got lotsa talent." Motioning toward her pad with his chin, he added. "You should do a lot more a that."

She smiled, although his comment caused a little pain to appear in the region of her heart. For a moment there, Gordie had sounded just like her father.

"Daddy always told me I should be an artist when I grew up," she mumbled.

"Smart man."

She jerked her chin a little in a nod, blinking back the moisture threatening to gather in her eyes. It was so hard being in the mountains again. And being here made it impossible to not think about her father, and how much she missed him.

"Yes. Yes, he was." She swallowed hard, struggling to control her emotions. "Whenever Daddy saw me drawing, I was almost always sketchin' the mountains. I've loved the mountains my whole life." Her lips lifted a little at the memory. It was nice to know not all her memories about this place were painful. "It even got to the point where he started callin' them 'Marcie's Mountains,' 'cause I drew them so often."

It was quiet between the two of them for a few moments. In the silence, Marcie stared out at the view and thought more about her father, and how much she still missed him—even after all these years.

"How long's it been since you've been back?"

Marcie flinched a little at Gordie's question, wondering what had given her away.

"I left ten years ago—when I went to college." She put her pencil away and snapped her sketchpad closed and stuffed it and her pencil box back into her backpack. Suddenly, the urge to draw was gone.

Not wanting to appear rude, but feeling she was all done talking to the man—at least about her past—Marcie stood and brushed sandwich crumbs off her lap, then gave him a little smile as she drew her backpack up over her shoulders.

"I suppose it's time we get back to work."

With that statement, Marcie turned and trudged back up the hill toward the trucks and the cabin, leaving Gordie behind. When she reached the top of the hill, she noticed Dean was headed in her direction. As he walked up to her, he handed something to her.

"I brought you a little fruit for dessert." He gave her a quick smile, and she couldn't help but notice the questioning look on his face as she reached for the banana.

"Thanks."

Marcie felt the scrutiny of Dean's green eyes on her as he fell into step and walked beside her. She hoped he'd leave her alone and not starting questioning her too. She really didn't want to talk to Dean McRae about her feelings any more than she'd wanted to talk to Gordie about them.

"You okay, Marcie?"

She chuckled, blinking back the tears just under the surface.

"You keep asking me that, Dean. Do *you* think I'm okay?"

He laughed outright, and Marcie couldn't help but smile in response, feeling a little of her sadness evaporate and her heart began to lighten. It was hard to be sad when you heard the pleasant sound of Dean McCrae's laughter.

When she came to a stop, Dean turned around and walked backward away from her, but his green eyes never left her face.

"Okay? I'd have to say I think you're much more than just okay, Marcie Starr."

4

"So….why Dutch and Mac? I mean, are those actually your real names?"

Marcie glanced across the table at Gordie. "I can understand Gordie's nickname—since his last name's Gordon. That makes sense, as does 'Mac,' I guess. But I can't quite figure out where the name Dutch comes from and why you'd want to use it instead of your real name."

The four men and Marcie sat around a corner table in a diner half-way between the Hawk's Ridge cabin and Dean's house. They weren't finished at the cabin yet and would have to go back the next day—possible even another one—but on the way down the mountain Dean had told her he was very pleased with the progress they'd made so far. Gordie had left the flatbed truck and forklift on the job site and had ridden to the café with the other two men. Dean had told her that the next day they'd tag the logs and Gordie would start loading the good logs and the rest of the salvageable wood onto the flatbed trailer.

But, before they'd left the work site, Dean had announced to the crew that they would stop and eat on the way home as he was hungry as a bear. Marcie didn't know if she were that hungry, but a hot dinner did sound good to her. It had been a long day, and she hadn't even been doing the physical labor the guys had been.

While Marcie waited for the answer to her question about the guys' names, she heard Dean's quiet chuckle, then Gordie laughed outright as if sharing a private joke. Marcie noticed the red creeping up Dutch's neck and wondered if he'd ever tell her the truth about his name. It couldn't be that bad, could it?

"Might as well fess up, Dutchie. Miz Marcie's a reporter. Reckon, she'll git it outa ya eventually." Gordie folded his arms across his chest and grinned at the young man who sat across the table from them, looking as miserable as possible.

"Oh come on, guys. It can't be *that* bad," Marcie finally mumbled, glancing over at Dean, who gave her one of his little winks. Suddenly she felt a little warmer than usual and seeing his eyes twinkle, she almost lost track of what they'd been talking about.

Finally, Dutch heaved a heavy sigh as if feeling the weight of the world on his shoulders. "For cryin' out loud." Then he released another sigh as if in surrender. "Okay. Well ya see, my momma named me for my great-grandpappy."

He ducked his head, then gave her a sorrowful look that reminded her of an old Bassett hound their neighbors used to have.

"My real name is Clemson Emanuel VanOosterhout. Growin' up, all the family called me Clem. The only one who still calls me that, ma'am, is my momma."

Dutch got a fierce look on his face as he stared at his co-workers in defiance. "Nobody else better call me that neither or they'll be sorry."

Then he gave Marcie a weak smile. "Dutch seemed to sound much better, considerin' my last name and all."

Marcie had to work hard to keep the smile off her face. She'd heard worse names in her life. But Dutch's full name certainly *was* a mouthful.

Clemson Emanuel VanOosterhout

"How about if I just refer to you in the article as Dutch VanOosterhout?"

He gave her what looked like a grateful smile. "I'm much obliged, Miz Marcie."

Trying to take the heat off the young man, she turned to Mac who was sitting to her left. "So, why 'Mac'? I mean, if I remember correctly, your last name starts with that, right?"

Mac wiggled a little in his chair as if he wasn't comfortable with suddenly being the center of attention.

"Yes, ma'am. My last name is Mackenzie. My great-great-great-grandpappy was one of the first settlers around these parts. He came over from Scotland on a ship—a long time ago." He gave her a shy smile. "I don't much like my first name either, so I usually jist go by Mac."

She gave him a little nod. "Okay. Duly noted. You'll be Mac Mackenzie when mentioned in my article." She paused a moment. "But just out of curiosity, what *is* your real name?"

She heard Dutch's giggle, and Gordie let out a little cough behind his hand as if trying to hide a chuckle. Marcie glanced over at Dean and was rewarded with yet another one of his winks.

Mac did a little more wiggling in his chair before he finally lifted his blue eyes to hers.

"It's Ellsworth, ma'am. But I don't never use that name. *Ever.*" He glanced over at Dutch. "Not even my momma dares to call me that anymore!"

Marcie nodded and chewed on the inside of her cheek to keep from smiling. "Got it, Mac. No worries. Your secret is safe with me."

Fortunately, about that time, the waitress brought their food to the table, and after a brief prayer to bless the food (said by Gordie) they all dug in. Now that their names had all been discussed and revealed, the conversation around the table ranged from their current job to what their favorite song was playing over the diner's speakers.

"So what do you think of our little operation, Miz Starr?" Dean asked her when they were about half finished with their meal.

She swallowed the bite of food she'd been chewing and looked across the table at him. His intense green eyes were studying her carefully, and the expression on his face was serious enough Marcie could tell he was genuinely interested in hearing her answer.

"Well, I have to say it's quite unique. I love how y'all have a job—one particular task you're really good at, and that's what you concentrate on doing. It's easy to tell you're a real team, and I have to say, it's a joy seeing you work together."

Marcie was thankful to see nods and smiles on the faces of all the men sitting around the table. She'd meant what she'd said. These four men had a special relationship. Dean was the boss—no question about that. But he treated them all as equal—as brothers. And they worked well together.

"Thank you, ma'am," Gordie finally said after clearing his throat. Then he chuckled. "We're kinda like that show you see on TV. You know, with those guys that go around and save big barns and cabins and rebuild them?"

Dean chuckled. "On a MUCH smaller scale, of course."

The other men laughed before Mac added, "And, of course, we don't have no TV crew followin' us around everywhere with cameras and microphones stuck in our faces all the time. I don't think I'd like that very much!"

Marcie saw all the men's heads nod as if in agreement. Then Dutch piped up.

"But, we're *much* better-lookin' than them guys, though. Don't ya think?"

Laughter rang around the table, and Marcie quickly joined in, feeling more comfortable with the four men accompanying her than she ever could have imagined. They really were good people.

It was nice to know honest and decent, hard-working men like this still existed in the world. She'd about given up hope.

DEAN leaned back in his desk chair in his office and attempted to stretch his back muscles. It had been a long day, but a good one. As long as everything went without a hitch the next day, they'd have another small cabin to add to the Wood Lot. Once they got the cabin back home and re-stacked, Dean would put a photo of it on the website and hopefully, they'd soon have a buyer. He'd already entered some of the information about it into a file on his computer and had tentatively named it the 'Hawk's Ridge Cabin.'

As he raised his arms and placed his hands behind his head, Dean gazed up at the barn trusses and rafters of his office ceiling and replayed how the day had gone. When he'd started pulling the siding off and discovered the cabin wasn't in as terrible shape as he'd first thought, he'd felt incredibly blessed. That didn't happen very often. More often than not, it went the other way and a cabin he'd counted on being one hundred percent, wasn't.

His mind automatically turned to the sight of seeing Marcie Starr wearing that cute little hard hat, walking around the work site with her camera in hand as she watched every move Dean and the boys made. As skeptical as Dean had been about having a woman on-site, he had to admit it had felt kinda nice having her there. Although he'd never admit that feeling to anyone else—especially her.

There was something about the lovely willowy woman that drew him to her and made him want to know her more— find out what made her tick. Dean was more than a little curious about that southern drawl that kept sneaking into her conversation every now and then. Marcie Starr might be living in D.C., but it was clear as day that she wasn't originally from there. If Dean had to guess, he would say Marcie was actually from this part of Tennessee. But, for some unknown reason, she wasn't admitting that.

Yup. There was much more to Marcie Starr than met the eye.

Dean briefly closed his eyes and whispered a quick prayer for the young woman who had been tossed into his life. He couldn't help but feel there was something painful in her life that haunted her. He'd seen a little of it that noon when she'd come back from her resting spot down the hill. Something had almost made her cry, and Dean couldn't help but want to know what that something was so he could make the pain go away.

He also prayed for wisdom to know how to help Marcie overcome whatever it was that had driven her away from these mountains—because somehow or other, Dean was sure she wasn't a stranger to these parts. And he prayed for wisdom for himself so he'd know how to react to the young woman who had caught his eye from the first moment he'd opened his front door to find her standing on his porch.

With a final amen, Dean opened his eyes and released a sigh, and then sat back up straighter in his chair. It would be best if he eliminated that last train of thought right away. Marcie was here on a work assignment for her magazine. That was all. She'd be with him and the boys for two weeks and then would return to her life and her job in Washington, D.C. She lived in the city because that was where she wanted to live. Dean had been down that path before, and there was no way he was ever going down it again because he was certainly finished with living in the city. He wouldn't move back there for anything—or anyone—no matter how cute they might look in a hard hat.

Besides, Dean wasn't a fool. He was reasonably sure Miss Marcie had a man waiting for her back home. He found it impossible to believe someone as cute and smart as she was wouldn't have a boyfriend. So there was no sense in him looking at her in any way other than what she was; a magazine writer here to do an article on his business.

Business. That was all it was. And all it would ever be.

Now if he could just get his brain to agree with him.

THE next morning dawned bright and warm. Before going to bed the night before, Marcie had been sure to set her phone alarm—this time making sure the volume was turned up so she wouldn't sleep through it.

When it went off, she noted it was plenty early, and when she took a deep breath of air through her nose, she didn't smell coffee brewing. Good. This morning, Dean McRae would *not* catch her sleeping late.

After a quick shower and dressing, Marcie was already in the kitchen and had the coffeemaker started when she heard Dean unlock the front door. Marcie couldn't hold back her smile as she stood and listened to him quietly make his way through the Great Room as if afraid he'd wake her. Waiting for his appearance in the kitchen, Marcie leaned with her back against the counter that faced the doorway that led from the main living area of the house to the kitchen. Arms crossed across her stomach, she allowed her lips to turn up in a huge grin.

This morning, she would surprise him.

"Do I smell coffee?" The sound of Dean's voice came through the door before he did, looking much more handsome than a man had a right to look so early in the morning. As he had been the previous day, Dean was dressed in brown work pants along with a worn tan-colored Tennessee Volunteers T-shirt, topped off with a blue and white plaid flannel shirt. His russet red hair was combed neatly, and his face looked like he'd just shaved.

Marcie grinned even wider. "Good morning, Mr. McRae! I actually got to the kitchen before you did this morning—*and*, I already made the coffee."

Dean gave her one of his dimpled grins and strolled over to stand close to where she stood. He reached up to pull a couple of mugs out of the cupboard directly behind her and

Marcie almost held her breath at the feeling of having him stand so close—close enough she caught a pleasant whiff of his spicy aftershave. His whiskers from the previous day were gone, which Marcie almost thought was a shame. She'd kind of liked the rustic look of his dark red whiskers. It had made him look like an untamed mountain man.

After pouring a mug full of coffee, he handed it to her, then poured a second one for himself before he stepped over to stand in front of the stove.

"So, what sounds good this morning, Marcie? Bacon and eggs? Sausage gravy and biscuits? Or maybe pancakes?"

She laughed at the thoughtful look on his face as he stared at the stovetop. Dean McCrae *did* take his food seriously.

"Pancakes sound good. But only if you let me make them."

His bushy right eyebrow went up as looked over at her. Did the man really think she didn't know how to cook? Or perhaps he just didn't trust her in his spotless kitchen.

She slid over closer to where he still stood in front of the stove, unable to resist the temptation to tease and flirt with him a little. Marcie knew she shouldn't. She was here in a professional capacity only—and had no business thinking about how good-looking Dean was. But she *was* only human, after all. And Dean McRae was quite the temptation.

"I'll make you a deal, McRae. You fry up the bacon and sausage, and I'll do pancakes. From scratch."

She stuck out her right hand. "Deal?"

He stared at her hand a few seconds still wearing that look of shock on his face, and for a moment she thought he wasn't going to accept her hand. Then he grabbed it in a firm shake, and the sparkle in his eyes and the dimpled grin on his face returned.

"Oh, lady! You have my permission to cook for me *anytime.*" He frowned a second before adding, "Assuming you *can* cook."

Marcie reached out and lightly punched him in the shoulder.

"I'll have you know my momma taught me how to cook and bake when I was knee-high to a grasshopper, mister."

His laughter let her know he'd only been teasing. Or maybe he was flirting with her just a little. But whatever had just happened between the two of them, Marcie had liked it. Probably a lot more than she should.

By the time Mac and Dutch made their way over from The Barn to the main house, Dean had fried up enough bacon and sausage to cover a platter. And Marcie had just started dropping the batter for the first buttermilk pancakes onto the sizzling griddle Dean had dug out of one of the bottom cupboards. The two men razzed Dean a little about letting a woman into his kitchen. But after Dean said a quick prayer to bless the food and the three men had a chance to take a bite or two of the fluffy thick pancakes stacked on their plates— slathered with butter and covered with thick maple syrup that Dean had told Marcie was made locally—they'd all changed their tune.

"Hey! Yer a pretty good cook, Miz Marcie," Dutch said around bites of sausage and pancakes.

Marcie laughed as she poured a generous amount of maple syrup over her own small stack of pancakes.

"Thanks, Dutch. I take that as a high compliment comin' from you. I *do* realize I have Dean's and his momma's reputations to live up to. So thanks!"

There was more laughter around the table as they all dug into their breakfasts. In a short time, everyone had full stomachs, and the kitchen had been cleaned up from the morning's breakfast preparations. Unlike the previous morning, when Marcie had been running late and had to go back to her room to get ready to leave, Marcie paid close attention to what Dean was doing as they cleaned up. She couldn't help but note that while she was putting the last of the leftover sausage into the refrigerator, Dean was making sandwiches and packing a cooler with lunches again—just as he had the day before.

"I could help with that," she said quietly as she walked over and stood next to him at the counter where he worked. He glanced up at her as he deftly wrapped plastic wrap around another sandwich made with a sub bun and stuffed with meat and veggies.

"I'm almost done with the sandwiches, but if you could grab those two jugs of ice tea out of the frig, that would be great."

Marcie pulled the two jugs from the refrigerator and placed them on the counter next to the stack of sandwiches. There was also a large paper sack she knew was filled with apples, oranges, and bananas. She stood and watched as Dean quickly filled the cooler on the floor with a bag of ice he'd brought from a freezer in a small room off the kitchen. Adding all the foodstuffs to the cooler, he closed the lid with a click, then looked over at her and grinned.

"Well, then. I guess we're ready to go."

With that, Dean easily hefted what Marcie knew had to be a heavy cooler and headed toward the door. She quickly scooted around him so she could get to the door first and hold it open while he walked through, then she ran down the porch steps and lowered the tailgate on the truck for him.

"Do you do this *every* morning?" she asked as he closed the tailgate with a slam.

"Naw. Most of the time we're far enough away from home we just grab a bite someplace at a local diner. But since this job isn't that far from home, I decided to pack our lunches and save us all a little money."

"That's nice of you," Marcie said as she opened the passenger door of his pickup and got in the truck.

Dean got in the driver's side and stuck the key in the ignition and started the truck, then turned and gave her a toothy smile, his eyes twinkling.

"You'll find I'm a really nice guy, Miss Starr—once you take the time to get to know me, that is."

With a chuckle, he put the truck in drive and pulled out of the yard. Marcie glanced back long enough to see the vehicle holding Dutch, Mac, and Gordie following them. Gordie had driven over from his place that morning and had arrived in the kitchen just in time to get the last two pancakes. Even though Gordie had told them when he'd arrived that Sally had already fed him, he'd added with a grin that he just couldn't see letting good food go to waste. It hadn't taken him long to finish off the leftovers.

Once they reached the main road, Dean turned in a different direction from where they'd gone the previous day. Marcie noted the other truck didn't follow them and glanced over at Dean feeling confused.

"I thought we were headed back to Hawk's Ridge."

He gave her a small smile. "We are. But I need to fill this baby up with gas first, or else we'll be walking down that mountain."

Marcie gave a nod, then relaxed against the back of her seat and decided to enjoy the view. Not doing the driving was rather enjoyable as it allowed her to really look at the beautiful scenery around her. As they drove down the mountainside and into a valley where a small town was located, Marcie sat up a little straighter as her heart dropped to her stomach. It was a small town she knew all too well.

Swallowing hard, Marcie steeled herself as they hit the road that would take them through the central downtown district—although it wasn't much of a downtown. Just a couple of blocks of tall brick buildings that housed an insurance office, a doctor's office, the community library, the hardware store her father had once owned, and several other shops and stores. She'd been gone ten years, and yet the small town didn't look much different from when she'd left. The two churches in town were still there—each one sitting on opposite ends of town almost acting as guardhouses to protect the community from the outside world. At one time, she'd loved the places she now saw outside the truck's window. But now…seeing it all again only brought her pain. She'd lost so much here.

"Kinda quiet over there. You okay, Marcie?"

Trying to swallow back the emotions threatening to spill over in tears, Marcie nodded.

"Just fine," she finally croaked out.

Dean pulled his truck into the small gas station at the other end of town, and Marcie felt like scrunching down in the seat, hoping no one would be around that might recognize her. It had been years since she'd left the area, so chances were no one would even remember her. Nonetheless, being back in her old hometown made her unspeakably nervous.

"I'll just fill 'er up, and we can get back on the road."

He gave her a glance that Marcie easily read. His mind was probably filled with questions about her strange actions, but thankfully Dean McRae was too much of a gentleman to ask them. Which was a good thing. Because there was no way Marcie was going to talk to Dean or anyone else about the gamut of emotions rushing through her at being back in her hometown again.

5

After paying for the gas, Dean exited the gas station, keeping his eyes trained on the woman sitting in the cab of his truck. Marcie had started acting strange the moment he'd turned toward town and was now scooched down so far in the seat, it was almost as if she was trying to hide from somebody. And perhaps she was.

As he reached his door and tugged it open, he gave a little shake of his head. He would never understand women, but thankfully, he didn't have to. This one was only along for the ride and would be gone and out of his hair in two weeks.

He also didn't have to be a psychic to notice that once they'd left the city limits and started to drive the roads leading back up the mountain to Hawk's Ridge, the woman seated beside him visibly relaxed. Dean could almost hear an audible sigh from her the further they climbed up into the hills. A part of him wanted to ask her what her deal was, but the other part of him understood it was none of his business. That didn't mean he didn't want to ask the question, though.

When they reached the work site, and he pulled in and parked the truck, Dean was glad to see Mac and Gordie already up on ladders, getting ready to tag logs. Dutch was inside the cabin pulling off the remaining floorboards, hauling them out, and stacking them to the side. Later they'd be hauled back to the Wood Lot. Dutch would also be working clean-up duty, picking up the pieces of wallboard and siding they'd ripped off the walls the day before and dumping them into the trailer the guys had hauled up this morning. The trailer load would be taken back to the Wood Lot and sorted through and what couldn't be used would be burned or taken to the dump.

After unfastening his seatbelt, Dean glanced over at Marcie, who turned her head and gave him a little smile. He smiled in return, noting the stress he'd read on her face earlier had disappeared.

"Ready for another exciting day, Miz Starr?"

"Ready as I can be. I promise I'll try to stay out of the way, but please keep me in the loop as to what you're doing and why so I can take notes."

He grinned. It looked like Marcie was back to business, which was just fine with him.

"Yes, ma'am."

TUGGING her hard hat out from behind the truck seat, Marcie plopped it on her head and followed Dean up the small rise to the grassy area in front of the cabin. The relief she felt at being back on top of the mountain was almost unbelievable. She'd been so stressed out while she'd waited in the truck for Dean to pay for his gas, Marcie had thought she was going to throw up.

It had been difficult enough for her to come back to this area of Tennessee, but Marcie had somehow hoped she'd be able to avoid actually seeing her old hometown. As she'd sat and waited for what felt like years for Dean to fill his truck with gas and pay for it, memories of Marcie's childhood had engulfed her.

She had some happy years in that town. And there had been some years that hadn't been so great. Those were the ones that had driven her away, and they were the reasons she'd never returned.

Taking a big breath of the fresh mountain air into her lungs, Marcie tried to calm herself by concentrating on the job ahead of her. Instead of thinking about her panic attack back in town, Marcie focused on taking photos of Gordie and Mac at work. They were both up on ladders, nailing numbered tags on both ends of each log of the structure. As they worked, the two men called down lengths of logs and tag numbers to Dean who appeared to be writing all the information down in a book he'd brought from his truck.

She snapped a shot of Dean from the side, then walked over and stood next to him, hoping she'd get the chance to peer over his shoulder without him noticing she was there. But that didn't work. As if sensing her presence, Dean turned and gave her a smile, his green eyes gazing into hers for a moment. After her paranoid behavior back at the gas station, Dean was more than likely trying to figure out if she was losing her mind. Well, she couldn't blame him. Her actions back in town had been slightly out of control. He probably thought there was something seriously wrong with her.

He finally shifted the open book he was holding so she could see what he was doing. A series of numbers and letters filled one page, and on the opposite page, he'd drawn a sketch of the cabin.

"I'll take photos too before we start dismantling it, but this sketch is crucial. It, along with the dimensions and tag information, will tell us how to put the cabin back together."

He grinned at her again, and Marcie couldn't help but smile back. His joy at doing his job was infectious.

"Imagine tryin' to build a Lincoln log cabin without any instructions. This is sorta like that—only on a MUCH larger scale."

Marcie nodded and smiled a little, then stepped away as the other two men continued to call out tag information and lengths of logs for Dean to write down. She didn't want to interfere in their work, but she *did* want to be aware of everything they were doing—and why. It was fascinating to watch the team work together. And Dean was correct; it was going to be like taking down a life-size Lincoln log house and moving it someplace else before reassembling it.

It took most of the morning for the guys to tag the logs. Once the tags were all attached to the logs and Dean had taken about a dozen photos of the structure with his cell phone, Gordie climbed into the cab of the forklift truck and fired it up. Mac and Dutch moved all but two of the ladders from the structure, remaining on those as they called out instructions to Gordie about moving the upper logs.

Marcie was standing off to the side, snapping as many photos of the proceedings as she could, when Dean strolled across the yard toward her.

"You'll need to back up some, Marcie."

She felt his hand come to rest on her back as he steered her away from the area. She went with him, although a part of her had wanted to be closer to the action. She guessed she understood Dean's concern, though. If anything were to happen to her or anyone else on the job, it was on his head. After they'd moved back quite a ways, he stopped and turned her back toward the cabin, his hand still resting on her shoulder as if to make sure he had her attention.

"Now pay close attention. This is where Gordie earns his keep."

She did watch, almost mesmerized as Gordie slowly and carefully removed the upper logs of the structure one at a time, placing them in turn on the flatbed of the big truck trailer he'd driven up the mountain the previous day.

"Is he going to be able to get all of them on there—and still get the forklift on there too?"

Dean turned toward her, shaking his head.

"Naw. He'll take a load down tonight, and him and the boys will come back in the morning and finish getting the shorter logs and clean up the rest of the site."

He continued to gaze at her a moment, and Marcie felt her face grow warm under his scrutiny, wondering suddenly if she had a smudge on her nose or something.

"And while they're doin' that, you and me are headin' out on a field trip tomorrow."

"What field trip?"

He gave her one of those heart-stopping smiles, then turned to look back toward the forklift as Gordie continued to move logs from the cabin to the flatbed.

"Yup." Dean gave her a little pat on her left shoulder before he walked away, calling over his shoulder. "Be ready to leave right after breakfast, young lady. You and me—we have places to go, and people to see."

DEAN finished packing the cooler with lunch and some snack food for the guys, then snapped the lid shut with a sense of accomplishment. Gordie, Mac, and Dutch were already at the door, pulling on their boots and readying to leave.

Miss Marcie Starr, on the other hand, had yet to appear at the breakfast table.

As early as she'd risen the day before—even beating Dean to the kitchen—he was starting to get worried about her. He was beginning to wonder if he should knock on her door and check if she was sick or something. After the strange way she'd acted the previous day when they'd been in town, Dean was starting to think something weird was going on with her.

The other three men quietly said their goodbyes and headed out the door, leaving Dean still standing and staring at her bedroom door, and wondering what to do next. He needed to get on the road too—even if Marcie wasn't going with him. The schedule for his day was very full.

The sound of the fellas starting their trucks must have finally awoken the sleeping princess, though, because the vehicles had no more than pulled out of the yard when the door to Marcie's bedroom flew open and a much-disheveled woman appeared. Dean stood leaning against one of the kitchen counters with his arms folded across his chest and watched Marcie's face as she stood in her bedroom doorway, still dressed in what looked like flannel pajamas with cute little pink bunnies on them. Her black hair hung in disarray, but Dean couldn't help but notice how even the first thing in the morning, the woman was gorgeous. More than gorgeous.

He watched as her expression quickly went from panic to embarrassment when she realized Dean was standing there staring at her.

"Oh, my gosh! Dean, I'm so sorry! I overslept." She pushed her long black hair out of her eyes, and the expression on her face went from embarrassment to looking like she was about to cry.

"Well, good morning, princess." He gave her a smile and tried to calm his heart rate as he stared at the beautiful woman standing barefoot in front of him. How could someone look that good after just rolling out of bed?

"You have exactly fifteen minutes to get yourself out here and eat some breakfast. We leave in thirty."

Dean knew his voice had been rather terse, but the sight of her looking so vulnerable and cute had totally unnerved him. He watched as Marcie gulped and her cheeks turned beet red. Then she gave him a quick nod before she turned and went back into her bedroom, quietly closing the door behind her.

After her departure, Dean finally allowed himself to smile. That had actually been fun, although he was sure Miss Starr wouldn't have agreed with him.

Ten minutes later, a very calm, collected, and entirely professional Marcie Starr opened her bedroom door, dressed and ready to go. She dropped her backpack on the end of the kitchen counter and strolled over and poured herself a cup of coffee and took a sip. Then and only then did she turn and look at Dean who was sitting at the table, reading through the notes he'd made on the cabin on Hawk's Ridge.

"I'm really sorry, Dean. I can't believe I overslept. There must be something about this mountain air that knocks me out."

He gave her a nod and forced himself not to smile as he took in the look of embarrassment she still wore on her face. Dean supposed he could make a big deal out of it, but it wasn't as if they had an appointment to keep someplace. He'd just wanted to get an earlier start than they were going to get.

"Those things happen." He cleared his throat, not wanting to appear too gruff, and pointed to the cabinet behind her. "There's cereal in there, or if you want toast, there's a loaf of bread on the counter. There are also energy bars in the cabinet—and some fruit in the frig."

She gave a little nod. "Thank you."

He watched Marcie fix two slices of toast before grabbing the jar of strawberry jam out of the refrigerator. It didn't take her long, and she'd inhaled her food. He was happy to see she also grabbed an apple and an orange from his supply of fruit and stuffed them in her backpack before she pulled it over her shoulder.

"I'm ready to go, boss man."

Dean held back his smile and grabbed his truck keys, hearing her boots clunking behind him as they left the house and went to get in the truck. His morning hadn't started out the way he'd planned, but that was okay. Somehow seeing Marcie standing in her bedroom doorway, wearing those darling bunny pajamas had been worth the late start.

It was silent between the two of them for several miles, but once they reached the main highway, he turned to find Marcie's gaze on him.

"So, where are we off to this morning, boss?"

He chuckled, loving the nickname she'd assigned him rolling off her tongue. Somehow it tickled him to hear her call him that.

"I need to check out a couple of possible future jobs."

He glanced over at her long enough to see she was looking at him as if she were genuinely interested in his answer. Then he turned his eyes back on the road, even though he'd really rather watch her. But driving down the road wasn't the time to do that. He stretched his shoulders and tried to get his mind back on his plans for the day.

"Every now and then, my business requires I leave the actual work to the guys and go hunt up other jobs. We don't have the resources to travel long distances, but whenever I get a chance, I drive the back roads, looking for old structures people might not want anymore. I've found some terrific bargains over the years by doing that. Or I follow up on calls people have made, telling me they have a structure they want me to come to look at and see if I would be interested in either buying it from them or tearing it down for parts. That's what we're going to do today."

"Are they all money makers?"

Dean chuckled. He wished.

"Unfortunately, no. Every now and then I guess wrong, and it's a painful lesson that reminds me to be more cautious in the future. Once in a while, though, a place really draws me in—wondering about its history—and I can't help wanting to save it."

"For instance…"

Marcie's eyes momentarily locked on his when Dean took a moment to glance over at her. More than likely whatever he told her was going to find its way into her article, so Dean wanted to make sure he explained it in a way that she would understand. But how was he going to do that? How was he going to tell this woman from the city sitting in the truck cab next to him the emotions that rushed through him when he first saw an old cabin—sitting out in the middle of the hills— untouched and ignored—often for decades? A cabin that once upon a time had been home to some family. A place that had meant everything to them.

"Well, there was this one job we did in West Virginia—it was shortly after I started the business. A young couple new to the area contacted me and told me they'd bought this old farmhouse and wanted to tear off a section of it to add a solarium. They knew there was an old log cabin underneath the siding, so I went and checked it out and thought we could do the job. No problem.

"When the guys and I actually got there and started tearing wallboard off, we discovered logs underneath all right. But what we discovered wasn't exactly what we expected. For one thing, those logs were fourteen inches wide and almost thirty feet long—*much* bigger than we thought."

He shook his head as he recalled that day. Dean couldn't even begin to imagine the work that man had done to build that cabin. Cutting down and cleaning those trees alone had to have been a huge job. And then to lift those monstrous logs into place…he couldn't possibly have done it alone.

Dean felt the warmth in his chest as he remembered the feeling he'd gotten the next day when he'd found the date '1820' carved into one of the logs around the fireplace. He'd traced the numbers with his fingertips, and it suddenly felt as if he'd traveled back in time. Dean had sat back on his haunches and said a little prayer of thanks for the opportunity that had been given him and the boys to save that magnificent structure.

"I did a little research and found out that cabin had been built by one of the earliest settlers in that area—back in 1820! And that date was actually carved into one of the logs. The owners did more research and learned the original cabin had been built onto four times. Because of that, it was so camouflaged we couldn't tell how big it actually was until we started tearing it apart."

Dean shook his head as the memories of that day came back to him. He'd never forgotten the feeling of standing in the middle of that cabin when they'd totally uncovered the logs. It had been like standing in a piece of history.

"I thought after we found out about the cabin, that maybe the owners would change their mind and decide they didn't want to sell it after all. But they didn't want it left there, so we took it down."

He smiled over at her. "When we resold that cabin we made the biggest profit on it than I've ever made on another one since. A retired couple bought it and had us restore it at a lake as a summer place for them and their family, not too many miles from where it was originally built. The woman was really into historic preservation and filled the cabin with pieces from the early 1800s—the time period when it was built. The boys and I went back and visited them and saw it once they had it finished and had moved in. That was an awesome experience."

6

Marcie watched Dean's face as he told her about the 1820's cabin they'd moved and restored. His green eyes sparkled with excitement as he recalled it all, and it was easy to tell Dean McRae loved what he did—with a passion.

She couldn't help the little stab of jealousy that shot through her at that realization. Would she ever feel that way about her job? Oh, most of the time she enjoyed the writing and the research, and she certainly appreciated the paycheck. But it wasn't like it was with Dean—she could tell. He *loved* what he did, and she would bet he bounded out of bed every morning filled with excitement—more than ready to do it all again.

Getting to where she was in life hadn't been easy for Marcie. She'd worked hard to get through college and gain her degree, but she'd managed to complete it and even double-majored in English and History with a minor in Accounting. The Accounting degree had been a decision she'd made in the middle of her sophomore year, figuring that would always be a skill she could fall back on if needed.

When she'd graduated, she hadn't really known what she wanted to do—other than she hadn't wanted to be a teacher. So Marcie had applied to several rather generic positions and then landed the job with the magazine. She'd thrown herself into it head first, and worked hard in an attempt to move up in the organization.

But to Marcie, it wasn't anything more than a job. And that was all it was ever going to be to her. A job. It wasn't a passion. The work she did for the magazine didn't set her heart racing in excitement or put a sparkle in her eyes the way Dean's business did for him. She'd never thought about it before until she'd met Dean and seen his work ethic and approach to his business, but there was a vast difference between having a job and loving a job.

"So, anyway," Dean's deep voice continued. "I'm always on the lookout for another place like that—a surprise just waiting for us to find it and re-tell its story." He glanced over and grinned at her with that beautiful smile that showed off his cute dimples to the max. "But, of course, those opportunities are few and far between."

"Of course," Marcie murmured, feeling she needed to respond—with something. She'd been quiet for the entire length of Dean's story—almost mesmerized as he retold how it had been that first moment when he'd discovered the date '1820.' How cool was that!

"How did you get into this business anyway? I mean, what happened that made you decide you wanted to do this the rest of your life? Surely there are easier ways to make a living."

"Well," Dean's deep voice drawled out the word as if he were trying to think how to start. Or maybe he was stalling as he tried to decide how much to tell her.

"I've already told you I worked in California for a couple of years before I came back here. I'll admit, I was a little lost when I first returned as I didn't know what I was going to do with myself. It was shortly after my dad had passed away, and I just knew I needed to be back in Tennessee. I brought my mom back to this area and settled her in, but I had no idea where to go or what to do next. And there aren't too many opportunities for architectural engineers—especially for modern structures—in this part of the country—even in the larger cities."

She watched as a gentle smile swept across his face.

"Then one day, my brother was visiting—that's Nick. He's married and lives in southern Indiana and owns a landscape business. Anyway, Nick and I were driving into town one day with my niece Katie—that's his littlest girl—who was riding in the back seat of Nick's car." Dean's eyebrows came together as if he were thinking. "She must a-been—oh, about four years old back then. Anyway, we were out on one of the back roads in the hills, and Katie pointed out the window toward this barn that was fallin' over and said, 'That's a terry barn, Uncle Dean, and somebody needs to be a-tear-ing it down.' Well, of course, Nick and I cracked up at her cute little sayin', but it got me thinking. What *was* going to happen to the hundreds of structures—old barns, and cabins, and sheds—that are strung out all over the valleys and mountains? Are they just going to sit there and deteriorate and rot until they all disappear? I found myself really bothered at that notion."

He glanced over at her long enough that Marcie could read the thoughtful expression on his face. There it was again—that passion she'd seen earlier.

"I mean, think about it; those buildings are this country's past—our history. And if we don't do something now to save them and the history that surrounds them, they'll be gone forever. And I just couldn't see lettin' that happen."

Dean turned toward her long enough to give her a crooked smile. "That was when I decided what I wanted to do when I grew up."

He chuckled. "It was pretty rough the first year or so while I got my feet under me. It's one thing when you work for someone else in a business. You go to work every day and do what you're told and go home at night and enjoy your weekends and forget it all. It's entirely different when you have to run the business yourself and deal with employees, and taxes, and payroll, and insurance, and all the worries and stress that comes with it.

"But now—I wouldn't want to do anything else with my life. I love it."

"I can tell," Marcie murmured, all the time wishing she'd thought to take a photo of Dean while he was telling her his story. The expression on his face as he recounted the beginnings of *McRae's Recycled Logs and Materials* told it all. She hoped she would somehow be able to recapture that passion for his business when it came down to writing the article.

"So, Miss Starr, turnabout's fair play. What got you started writing for this magazine you work for?"

Marcie gave him what felt like a weak smile and struggled to swallow the lump that had suddenly appeared in her throat as she tried to come up with something to say. How could she tell Dean about her choice to get into the magazine business without sharing where she had formerly come from?

"Well, when I graduated from college, I knew I wanted a job in the city. Someplace where I could make a name for myself."

She almost snorted when her brain replayed her words. It sounded like she was saying this job at the magazine was big-time or something. But Marcie knew she was just a minor cog in a wheel made up of other people with much more influence and experience than she had. Most days, she was thankful to have a job at all—one that more than supplied income to pay for the expensive little apartment she had outside D.C. and the nice vehicle she drove. When she'd gone to college, she'd been determined to make it, though—and live someplace in a city, far away from everything her former life had represented, and Marcie guessed she had accomplished that.

"So, have you?"

Dean's voice brought her back to the present, and it took her a few seconds to remember what she'd told him about making a name for herself.

"Well, I do get my name on articles every now and then. Getting a byline is a big deal, and I'm very thankful to Mr. Avery for allowing me this current opportunity."

She gave Dean a smile, hoping to sound professional. "I promise to do a good job for the magazine and you on this piece, Dean. I want to let people know about your business—why you do what you do, and why you're so good at it. Hopefully, our readers will find my article inspiring and informative, and will bring you even more clients."

His green eyes studied her for a few seconds before turning back to the road.

"Thank you." Dean's voice was hushed as he responded to her rather flippant-sounding speech. Thinking back on what she'd said, Marcie felt her face grow warm. She had made it sound as if the article was more about her than what it could do for his business—and that wasn't her intention at all. She hoped Dean didn't think she was really that kind of person, but she couldn't erase the words she'd already spoken.

It was silent between the two of them for several more miles. Then Dean flipped on the turn signal and took an exit for Sweetwater.

"I'm goin' here to look at a barn nearby—check it out and see if it's a possibility for us or not. The owner called me a couple of weeks ago and said I could tear it down for parts if I wanted. But I have to see if it's financially feasible first."

He released a deep chuckle. "That's a lot of 'f's' in one sentence."

Marcie laughed along with Dean, feeling the earlier seriousness of their conversation dissipate. Dean was back in entertainment mode. Well, there was no way he needed to know it, but Dean McRae was definitely an entertaining man, and he certainly had her attention.

DEAN drove his truck into the driveway of an old farm—noting the faded white paint on the two-story farmhouse in front of them. The owner had sounded like he was in his retirement years and was readying the farm to sell. Thus, he'd called *McRae's* and wanted to know if Dean would be interested in taking down their old hip-roof barn. Dean could see the barn in the distance—sitting way back behind the house. Even from the driveway, it looked in pretty bad shape, and Dean's heart immediately dropped. The photo Mr. Cavanaugh had emailed him apparently hadn't been a recent one.

The truck's engine had no more than stopped when Dean saw the back door of the house open. An elderly gentleman wearing faded bib overalls and walking with a cane carefully came down the back steps. Dean looked over at Marcie who gave him a questioning look. He reached down with his left hand and started to open his truck door.

"You can wait in the truck if you'd rather, Marcie."

At her quick nod, Dean got out of the truck and turned to meet the homeowner who was approaching him with his hand outstretched.

"Mr. McRae?" the older man asked, his voice as shaky as the rest of him.

Dean smiled at the silver-haired man and shook the offered hand. "Dean McRae, sir. You must be Mr. Cavanaugh. It's a pleasure to meet ya."

Mr. Cavanaugh smiled, the wrinkles around his eyes crinkling even more. "Thanks for comin' out and givin' the old barn a look-see." He pointed in the general direction of the structure. "It's not in the besta shape, but maybe you can get somethin' out of it."

Nodding, Dean glanced over his shoulder at the structure and flinched inwardly, knowing he was more than likely going to have to disappoint this nice man by telling him he couldn't afford to tear it down for him. But Dean prayed he was wrong.

"Well, let me take a look at it, Mr. Cavanaugh. I can't tell from here whether it's worth me tearing it down or not, but I'll go check it out and then I'll give ya my decision. Okay?"

"Fair 'nough, young man. I 'ppreciate it." The elderly man gave a little wave as he slowly headed back toward the house.

"I'll be inside. Just give a knock on the back door when yer done."

Dean nodded and hurried back to the truck. Perhaps he was wrong. Maybe when he actually saw the barn, it wouldn't be as bad as he thought.

He shot Marcie a quick smile as he got back in the truck and drove down a narrow lane leading behind the house and through the barnyard and brought the truck to a stop. It was as close as he could get to the structure which sat in an open field. At one time, the area around the barn had probably been more easily accessible, but it was easy to tell this barn hadn't been used in many years and with livestock and fences long gone, nature had quickly reclaimed the area.

Dean glanced over at Marcie who had been sitting quietly in her seat all this time.

"You ready to wade through some weeds?"

Surprisingly, she gave him a big grin and a nod, her dark eyes sparkling. "Yup. Just let me don my hard hat, and I'll be ready to follow you anywhere."

Dean got out of the truck and waded through the high grass, praying he and Marcie wouldn't run into any snakes. She might have said she'd follow him anywhere, but this looked like it was going to be rather rough going. Obviously, no one had recently been trekking back and forth from the house to the barn in a long time—probably years, by the looks of the brush and tall weeds taking over the area. He glanced behind him once long enough to see Marcie trailing close behind him, following his steps carefully and keeping her eyes glued to the ground—probably watching out for the same thing he was.

Once they reached the structure, Dean paused in front of the open doorway and waited for her to catch up.

"Let me go in first and make sure it's safe. Sometimes the floors are unstable, and by the looks of this barn, I'm a little skeptical about you wandering around too much on your own."

She pushed a few stray strands of hair off her face and gave him a nod, and Dean turned around and pushed the old sliding doors open and stepped into the barn. The smell of straw and wet wood immediately tickled his nose as he entered the old structure. He cautiously trod on several of the floorboards to test them, and since they seemed sturdy enough, finally motioned for Marcie to follow him in.

"Just stay right behind me, okay?"

Marcie gave him a nod, her eyes already looking around the inside of the structure.

"Kind of exciting, huh?"

Dean snorted. Exciting wasn't the word he would use—especially if one of them fell through a rotten board someplace.

"Just be careful, Marcie. Please."

He heard Marcie giggle behind him and curbed the temptation to roll his eyes, then grinned—even though he knew with her behind him, there was no way she'd be able to see him do either. Dean stopped in the center of the main floor of the barn to get a better look at the interior of the old barn. Half the roof was gone, allowing plenty of light into the building which painfully showed the years of neglect. It wasn't a large barn, but it was big enough it would be a lot of man-hours and muscle to take it down.

"Okay," Dean turned around, almost toppling Marcie who was directly behind him—much closer than he'd thought. He automatically reached out and grabbed hold of her arms and helped her regain her balance.

"Sorry." He gave her what he hoped was an apologetic look, then directed her to follow him back out into the sunshine.

"I've seen enough of the inside, now I need to walk around the perimeter." Dean frowned. "You're welcome to wait here, Marcie. The weeds and brush are fairly thick all the way around it, and I don't want you to get bit by a snake or attacked by a hive of angry bees or anything."

Dean watched her chew on her lower lip while she listened to him tell her just some of the dangers of following him.

"I'll wait here if that's okay with you."

He nodded. Good choice. At least he'd be able to concentrate on what he was here for and not have to worry about something happening to her.

"It won't take long."

Pulling a small notepad out of his shirt pocket along with the stub of a pencil, Dean walked around the outside of the barn, noting approximate square footage and how much of the siding was salvageable and how much wasn't. The more he saw, the more Dean's spirits sank. He hated to disappoint Mr. Cavanaugh, but tearing down this barn—even for parts—wasn't going to be feasible. It would be too costly for what little useable material they'd get out of it. Probably two-thirds of the siding wasn't salvageable, and even the large beams inside looked as if termites had moved in. The old building just wasn't worth it. How he wished they'd contacted him several years earlier. Perhaps it would have been worth saving back then.

Dean finished his walk around the barn and met Marcie, where she waited near the truck. Shooting a quick smile to her across the vehicle's hood, he tugged open the driver's side door.

"Guess I'm ready to go give Mr. Cavanaugh the verdict."

Marcie got in on her side of the truck and glanced over at him, her face filled with concern.

"You aren't going to be able to take it down for him." It was a statement, not a question.

Feeling disappoint—not only for a wasted trip but also for not finding something worth their time—Dean shook his head, his jaw clenched.

"Nope. It's just in too bad a shape. It would cost us more to tear it down and transport what little we could get out of it than what it's worth. I wished he'd called me a couple of years ago. We might have been able to save it back then."

"That's too bad," she murmured, echoing his feelings.

As he drove back through the weeds toward the farmhouse to tell Mr. Cavanagh his decision, Dean nodded in agreement, feeling a small spot of pain in his chest. It was one old structure he wouldn't be able to save.

"Yeah, it is."

7

After a quick lunch at a small restaurant in Stillwater, Dean and Marcie were back on the road. Dean informed Marcie that this time they were going to check out a small cabin the owners wanted to sell.

"So, tell me what you like about being a magazine writer?"

Marcie turned her gaze from the scenery passing by to admire Dean's profile while she thought about how to best answer his question. He was a good-looking man, and the best part was, unlike most of the handsome men she knew back in D.C., Dean McRae didn't appear to realize it. He was either completely unaware of how attractive he was or it just plain didn't matter to him. If she had to guess, in Dean's case, it was the latter.

"There's not much to tell," she finally replied. What she did at the magazine wasn't all that exciting. It was just a job. It certainly wasn't as impressive as what Dean did for a living.

"Sure there is," he said after tossing her a grin. "Is that what you always wanted to be when you were growing up—a writer?"

Marcie paused a moment before answering and chewed on her lower lip as a faint wisp of a memory came to her. She had been sitting at the edge of the woods back of their house, drawing the mountain ranges in the distance on an old sketch pad she'd bought at a garage sale for a dime. She'd probably been about ten or eleven years old at the time. That was the day she'd discovered how much she loved to draw. And until she'd sat up on Hawk's Ridge the previous day and pulled out her sketch pad and pencils, she'd forgotten exactly how much she loved it.

I'm going to be an artist when I grow up, Daddy.

"Not really."

Marcie sighed and tried to make the pain in the region of her heart go away, all the time wondering how to get Dean to let go of this train of questioning. She knew he was more than likely just making polite conversation, but it was leading down a road she didn't want to go.

"So what *did* you want to be?"

She sighed again. The man was relentless. Couldn't he tell she didn't want to talk about this?

"If you really must know, I had a crazy notion that I wanted to be an artist when I was little, but now it really doesn't matter. Our childhood dreams don't really mean anything." She glanced over at him. "I mean, you didn't want to own a log restoration business when you were a little boy, did you?"

He laughed, and the sound lessened some of Marcie's unease with the direction their conversation had been going.

"Believe it or not, Marcie Starr, I wanted to be an NFL football player."

Marcie couldn't hold back her grin, causing her to wonder what little red-headed Dean McCrae had been like as a child. Probably a handful of energy and trouble. She truly hoped she'd get the opportunity to meet his mother before she went back home. LizBeth McRae had to be somebody special to have raised this man.

She chuckled. "I can believe that. So, you didn't follow that dream, did you?"

He turned his head long enough to give her one of his winks.

"Not yet, but there's still time, Miz Starr. There's still time."

She released a nervous laugh that came out sounding more like a snort, then covered her mouth with her hand as embarrassment swept over her. She hadn't laughed like that in years. What must the man think of her? But Dean just grinned at her like a silly schoolboy and kept driving, while Marcie gulped and tried desperately to disappear into her side of the truck cab.

A short time later, Dean turned the truck onto a narrow dirt lane to the right of the road that led down a hill into a small hollow. Marcie gazed out the window as a sense of nostalgia swept over her. There was a main house with a few small outbuildings and a little fenced-in pasture where a couple of worn-out looking horses grazed. The scene actually reminded Marcie of her grandparent's place back in the mountains where they used to visit when she was a little girl. They'd gone to her Granddad's and Memaw's small farm every Easter, Thanksgiving, and Christmas. And Marcie had spent at least a week of every summer there until she was twelve. Then her grandad had passed away, and her grandmother had moved into a small house in town. Memaw had passed away the year Marcie had graduated from high school.

Dean slowed the truck when they reached the small white clapboard house at the end of the drive and put the vehicle into park and shut off the engine. As he had at the farmhouse, he glanced over at her before he exited the truck.

"I'll be just a minute."

Marcie gave him a nod, more than willing to wait in the truck when she saw the large hound dog come running around the side of the house, barking like crazy. Dean kept walking up the front steps of the house onto the little porch as if he wasn't even aware of the dog that sniffed and circled his legs. Marcie shivered and stared and wondered how he managed to not be afraid of anything.

Dean McRae was something else.

A man about Dean's age finally came to the door, yelling at the dog which caused it to jump off the porch and slink behind the house again. Once the dog had left the area, Marcie released a sigh of relief, although there was no way she was getting out of the truck as long as that dog was still around. Big dogs terrified her. For that matter, so did little dogs. She'd never understood why she was so frightened of them, but it was a real fear, and so far she hadn't been able to overcome it.

She watched the man as he stood and talked to Dean. He was wearing worn jeans and an old T-shirt that barely covered his belly. His hair was cut neatly though, and at least he was wearing shoes. Marcie shook her head as she realized how terrible her thoughts sounded—even to herself. She was judging the man by the way he was dressed, and she had no right. She didn't even know him.

The other man continued to wave his arms around and pointed in back of the house a couple of times. Marcie sighed as she continued to wait while she assumed the gentleman gave Dean directions to wherever this cabin was located they were here to see.

While she waited, Marcie thought more about the process Dean went through to find cabins and barns. It was a lot of work, and like it had been at the last place, they didn't all pan out. She still felt terrible for the Cavanaughs but understood Dean's decision to not tear down their barn. He was running a business, after all.

A few moments later, Marcie saw Dean reach out and shake the other man's hand, then watched as he strode back to the truck in that self-assured way he had—his shoulders wide and his back straight.

Dean threw her a grin and a wink as he got in, snapped on his seatbelt, and started the engine.

"It's a good thing this truck has four-wheel drive. I'm thinkin' we're gonna need it."

Marcie held onto the dashboard as Dean drove back of the house, following a faint grass-covered path running along a line of woods. He drove slowly, and she could tell he was trying to avoid the deeper ruts and rocks in the track, but it didn't seem to matter. Even as slow as they were going, the truck rattled and shook and Marcie felt out of control as she bounced around every time the truck hit a bump.

"How far is it?" she finally managed to ask through clenched teeth.

Dean chuckled and took a second to glance over at her.

"Farther than I'd like, but I'll try and take it slow. Just hang in there. We'll make it." He gave her another crooked grin. "Sometimes you gotta take the old roads, sit with the old dogs, and listen to the old folks. It reminds you to slow down in this hurry-up world of ours." He gave her a toothy grin and added, "And you never know what's waitin' for ya 'round the next corner."

Marcie gave Dean what she was positive looked like a weak smile, then held onto the door handle a little tighter. He could be as philosophical as he wanted, but he wasn't the one being jostled all over the place. Just when she thought her teeth were going to rattle out of her mouth, the path turned sharply to the left and they entered a small clearing in the trees.

That was when Marcie saw it. Sitting in a shaft of light shining down through the treetops sat the sweetest little log cabin Marcie had ever seen.

Dean hit the brakes, and as the truck came to a sudden stop, Marcie heard his intake of breath.

"Wow."

He turned to look over at her at the same time she turned to look at him—and she was sure her face held the same look of awe and disbelief his did.

"Are they *giving* it to you?"

Dean shook his head as he took his foot off the brake and drove the truck a little closer, put it in Park, and shut off the engine.

"No. But the price they're asking is low. If it turns out to be as good as it looks, I think this one is a job we can afford to take."

He took a deep breath, and then she heard him release it slowly. It was almost as if he was trying to temper his excitement—just in case. She saw Dean close his eyes for a moment, tipping his head back as if in prayer. Then his eyes popped open, and he turned toward her, giving her one of his signature winks and a huge grin.

"Let's go check it out!"

DEAN unbuckled his seat belt and hopped out of the truck, the adrenaline of seeing the cabin for the first time still rushing through him. The structure appeared to be in great shape, but he tried to rein in his enthusiasm. He needed to check it out carefully before he got too carried away. He'd learned the hard way that things weren't always as they appeared.

Sensing Marcie behind him with her ever-present camera in her hands, Dean strode the short distance to the front door of the cabin. Before he reached it, though, Dean glanced up at the roof, noting it was metal. That was more than likely one of the reasons the cabin had survived this long.

The door was slightly ajar. That probably wasn't a good thing. Animals could have gotten inside, along with rain and moisture.

Calvin Potter, the owner and the man he'd talked to back at the main house, had told him the cabin had been vacant the past ten years. It had been Calvin's grandfather's cabin, and he had staunchly refused to leave it until his health had gotten so bad Calvin and his wife had finally convinced him to move in with them. At that time, they'd cleaned out the cabin. Then the old man had passed away a year ago, and Calvin told Dean he'd decided it was time to get rid of the place.

Well, there was only one way to find out if it was something Dean wanted or not.

Taking a deep breath and slowly letting it out, Dean pushed the door the rest of the way open, pausing on the threshold long enough to let his eyes adjust to the dark interior. There was a possibility a critter might still be in the cabin, so he knew he needed to be cautious. He'd had his share of run-ins with raccoons and other varmints over the years, and wasn't interested in having another one. And there was also the possibility of a bear being inside. That wouldn't be a fun encounter.

He felt Marcie peeking around his shoulder.

"This place is awesome."

The awe in her quiet voice matched his own, and he couldn't help but smile upon hearing it. He couldn't believe the Potters weren't asking more for the place.

"It sure is."

He stepped the rest of the way into the cabin—estimating it to be approximately twelve feet by eighteen feet. A small rusting woodstove still sat in one corner, more than likely the only heat the elder Mr. Potter had in the cabin when he'd lived there. A built-in wooden bedframe sat in another corner—the mattress long gone. The floor was made up of wide oak planks, but even covered in dirt and trash and thick layers of dust, Dean could see the quality of the wood. Someone had put a lot of love and hard work into building the place.

"Did someone live here recently?"

Dean turned his attention back to Marcie who had strolled into the cabin after him and was holding what looked like a torn section of a newspaper she'd picked up from the floor.

"The date on this is 2007. That's not so long ago."

He nodded. "The owner's grandpa lived in this cabin until about ten years ago." He smiled as he tipped his head back and took in the sight of the hand-hewn beams and rafters above them.

"Can you imagine? According to Calvin Potter—that's the owner—this cabin was built by his great-grandfather in the early 1880s."

Marcie looked at him and grinned. Dean could read the emotion on her face and knew without her saying a word that she was feeling the same thing he was. Stepping into this cabin had been like walking back in time. Dean felt this rush every time he found a previously unknown cabin. But this time he wasn't alone, and it was different having someone else with him to experience that first excitement of a good find.

Putting his hands on his hips, Dean released a breath or two as he tried to refocus. Okay, enough daydreaming. It was time to get to work and discover whether this place was just a pipedream, or if it was really as good a deal as he thought it was.

He glanced over at Marcie, who was taking photos of every nook and corner of the place. She appeared as enthralled by the old cabin as he was.

"I'm gonna go check the outside. The inside looks good, but I need to make sure there isn't any hidden damage— particularly on the back of the house that sits in the shade of the woods."

Marcie nodded. "I'll wait for you in here if that's okay." She smiled. "I'm a little leery of wandering through the weeds." He saw her visibly shudder. "I really don't like snakes."

He laughed. "I'm not a fan either, but it goes with the territory."

She stared at him with those dark eyes of hers for a few seconds before adding in a quiet voice, "Please don't get bit, Dean. I don't know CPR."

He gave her what he hoped looked like a confident smile and went back out the door, taking note that all of the windows still had glass in them, although a couple of the panes were cracked. That was an easy enough fix. The framework around the windows looked a little rough too. There was some rotting in the bottom wood of the frames, but that also could be repaired or replaced. Gordie was a pro at that.

When he came to the rear of the cabin, Dean squatted down in the weeds and dug around with his hands so he could get a closer look at the bottom-most logs. Even though the foundation—an old stone foundation—still seemed intact, it looked like the lowest log in the stack might not be in the best shape, although it didn't look like there was any termite damage. And they should have another spare log or two back at the Wood Lot that could replace any that were rotten. Thankfully, they had a relatively large inventory of odd lengths of logs from other teardown jobs, and Mac was a pro with the chainsaw at cutting the notches for a perfect fit.

Dean stood back up and rubbed his hand across his chin while his mind raced. All in all, the cabin appeared to be in great shape, and even if there were a few bad surprises, the place was worth his attention.

A feeling of happiness swept over Dean at the realization that this little beauty wouldn't just sit here in a field and fall to pieces over the years, but instead could be salvaged and used for many years to come. He even had a prospective buyer already in mind—someone who had contacted him the week before, looking for a cabin about this size. But even if that client didn't want it, Dean knew he had to save it. There was no way he was letting this cabin get away.

Dean strode back through the weeds to the front of the cabin and found Marcie sitting on the flat stone front stoop, gazing out over the field toward the woods on the opposite side of the clearing. She looked up at him and gave him a smile.

"Can you imagine what it must have been like to live out here?" She chuckled. "Although I *did* notice the little outhouse out back, and the fact that there's no running water or electricity in the place." She wrinkled up her cute little nose as if she wasn't a fan of those inconveniences.

He plopped down on the step next to her, close enough he could easily touch her arm if he wanted—or dared—to. But he knew better. He'd been burned by a woman before and wasn't about to head down that road with this one. All Dean needed to remember was that she was only here in his life for a brief time and then would go back to the city. But as much as he fought it, Dean still found himself enthralled by Marcie Starr. In some ways, she was a tough-skinned personality, and at other times, she was all warm and soft like the inside of one of his mother's homemade chocolate chip cookies. And when they were out in nature like they were today, it was as if she lost her city-fied edge and allowed herself to let her hair down. He couldn't help but wonder which Marcie Starr was the real one.

It had interested Dean more than he would have thought when she casually mentioned wanting to be an artist when she grew up. He could see that. She seemed to shine when she was working on her little sketches during the crew's break times. So, why hadn't she pursued her passion?

Dean took a deep breath and released it, enjoying the smell of trees and plant life around them. He needed to get back to business and think about the cabin more than Marcie Star.

"I need to find out the history of this cabin. There's a story to this place, I'm sure, and I'd love to be able to share it with the new owner."

He sighed and stared across the field toward the woods where he could hear a squirrel chattering as if scolding something.

"I believe I may already have a buyer for it, so I'm thinking about offering the Potters a little more than what they're asking me to pay."

Marcie swiveled her head and gazed at him. "Why would you do that? I mean, why not just take the additional profit. Most people would."

Dean turned up his lips into a small smile as he returned her stare. As he gazed into the dark pools of her eyes, he once again felt drawn to her in that way that unsettled him a little bit.

"Because, Miz Starr. That's not the way I do business."

He wasn't sure what she'd make of that statement, but it didn't really matter to Dean. He was who he was, and being honest and having integrity was how he'd been raised. That wasn't going to change no matter what.

Now that he'd made up his mind, Dean put his hands on his knees and stood up, then turned around and reached out his right hand and pulled Marcie to her feet. At the touch of her hand in his, a small jolt of something went up his arm, but as soon as she gained her footing, he quickly released her. Whatever it had been, it had shaken him more than he wanted to admit. One more reason to keep his distance from the woman.

"Well," he said, after clearing his throat and attempting to steady his heart rate. "Let's head back and see if I can strike a deal with Mr. Potter."

Once they were back in the truck, Dean put the truck in gear. He glanced once more at the woman at his side, and in an effort to lighten the little pain in the region of his heart, decided it was time for some levity.

"I can already hear Gordie complaining about havin' to drive the big rig through this mess."

Marcie joined in his laughter as the two of them headed back to the main house.

8

Marcie sat across the table from Dean McRae and studied the laminated menu in her hands. He had demanded he was going to faint dead away if they didn't stop for lunch, and had pulled into a small café they'd found along the side of the highway. It looked to be a family owned establishment, and was even called 'Mom's Place.' Marcie couldn't help but notice that all the items listed on the menu reminded her of her own grandma's cooking. Once the young woman, who looked to be in her late teens, had taken their order and returned to the kitchen, Marcie leaned against the back of the booth they were in and studied the man sitting on the other side of the table.

Dean McRae continued to amaze and surprise her. She'd never known anyone who would actually pay more for something just because he thought it was worth more than what the owner was asking. He was one of those old-fashioned men like her father had been—a man of his word, and determined to treat his fellow human beings with integrity and fairness.

But was he for real? She'd known men before who could put on a good show at being something they weren't. Was that what Dean was doing—just putting on a show for her so she'd write good things about him in the article?

Her mind ticked through everything she knew about Dean so far. He'd grown up in the mountains, gone to college, and ended up working for an architectural firm in Los Angeles, California. So, what would make a man give up a good paying job in L.A. to come back here and restore cabins and barns for a living? What had really happened to Dean McRae in California? And could it have involved a woman? She didn't know why it mattered, but Marcie suddenly had to know.

"So, why aren't you married, Dean?"

The words she was thinking in her mind tumbled out of her mouth before she had a chance to stop herself. Marcie immediately put her hand over her mouth as if that would erase the words she'd already spouted and actually flinched as she saw Dean's head fly up. His intense green eyes locked on hers, and she saw a brief flicker of something in those eyes...perhaps pain or maybe remorse. Then Marcie watched as his lips curled into a half-smile and he gave her one of his trademark winks.

"Are ya asking for yourself darlin', or is this for that little article you're writing?"

Marcie felt the heat rush to her face, and she stammered and stuttered as she tried to figure out how to answer his question. She couldn't believe she'd actually asked the man something like that. What was the matter with her?

"No. Yes. I mean, I was just curious, that's all. It's got nothin' to do with the article. Honest."

Dean was saved from answering her question right away as the waitress appeared at the table with their meals. A hamburger and fries for Dean, and a chef's salad for Marcie.

Marcie picked up her fork but then paused as Dean cleared his throat.

"Let's take a minute to bless our food."

Feeling embarrassment again at forgetting Dean's habit of praying before each meal, Marcie nodded and quickly dropped her head. Evidently, Dean McRae prayed everywhere—even in restaurants. That was the type of man her daddy had been too, but it was going to take her a while to get used to the fact that this man she was sitting with was also like that. She'd never known another man like her daddy before.

After Dean's brief prayer, Marcie took a bite of her salad, refusing to look across the table at the man. And she wasn't about to try and start a conversation with him again. She was done sticking her foot in her mouth. She hoped.

Dean's deep voice surprised her.

"To answer your previous question, I *was* married—once upon a time."

Fork held midair, Marcie stopped chewing and lifted her eyes from her salad to stare at him. That hadn't been the answer she'd expected.

"So, what happened?" She closed her eyes and dropped her head again. Hadn't she just promised herself to keep her mouth shut and not ask him any more personal questions? What was wrong with her?

Marcie watched as Dean reached out and snagged the bottle of ketchup off the end of the table, unscrewed the cap, and poured a generous amount over his French fries. Just when she was sure he wasn't going to answer her latest tactless question, he leaned back in his seat and looked across the table at her.

"I came home from work one day to discover an envelope with divorce papers sitting on the kitchen counter and my wife walking out the door with suitcases in her hands."

Marcie watched him drop his eyes to stare at the tabletop and heard his sigh, the sound of it ripping away a corner of her heart.

"The saddest part was, I never even saw it coming."

She swallowed hard, feeling the pain he must have felt at his wife's rejection. But then again, maybe she did know a little what that pain was like.

"I could say I can't imagine what that felt like. But I'm sorry to say, I can."

DEAN studied Marcie's face while he chewed and swallowed the bite of hamburger in his mouth. From her last statement, it almost sounded as if she'd been married too.

"Really," he finally stated, reasonably sure she had *no* idea what it was like to trust someone you thought you knew, only to find out they had never loved you. That the woman you had given your heart to had, in fact, been having an affair almost from the moment you'd returned from your honeymoon.

"Really."

Her voice was hushed as she echoed his last statement, but nonetheless, Dean heard the pain in it.

"In my case, at least I hadn't married the jerk yet." She raised her dark eyes, and Dean read the sorrow there. This guy, whoever he was, had been a first class jerk to mistreat someone as sweet as Marcie Starr.

"David and I were engaged, though—had been for almost a year." She laughed, a brittle little laugh that sent a stab to Dean's heart. "I thought everything was great between us. We'd been making wedding plans and everything. Then I caught him and a sweet little blond making out in his car one night in front of her apartment complex."

Dean wrinkled his brow as he tried to figure out why Marcie had been at the other woman's apartment complex. But her next words spelled it out for him—all too clearly.

"The sweet little blond happened to be my neighbor, and a woman I believed was my best friend." Marcie groaned. "I thought seriously about killing them both. Right there. In his car." Then she took a deep breath and pushed her lips tightly together, and lifted them in what looked like a sad smile.

"Instead, I threw the engagement ring he'd given me at them both and stormed up to my apartment. When Kelsey tried to get me to open the door later, I told her to get lost.

That she could have the jerk, and that David was welcome to her.

"David never even tried to call me or contact me." He heard the little catch in her voice as she added, "Showed how much he cared, huh?"

Dean wanted nothing more than to reach across the table and take her hand...to do something to take away the intense pain etched on Marcie's face. But he didn't know her that well, and there was really nothing he could do to make her feel any better anyway. Dean had to go through his own pain, and Ms. Starr would have to go through her own.

"How long ago did this happen, Marcie?"

He saw her swallow back some tears, and she wiped her eyes quickly with the corner of her napkin.

"A year ago." She gave another little laugh. "You'd think I'd be over it by now, wouldn't you?"

He shook his head, knowing full well that even though it had been five years since his divorce, it was something that haunted you for a long time.

"It *will* get better, Marcie. I promise. Just give yourself time. God has someone out there for you—someone much nicer and better suited for you than David The Jerk."

Marcie lifted her chin and shook her head.

"It's okay. I'm fine on my own. After all, I've been totally on my own for years, and I know what's best for me. I've learned it's better if you don't count on anybody else. Because one thing I know is that other people can't be depended on. They'll only end up hurting you."

Dean didn't respond. It was evident that Miss Marcie Starr had closed herself off from the possibility of another relationship to protect her fragile heart. He'd been there too, and it had taken hours of talking to the pastor of his church and studying the scripture before he'd finally forgiven himself for his marriage's failure. Patty had made her choice when she'd filed for divorce. Dean hadn't wanted the marriage to fail after only two years, but she was determined she wanted to be free of him. For months he'd mentally berated himself, wondering what he'd done to make Patty hate him so much. After counseling, Dean had finally understood that it had never been about him. It had all been about Patty and what she wanted—and Dean McRae hadn't been what she wanted.

So, he'd let her go.

The last Dean had heard, Patty had married some big-time executive in the film industry in California and was living it up. Dean didn't know if she was happy now or not, but he was content in the knowledge that she would never have fit in with his life now he was in Tennessee. Even the thought of Patty visiting here was enough to make him laugh. And the truth was, Patty hadn't been a Christian so he never should have married her in the first place.

"How long were you married?"

Marcie's soft voice brought him back to the present.

"None of this is going to go into your article, is it?" Dean chastised himself for opening up to her as much as he had. He needed to remember Marcie worked for a magazine and was here to write an article about him. He just should have kept his mouth shut.

Her dark brown eyes widened as she stared across the table at him. Then she shook her head.

"I would *never* use anything personal in the article, Dean. I hope you know I'm not that kind of person...."

Her voice dropped off, and he sighed. Of course, he knew that. Marcie Starr wasn't Patty. She obviously had some level of integrity and decency.

"I'm sorry." Dean frowned. "I know you wouldn't use anything personal, Marcie. It's just...I guess I still have a hard time trusting people at times. And to answer your question, we were married a month shy of two years."

Marcie nodded. "Is that why you came back here? To get away from the memories? "

"Maybe, although not entirely."

Dean frowned. Why was he telling this woman all his deep dark secrets? He hadn't even talked to his mother about most of this.

"I guess I came back because my job in the city didn't have the same appeal to me after the divorce. I sat there at my desk one day, and it suddenly hit me that it wasn't the real world there in L.A." He looked across the table at her. "That probably doesn't make any sense, but that's how it felt at the time."

Dean glanced around the small café, noting the tables filled with real people—farmers in their worn overalls and work boots on their feet and more than likely cow manure on those boots. Young mothers sat with their children, looking harried and tired, but the love evident in the care they gave their youngsters.

This. This was real.

When he turned his eyes back on Marcie, it was to find her brown eyes had brightened as if in understanding.

"Actually, I *do* understand. That's how I sometimes feel back in the city. Everyone rushes around in a hurry to get someplace, never taking the time to just stop and enjoy the moment. It's different than the way things are here."

He heard her release a little sigh. "If nothing else, this assignment has reminded me to stop and smell the flowers every now and then, listen to the birds sing, and appreciate how blue the sky is on a sunny day."

"Good."

Dean took the last sip of his iced tea and picked up the check the waitress had placed on the table earlier.

"You ready to head out?"

Marcie folded her napkin and placed it on the table before giving him a nod.

"Ready when you are, boss."

WHEN Dean and Marcie arrived back at Dean's house, it was to discover the other three men had been busy in their absence. Gordie had hauled home two loads of logs from Hawk's Ridge, and when Dean pulled the truck in and parked next to the house, Marcie could see the men were working on getting the last load of wood off the flatbed.

Marcie grabbed her camera off the seat of the truck and hurried after Dean as he made his way behind the house toward the Wood Lot, wishing her legs were just a little longer. Even as tall as she was, the man walking in front of her had a long stride, and it was challenging to keep up with him

"Hey, the boss man's back!" Dutch called out from where he stood as he and Mac straightened up a log Gordie had just added to the stack with his forklift.

She watched Dean walk toward where the other men were working, noting again the friendly relationship they had with each other. A part of Marcie wondered if they ever argued or got upset with each other. So far, she'd never seen anything but mutual respect between them, and a deep regard for Dean's wishes. They were definitely a team.

Gordie shut off the forklift and got down from the seat, and it immediately became much quieter on the Lot. Marcie gave Gordie a little wave as he looked her way.

"And our Miz Starr has also returned—not lookin' too worn out. Did Deano drag you all over the mountains lookin' for old fallin' down cabins, Miz Marcie?"

She laughed and glanced over at Dean, who was looking at her with a grin on his face. Before she had a chance to answer Gordie, Dean responded.

"As a matter of fact, Gordie—I *did* drag Miz Marcie all over the mountains. And for your information, this most recent cabin we looked at is a jewel. I'm tellin' ya, fellas, you're never gonna to believe it."

Dean gave Marcie another smile. "Hopefully a little later, Miz Marcie will allow the rest of you to see some of the photos she took of the place. I have to tell you guys, I think it's the nicest cabin we've ever found."

Mac had by this time walked over to join them. "Really? Is this the one you were unsure if you even wanted to waste your time goin' to look at?"

Dean nodded. "Yeah."

Then Marcie saw him frown. "That barn I told ya about was a total loss, though. But then there's this sweet little cabin. I think we may only need to replace a log or two on the back. The rest of it's in great shape.

"And I have a phone call to make later. I'm hopin' and prayin' we may already have it sold. I have a buyer that's been looking for something like this for quite a while."

By this time, Dutch had joined the rest of them, and Marcie stood nearby while they chatted. The other three told Dean about how it had gone getting the logs down from Hawk's Ridge, Gordie doing a little grumbling about the rotten road in the process. Dutch told Dean he'd already taken a load of the scrap wood to the dump earlier, and they'd finished cleaning up the worksite, so it was ready for the owner.

Marcie saw Gordie pull a folded piece of paper out of his shirt pocket and hand it to Dean.

"There's the check. Bill said to tell ya 'thanks' and that he's thrilled to have it out of there. He stopped in just as we were loading up the last logs. He also told us he has excavators coming in next week to start getting things ready to pour the foundation for his new house, so he said our timing was perfect."

"Great."

Marcie saw Dean glance at the check briefly before folding it up and sticking in his own shirt pocket.

"Well, I'll let you guys finish up here. I need to go make some phone calls before it gets any later." He paused and turned back to the pile of logs from the Hawk's Ridge cabin. "Do you think we'll be able to get this thing stacked tomorrow? It's supposed to rain this weekend, and I'd like to have it back up before bad weather moves through."

The three men looked at each other, then back at Dean, all nodding their heads.

"Don't see why we can't; Good Lord willing and the creek don't rise," Gordie said.

9

Dean took the stairs that led to his office in the upper level of The Barn two at a time. He'd left Marcie in the Wood Lot with the guys. She was busy taking photos and asking a million questions, as usual. The fellas would just have to deal with Miss Starr's magazine reporter mode. Right now, he had some important business to take care of.

Tugging open the middle desk drawer, Dean pulled out a small notebook holding all the information and inquiries he'd received from people looking for specific structures. His finger ran down the list and stopped at the one he'd most recently entered.

There it was. Drew Marshall, an attorney in Wears Valley was interested in purchasing a cabin to use as a home office. He wanted to place it behind his residence and was particularly interested in something about the size of the Potter cabin. Dean looked at the maximum price the man had said he'd be willing to pay and smiled. They were well within the man's budget, even with the cost of putting it all back together for him on his property, chinking it, and hiring a sub-contractor to install electricity. Dean picked up the phone and placed the call, hoping he'd be able to catch the man before he left his office for the day.

Twenty minutes later, the deal was set. The man was ecstatic that Dean had already found a cabin for him, although Dean promised to shoot him an email with a couple of photos so he could see the cabin for himself before he'd totally commit to it. Dean had a couple of photos he'd shot of the front of the place with his cell phone, and he quickly emailed them to the attorney. Dean was sure Marcie's photos would have been much better quality, but he didn't want to wait until she took the time to upload them to her computer. Dean wanted the deal wrapped up now.

Five minutes later, Dean's office phone rang. As he answered it, he silently prayed for good news.

"Is this for real?"

Dean laughed. "It sure is. I'm telling you, Drew, I couldn't believe how great a shape it's in. Someone was actually living in it until ten years ago, so it's been well taken care of."

After a couple more minutes, the deal was finalized. The gentleman expected them to start rebuilding the cabin on his site no later than Thursday of the next week. Dean figured that would give them enough time to make the replacement logs for the bottom course, then take the stacked cabin back down the first part of the week, and get it loaded to go.

Once he was off the phone and before he did anything further, Dean leaned back in his chair a few moments and said a prayer of thanks. This job would place them financially in much better shape than the company had been in quite a while. He had another more significant job already lined up for them the end of the month, but this one would fill in the empty spots on the calendar until then.

Once he finished his prayer, Dean picked up his phone again. There was one more phone call to make.

"Dean, is that really you callin'?"

The sweet sound of his momma's voice sent a rush of love through him.

"It's me, Momma. How ya doin'? Everything okay there?"

"I'm just fine and dandy, Dean. What's goin' on? I didn't expect to hear from you 'til Sunday afternoon when you usually phone."

Dean leaned back in his desk chair and smiled as he watched the muted late afternoon sunshine coming through the stained glass windows of his office, giving a colorful glow to the paperwork spread over his desktop.

"How would you like to have some company next week, Momma?"

"Y'all comin' for a visit, Dean?"

"Well, it would be all four of us, Momma—plus that woman from the magazine I told ya about. The one that's here collectin' info for that article she's writin'."

"They sent a woman?"

Dean smiled at the surprise in his momma's voice. Wait until she actually met 'the woman.'

"Yeah, Momma. They did. She's really nice, though, and I think you'll get along with her just fine. Do ya think you'll have room for us all?"

"Why sure, Dean. Y'all can come. That's no problem. You boys can bunk over in the barn like you always do, and I'll fix up the guest room real pretty for the woman—what did you say her name was?"

Dean chuckled. "I didn't, Momma. But if you must know ahead of time, her name is Marcie. Marcie Starr."

"Well, you just bring Miz Starr along, Dean, and I'll make her welcome. Not gonna fuss, mind you. She'll get treated just like the rest of y'all."

That made Dean smile even wider as he knew his momma well enough to know what that meant. Marcie would be fed exceptionally well, fussed over, and treated like she was one of Momma's own chicks. Because that's the way LizBeth McRae treated everyone.

They said their goodbyes and Dean went back to work on the computer. This time he had to deal with the bookkeeping side of his business. He wasn't a fan of having to write the checks and pay the bills—not because there wasn't enough money to do so. God had truly blessed his business the past few years, so thankfully that wasn't a concern.

No, it was more the matter of trying to keep track of it all. Dean had purchased a new computer accounting program for his business six months earlier, but other than installing it, Dean hadn't spent any further time with it. Doing everything the old-fashioned way took long enough. He couldn't imagine having to painstakingly punch all the numbers and information into the computer all the time. Maybe he'd break down and learn how to use it eventually, but currently, he just didn't have the time to mess with it.

THE next morning before joining the rest of them for breakfast, Marcie shot off an email to Bob Avery at the magazine with an outline of her article, along with a couple of her favorite photos of Dean and the crew at work. She wanted to wait until she got more information and saw them work at least one more job before she actually sat down and wrote the full article, but at least this would prove to her boss that she *was* working and not just goofing off. Once the email was on its way, Marcie shut down her laptop and headed out to the kitchen for breakfast.

Today there was no bright sunshine pouring through the large windows of Dean's house. Glancing out a window as she walked passed, Marcie frowned. It looked like it was already beginning to drizzle. It certainly wasn't going to be a very nice day to work outside.

When Marcie walked into the kitchen, the men were already seated around the table. As they always did, all four of them quickly came to their feet until she'd grabbed a mug and poured herself a cup of coffee. Once Marcie was seated, the rest of them resumed their seats and evidently picked up their conversation where they'd left off when she'd entered the room.

"I reckon we can get the Hawk's Ridge cabin stacked before the heaviest part of the rain comes through, Dean. We already debarked most of the logs that still had some old bark on 'em." Gordie finished what he had to say before Marcie saw him take another bite of the donut on his plate.

"I agree," Dean said. "I looked at the local radar a bit ago, and it doesn't look like the heavy stuff's gonna get here until this afternoon."

Marcie saw him glance over at her.

"We were just talkin' about workin' in the Wood Lot today. If you'd rather stay in outa the rain and work on your article, that's all right with me."

She quickly shook her head as she forked two pieces of sausage from the platter in front of her and placed them on her own plate.

"I promise, I'm not gonna melt if I get wet, boys. And if y'all are gonna be out there workin' in the rain, then so will I."

The men all chuckled, and Marcie couldn't help but notice Dean's eyes rested on her as if he were studying her. She knew she'd allowed her old drawl to sneak back into her voice this morning, but it had come out almost naturally. When she was hanging around with these guys every day, it was difficult to remember how to talk 'city.' She just hoped when she returned to D.C., the drawl would stay here in the mountains.

Once the breakfast dishes were cleaned up, Marcie returned to her room long enough to brush her teeth and pull on a hooded sweatshirt. So far, the rain was more of a mizzle— a misty drizzle. But she knew later it was likely to turn into a real downpour. She hoped the guys could finish their work before that happened. But either way, she was going to be there to take photos of them working. It would be the first time she would experience seeing a cabin being stacked, and she was so excited at the prospect she could hardly wait.

By the time she arrived at the Wood Lot, Dean and Mac had measured out the area where they intended to stack the cabin and had placed wooden blocks down for the foundation. Even though it was going to be temporary, Marcie watched as Gordie checked and double-checked to make sure everything was level. She knew from talking to Mac earlier that this was standard procedure. If things weren't level when they started, the cabin wouldn't fit back together well, and they could run into all kinds of trouble squaring things up the higher they went.

Before they started moving logs, Dean called Marcie over to a massive stack of logs and pointed.

"Do you remember we had two logs from the rear of the cabin that weren't any good? Well, we have spares here, and we're going to find two that are the right dimension and length, and cut them to fit."

Marcie nodded as she pulled up her camera and took a few shots of Gordie and Dean as they looked over the logs, measuring them carefully with their tape measure. It didn't take long, and the two of them found two they said should work. Gordie quickly moved them with the forklift over to a couple of sawhorses where Dutch and Mac were waiting.

"What are they doing now?"

Dean had walked over to stand next to Marcie, and she immediately turned toward him for more insight into the operation. Marcie saw Mac pick up a metal tool and place it on the old damaged log first, then move it over to the replacement log.

"He's usin' an angle finder to find the right angle of the notch from the old log. Then he'll replicate it on the new one using the same tool, and then use the chainsaw to cut a new notch. The cut has to be exact, or the logs won't fit together tightly. It's an art to be able to do it, and he's one of the best I've ever seen."

Marcie continued to watch and take photos as Mac moved the metal tool and placed lines on the new log with the stub of a pencil he pulled out of his shirt pocket. When it appeared he was satisfied, Mac tugged on the rope of the chainsaw to start it and went to work. Seconds later, the cuts had been made, and he shut off the noisy saw.

Dean spoke again before moving away.

"If we were gonna have to saw a bunch of them we knew were all the same angle, we'd build a jig to use as a pattern to make it easier. But in this case, it's only a couple of logs, and they have to match the original, so he does it all by hand. Like I said, Mac's one of the best I've ever seen with a chainsaw."

Then Gordie crawled into the forklift and fired it up, and things really started to happen. Piece by piece, log by log, Gordie slowly picked up the individual logs to move them over to the site, Mac and Dutch were there to help push them into place. All the while, Dean was checking each tag carefully to make sure they had the correct logs. Marcie was fascinated with how quickly the first few front and side logs slipped back into place—their dovetail notches lining up again perfectly.

She turned to watch again as Gordie lifted one of the replacement logs up with the forklift and moved it around to the rear of the cabin. With Dutch and Mac on either side of the log, it appeared to slip into place as if it had been made for the spot.

Amazing.

One after another, the logs were stacked onto the structure, and right in front of Marcie's eyes, the cabin seemed to come back to life. Oh, it didn't look like it had originally as there was no chinking between the logs and it had empty holes where the windows and door would go, and it had no roof. But Marcie knew Dean would easily be able to take care of those items once the cabin was sold and they rebuilt it for a client. In her mind's eye, though, Marcie could see the cabin as it would be when it was finished—a shining example of hand-hewn logs made to last another hundred and fifty years.

An hour earlier, Marcie had pulled her hood up over her head to protect her hair from the drizzle which had slowly become heavier and heavier. By the time Gordie had placed the last log on the top course, and the other two men had pounded double-headed nails into boards meant to hold the structure together, the light drizzle had turned into a steady rain. After standing out in it all morning, Marcie was beginning to feel the wetness seep through her clothing. She gave Dean a little wave and made her way back toward the house. She had plenty of photos and information to add to her article, and now it was time to get inside where it was drier—and warmer.

By the time Dean and the other three men stomped their way through the back door of the house—removing their wet boots as they came in—Marcie had a saucepan of old-fashioned hot chocolate simmering on the stove top along with a fresh pot of coffee brewing in the coffee maker. She had also dug through the cupboards and found a package of chocolate chip cookies which she put on a plate and placed in the middle of the table.

Dean looked across the kitchen at her and gave her a gentle smile.

"You didn't have to do that, Miz Marcie, but we fellas sure do appreciate it."

Dutch rubbed his hands together and gave her a big smile. "Yup. Sure do 'ppreciate it, Miz Marcie. Do y'all have marshmallows for that thar hot chocolate?"

Marcie laughed. "Well, I honestly don't know, Dutch. You'll have to ask the boss man. I was lucky I was able to find the makings for the hot cocoa."

While Marcie poured coffee for Gordie, who insisted hot cocoa was for kids and sissies, Marcie poured mugs of hot cocoa for herself and the other three men. Dean did manage to find a bag of mini-marshmallows in the cupboard, which brought a huge smile to Dutch's face, and he quickly dumped a handful of them into his hot drink.

"There. Now it's done."

They all sipped their warm drinks and sat around Dean's kitchen table, chatting about the bad weather and munching on the cookies, discussing how thankful they were that at least it had held off until they'd finished stacking the cabin.

Gordie spoke up during a brief break in the conversation. "I think the boys and I'll spend the rest of the day in the workshop, Dean if that's all right with you. We can update the inventory and sharpen chainsaws. It's been a while since we've done that."

Dean nodded.

"Sounds like a plan." Dean grimaced as if what he was about to say was distasteful. "And I will spend the rest of my day in the office working at my desk as I imagine you yahoos want your paychecks."

Marcie saw Dutch's eyes light up and Gordie nodded.

"Mrs. Gordon thanks ya in advance, Mr. McRae."

She sighed as she sipped the last of her chocolate treat.

"And I," she said quietly—more to herself than anyone else. "Have to get to work on writing this article."

10

ean gave a little wave to the other three men as they headed out the back door through the rain toward the workshop. He rinsed the last mug and stuck it in the dishwasher, then turned around to find Marcie Starr's eyes following his every move.

"What?"

"I'm tryin' to decide if you're really as nice a guy as you appear to be, or if you're just puttin' on a show for me 'cause you know I'm gonna write an article about you and your business."

He turned around and leaned against the kitchen counter, drying his hands on the towel in his hands as he grinned at her.

"Guess you'll have to keep hangin' around me so you can find out."

When Marcie rolled her eyes, Dean couldn't hold back his chuckle. "Tell ya what; when we're at my momma's house next week, you can ask *her* if I'm as nice as you think I am."

Marcie laughed out loud at that.

"Oh, yeah. Like your momma's gonna say anything other than you're 'the sweetest thing this side of sourwood honey.'"

Dean stared at her a moment, wondering again about her origins. He hadn't heard that expression in years, but it came right out of the mountains surrounding them. And it had rolled off Marcie's tongue as if it had been something she'd said or heard many times before.

Then he noticed her cheeks turning red, and she instantly dropped her eyes from his. The more time he spent with the woman, Dean was even more positive than ever she was trying to hide something. Why, if Marcie was originally from these parts, was she so afraid to let anyone know? Why had she completely turned her back on her roots?

Then Marcie's chin came up, and her dark eyes gave him what could only be described as a look of challenge.

"You keep talking about going to your mother's house next week. Why exactly are we going there again?"

Dean released a breath, thankful Marcie had apparently recovered from whatever he'd said, or she'd said, that had embarrassed her. He didn't want to drive her away. Quite to the contrary, Dean wanted the opportunity to get to know her better.

"Well," he turned back to the sink and quickly rinsed it out with the spray attachment for the faucet. "We have that job to do over there—the Potter cabin. Since it's not far from Momma's house, I figured we'd crash at her place a couple of days to save on travel time."

"Isn't that rather rude? I mean, I can't imagine your mom is too happy with having a bunch of characters like you show up at her house."

He chuckled as he hung the towel back on the towel bar and turned back around to face her.

"Well, that's where you'd be wrong, Miz Starr. Momma loves havin' company, and I've already told her you'll be comin' too, so don't get all worked up about it. She's lookin' forward to meetin' this lovely lady from the city I've been telling her about."

MARCIE bit her lower lip and tried not to smile. Dean had just called her 'lovely.' Did he really think of her that way, or was he just making conversation? And had he really been talking to his momma about her? She wasn't quite sure how she felt about that. She knew how mothers' minds worked, and she certainly didn't want Dean's mother to think there was anything romantic going on between the two of them.

"I don't know, Dean. I feel funny staying in a stranger's house. Maybe I should just get a hotel room someplace close by. That might be best for everyone."

He grinned and shook his head. "Not gonna happen, Marcie. As I told ya before, if you're gonna get a good feel for what we do in this business, you're gonna have to follow us around like a little puppy dog. And that means, you're gonna have to stay at Momma's house along with the rest of us."

She finally sighed and nodded. "Okay. If you're sure it's really all right."

Dean gave her a wink. "Yes, ma'am. Besides, by staying at Momma's, you'll have an opportunity to find out all the secrets about me and my past that no one else has ever discovered. Just remember you promised not to put the personal stuff in that article of yours."

Marcie had to laugh along with him at that statement, all the while wondering if there were actually any secrets to discover. Dean McRae appeared to be exactly who he was—a great guy, a good friend, and an awesome boss to his employees. She guessed if she stayed with his mother, she'd be able to find out what kind of a son he was too. Not that it had anything to do with the magazine article, but more to do with her own curiosity.

Dean McRae was becoming an enigma to Marcie—one she intended to figure out.

MARCIE spent the rest of the morning working on her magazine article. Once she'd spent a short time in her bedroom, she finally carried her laptop out and set it up at the dining room table. It would give her a better view of the outside—although there wasn't much to see other than rain running down the windowpanes in a steady stream.

After their earlier conversation, Dean had gone over to his office in The Barn, where he told her he had a mound of paperwork to take care of. Marcie had to assume the rest of the guys were out in the pole barn working on inventory as they'd discussed.

When the clock on the wall showed that noon had come and gone, Marcie was wondering what to do about eating lunch when Gordie, Dutch, and Mac came tromping through the kitchen door. They quickly removed their boots and plopped down in the other chairs scattered around the dining room table.

"I hope you guys aren't planning on me feeding you. Dean didn't say lunch was up to me today."

Mac grinned, and Dutch shook his head.

"Nah. The boss gave us a call earlier and said he was going into town and would be back directly. He also said he was bringing us somethin' for lunch."

Gordie nodded. "Not sure what it's gonna be, but he told us to show up, and he'd be here…eventually."

Marcie finished typing in another sentence on the article, then saved her work on the laptop and closed it, placing it on one of the bookshelves behind her.

"Well then, boys. I guess I'll go find some plates and silverware." She raised her eyebrow as she glanced around the table. "Maybe one of you guys can find glasses and pour the iced tea?"

In a matter of seconds, all three of the men were back up on their feet, trailing after her as she went into the kitchen. Mac found glasses while Dutch dug a tall pitcher of iced tea out of the refrigerator. Marcie pulled plates and silverware out of their respective cupboards, and Gordie dug around in the drawers and found a handful of napkins. The four of them had just finished setting the table in the dining room when the front door opened and Dean came strolling in with several large boxes of pizza.

"You went to McPherson's!" Dutch's eyes grew large, and he looked as if he might drool.

Marcie felt her own eyes widen as Dean placed several large boxes of what smelled like delicious pizza on the table in front of her.

"McPherson's? That doesn't sound very Italian," she mumbled.

Dean chuckled as he pulled out a chair next to Marcy.

"Mrs. McPherson's granny was Italian, and the secret family recipe has been passed down for generations." He gave her a wink. "Just wait until you taste it before you make any snap judgments, Miz Starr."

They all bowed their heads while Dean blessed the food, then the large slices of pizza began being passed around on the plates. Marcie took a bite of the meat-lovers pizza slice Dean had given her, then groaned as the spicy flavors hit her taste buds.

"You're right! This is good!" she mumbled around the food in her mouth.

Mac laughed as he attacked his own slice.

"We told ya."

It was silent for several minutes as they each scarfed down several slices of the tomato-ey delicious pizza pie. Marcie had eaten two slices before she even realized it—choosing pepperoni for her second slice.

She watched Dean wipe some wayward sauce from the corner of his mouth with his napkin, then he gave her questioning look.

"Well, whatcha think, Miz Marcie? Does it live up to your city-type pizza?"

Marcie felt her lips turn up into a smile.

"I have to admit—I think it's the best pizza I've ever had."

"I had to go to the bank, and on the way out of town, I passed McPherson's and made a snap decision that we couldn't let you go back to D.C. without knowing what *real* pizza tastes like."

Dean gave her one of those beautiful smiles of his that almost took her breath away. She immediately dropped her eyes from his and made a pretense of needing to wipe her face with her napkin. What she really wanted was to hide from the man's probing eyes. Dean McRae's sparkling green eyes seemed to see right into her soul, and Marcie was afraid if he kept looking, he might see how much she was dreading going back to the city. As much as she'd hated the thought of coming here, Marcie was finding her stay way too enjoyable.

"Well, we do appreciate it, boss," Dutch piped up. Those were the first words they'd heard out of the young man since the pizzas had appeared. The other two fellows quickly agreed and gave their boss equal thanks.

Marcie raised her eyes back up to find Dean still gazing at her with that intense look he sometimes had. She swallowed her last bite of pizza and gave him a smile, all the time wondering how the man could affect her so much when she'd only known him a few days.

"I agree with the boys, Dean. Thank you. That was a nice thing to do."

He grinned and gave her one of his little winks, then reached out to snag another piece of pizza from the box in front of him.

"I keep tellin' ya, I'm a nice guy, Marcie Starr. Maybe one of these days you'll believe it."

THAT evening, Marcie rode in Dean's truck with him while Mac and Dutch drove behind them in Mac's pickup truck as they all headed over to Gordie's and Sally's house for supper. Sally had called earlier in the week and insisted that she have an opportunity to show that magazine writer how good a cook she was.

Marcie wasn't sure what to expect when they pulled into Gordie's driveway. She knew from the way the Gordons' boys had been dressed that first evening in worn out jeans and shirts that the family wasn't exactly well-to-do. But she also didn't think Dean would allow one of his employees and friends to live in an old shack someplace in the hills.

She'd been right. Their home wasn't a log house, but it was a newer manufactured home, and the yard around it looked tidy and well-groomed. Somebody had put a great deal of time and effort into planting a large vegetable garden just to the left of the driveway, and Marcie had to smile at the comical looking scarecrow set in the middle of it. He was decked in a fluorescent pink flowered blouse and lime green pants and was sporting an extra-wide brimmed straw hat with red, white, and blue ribbons flowing from it. If the birds and other varmints couldn't see that scarecrow, they were blind.

The four of them climbed out of their respective vehicles and had no more than taken two steps in the direction of the house when the door opened, and Gordie came out to greet them, along with two hound dogs and the three boys Marcie now remembered were named Matt, Mark, and Luke. Marcie couldn't help but notice that this evening the boys were dressed very nicely in dressier jeans and cotton shirts, and had even combed their hair. She also noticed that everyone shook hands and greeted each other like they hadn't seen each other in weeks instead of just a few hours.

Marcie shyly followed Dean and the other guys as Gordie led his guests into the house.

"Come on in and set a spell," his deep voice admonished as they trailed him through the back door.

She took the time to look around as they walked through what looked like a small mudroom off the kitchen. It also appeared to be the laundry room as a washer and dryer sat in one corner. Just inside the door sat a wooden bench made from what looked like old barn siding and salvaged wood. Under the seat were three tan-colored wicker baskets. Each basket was tagged with one of the boys' names on it, and jackets hung neatly from hooks on the wall to the right of the bench. Sally Gordon was apparently a very organized woman.

Sally herself greeted them each as they filed into the kitchen, giving Dean a hug and a kiss on the cheek, then pulling Marcie into what felt like a bone-crushing hug that took her breath away.

"I'm *so* glad y'all came tonight, Miz Marcie! I've been lookin' forward to havin' a woman to talk to all week."

Gordie overheard his wife and gave Marcie a nod, his face growing pink with embarrassment. "She's done talked my ear off about you visitin' us, ma'am. In a house full of menfolk, she doesn't get much time talkin' to women about women things, you know."

Marcie smiled in response and gave Sally's arm a little pat. She wasn't sure what Sally and she would talk about, but surely they'd find something.

Sally pointed her guests in the direction of the small dining room where Marcie quickly noticed their hostess had outdone herself. The table was covered with a pristine white tablecloth, and it looked to Marcie as if Sally had pulled out all the stops and used her best china. Marcie smiled at that, wondering how many occasions the poor woman had to use her fancy stuff in a household with three rambunctious boys.

They all found chairs around the large table, and Marcie found herself seated between Dean and Dutch with the three

Gordon boys seated across from her. It grew quiet as Gordie stood and asked a heartfelt blessing on the food.

"Thank you, Lord, for everyone sittin' around this table tonight. You've blessed us greatly with the food we're about to eat, Lord. Bless the hands of the sweet gal that cooked it all, and thank you again for givin' us salvation through your Son and also for your everlasting love. Amen."

Everyone echoed Gordie's amen, and soon, platters and bowls started being passed. Marcie had been at a lot of fancy meals in fine restaurants and banquets in Washington, D.C., but the aromas of the food being passed her way far surpassed anything she'd eaten in the city. There was Swiss steak, buttered squash, corn on the cob, mashed potatoes and gravy, some sort of fruit salad with apples, carrots and walnuts in it, and for dessert, Sally had baked three kinds of pies: cherry, apple, and pecan. Marcie almost groaned as she saw the pies being passed, but couldn't help but grin when she noticed Dean take a piece of each.

She leaned over to whisper to him. "How can you eat like this and stay so trim?"

He turned his head to give her a confused look. "Eat like what? You mean, you don't eat like this every day?"

She almost snorted in response but caught herself in time so that it came out sounding more like a little laugh.

"If I ate like this all the time, Dean McRae, I'd be so huge you wouldn't be able to get me through the doors."

The youngest of the Gordon boys seated across the table seemed to find Marcie's comment funny as he laughed out loud, then ducked his head as if he were embarrassed at being caught laughing at the guests. Marcie gave him a grin and a wink, hoping that would put the young man at ease, and he gave her a small smile in return and went back to attacking his own piece of pecan pie with a vengeance.

Dean swallowed his bite of food and turned back to her, shaking his head. "If you worked as hard as these guys did every day, you wouldn't have to worry about it."

He reached down and patted his stomach with his left hand—the one currently without a fork in it. "As long as I keep doin' the physical work, I can keep eatin' like this." He winked at her with a twinkle in his eye. "But I for one, don't think you have to worry about getting so big we can't get you through the door, Marcie."

His eyes continued to look at he, and Marcie found she couldn't look away from them.

"I don't?"

He shook his head. "Nope. You're perfect, just the way God made you."

Marcie felt her lips slowly raise into a smile as she continued to gaze into Dean's eyes, noting the tips of his ears were starting to turn pink like they did when he was embarrassed. Well, the man didn't need to feel bad about saying such nice things to her. Especially if he meant them.

"Thank you."

His lips were still smiling when he turned to answer a question from someone down the table, and Marcie went back to enjoying her piece of cherry pie. It had been a long time since she'd had home-made cherry pie and she intended to savor every bite.

After everyone was stuffed, the men stood and followed Gordie out the back door, stating they were going out to the garage/barn to look at his latest project. According to Sally, who explained it all to Marcie as they carried leftovers and dirty dishes to the kitchen, Gordie was building her a hutch for her dining room, using salvaged wood from a barn the guys had torn down several months earlier.

"I can't wait for him to finish it so I have someplace to keep my fancy dishes."

Marcie carefully placed a stack of dirty plates on the kitchen counter next to the sink. "These are beautiful dishes, Sally. Where did they come from?"

Sally answered over the noise of the hot water running into the sink, quickly filling with soapy water.

"They were my great-grannie's dishes, and came all the way with 'em when they come from England."

She held up one of the plates with the pretty English floral pattern around the border and in the center. Each dish also had a scalloped edge. "I checked out online, and they were trying to sell some pieces of this same pattern. One of these here plates was sellin' for twenty dollars. Can you imagine?"

Marcie carefully ran the dishtowel across the plate in her hand, holding tightly to it as she did so. The last thing she wanted to do about now was to drop one of the dishes.

"I can believe it, Sally. These dishes are heirlooms to you, but because of their age and where they came from, they're probably worth that much or more to collectors."

Sally gave her a surprised look, then gazed back down into the dishwater. "I never thought about it much, but I suppose you're right." She grinned. "I don't use 'em often."

She rolled her eyes as she looked over at Marcie, who couldn't repress her grin in response.

"Can you imagine trying to use these every day with *my* boys?"

Marcie chuckled as she picked up the next clean plate.

"No, I can't. But the boys were very well behaved this evening, Sally. You're doing a great job of raising them."

The other woman snorted. "Their Pa threatened them with a tanning if they so much as sneezed wrong." Then she got a wistful look on her face. "They are good boys, though. Most of the time."

She rinsed the suds off the next plate and handed it to Marcie.

"Matthew is growing so fast. He's already taller 'en his Ma, and *so* smart. Why he knows so much stuff I can't keep up with him when he comes home from school—talkin' about all that science and biology stuff."

Sally's face filled with pride. "He says he wants to go to college, and Gordie and me, somehow we're gonna make that happen. We've been savin' for the boys' college costs, and Matt's grades are good enough—hopefully, he can get a sports scholarship of some sort to help out."

Marcie turned her head and glanced out the kitchen window that looked toward the garage at the sound of a ball bouncing. Sure enough, the three boys were out there shooting baskets into an old rusty basketball ring that hung on the front of the garage.

"I'm sure he will do great, Sally."

The conversation turned to Marcie's life in the city, and Sally asked all kinds of questions while they finished up the rest of the dirty dishes. Marcie had feared that she'd feel awkward or uncomfortable when the invite to Gordie's house had been made, but when they all said their thanks later, it was with a heavy heart that she hugged Sally goodbye.

"I won't be able to come over in the morning to say goodbye before you leave to go to Miss LizBeth's house, Marcie, since I gotta be to work at six. And since yer not gonna be comin' back to this side of the mountains before you head home, I guess this is goodbye."

Marcie knew Sally was a waitress at a local restaurant and worked long hard hours because of it. When Marcie thought about what an easy time she had in her job and her life, she couldn't help but look on Sally Gordon as an amazing woman.

"Thank you so much for havin' me over tonight, Sally. Everything was delicious," Marcie said as she hugged the older woman. "And I really enjoyed our talk."

She couldn't help but notice Sally wiping a couple of tears from her eyes. "I enjoyed it more than I can tell ya, Miz Marcie. You're welcome back here *anytime*. Don't you forget it."

In the growing shadows of evening falling, waves and goodbyes were called out as they all made their way to their trucks to head back to Dean's house. Marcie felt a real sense of loss, knowing she'd probably never see Sally Gordon again.

11

Saturday morning, Marcie rose early and finished packing her suitcase. Today they'd travel across the mountains to Dean's mother's house in preparation for the crew's next job. The plan was for Marcie and the guys to stay at LizBeth McRae's house the next week as they worked to dismantle and move the Potter cabin to its new location near Wears Valley.

After another hearty breakfast prepared by Dean himself, Marcie wheeled her suitcase and carried her laptop bag and her purse out to the front porch. While she waited for Dean to come back from The Barn, Marcie sat in one of the weather-worn wooden rocking chairs on the porch and tried to finish waking up.

They had a beautiful day ahead of them. It was still early enough that the sun hadn't totally reached over the tops of the trees yet, but the birds were beginning to sing their morning songs in the woods all around the house. Sitting and listening to the mountains wake up, Marcie couldn't help but relax. It had been good to come back to the hills of her childhood—even though she'd been terrified to return.

As she sat in the rocker and rocked, Marcie pondered her situation. A little part of her—way deep down—still wondered if she should try and visit her mother while she was there. But whenever her thoughts started wandering in that direction, Marcie immediately pushed those ideas aside.

There was no reason for her to look up her mom. The past was the past and was done and other with. When Marcie had driven away in her old beater car ten years earlier, it had been to leave.

Forever.

There was nothing for her here in these mountains anymore. It was a great place to visit and unwind for a couple of weeks, but then she would return to her life and her successful job in the city. That was where she belonged now.

But somewhere in the back of her mind, Marcie still couldn't help the thoughts that continued to haunt her. Was her mom okay? It had been at least two years since Marcie had heard from her.

I don't even know if momma is still alive.

At that thought, feelings of guilt wormed their way into Marcie's mind, but again, she quickly pushed them aside. Instead, she reminded herself of the reasons she'd left home in the first place. There was no undoing the losses she'd suffered. There was no going back. Momma had made her choices in life, and so had Marcie.

Marcie was so involved with thoughts of her mother and her past that she didn't even hear Dean's footsteps on the gravel driveway until he was standing at the base of the porch steps, staring up to where she sat, now motionless in the rocker.

"You gonna fall back asleep?"

Her eyes flew up and her eyes locked on his, and Marcie's first thought was she hoped Dean McRae couldn't read her mind. If he did, Dean was going to be as confused as she was.

She shook her head as she stood. "Sorry. Guess I kinda zoned out for a minute."

She shot him a smile, hoping to erase the look of concern on his face.

"I'm ready to go when you are, boss."

She was sure Dean was anxious to get on the road. Mac, Dutch, and Gordie had already left fifteen minutes earlier. Dean helped her get her luggage in her car. She would be following Dean in his truck as they drove to his mother's house.

What would it be like to meet Mrs. McRae?

As Marcie fastened her seatbelt, she tried to remember everything Dean had already told her about his mother. It sounded like she enjoyed taking care of people. That wasn't unusual for a mother. Well, some mothers.

Dean stood next to her open car window as if waiting to make sure she was ready to go so she decided to ask some questions to better prepare herself for meeting his mother.

"How far is it to your momma's house anyway?"

He shot her a quick smile.

"It'll take us a little over an hour. She lives up in the mountains near Cosby."

Marcie nodded, mentally thinking about what roads they would take to get there. It was surprising how quickly the mental map of Tennessee had returned to her memory—even after being gone for ten years.

She noticed Dean shuffle his feet and he dropped his eyes from her for a moment. Marcie couldn't help but worry what was bothering him. Perhaps he wasn't all that anxious for her to meet his mother after all.

"Jist to warn ya, Momma's really lookin' forward to meetin' you. She'll be tickled havin' a female to fuss over instead of it just being us guys. I think we tend to get on her nerves sometimes."

"Well, I certainly hope your mom's not goin' to a big fuss just for me, Dean. I'm just taggin' along, you know."

He nodded, the big grin still plastered across his face.

"Yeah, well, you don't know my momma. She doesn't allow anyone to come into her house without them feelin' like family by the time they leave."

A few moments later, as Marcie followed Dean's truck, she thought about what she had learned about him the previous evening. He'd been telling her stories about his childhood and how it had been for him growing up in the mountains. His experiences seemed much different than hers had been, and it was easy to tell Dean had a great childhood—although it sounded as if he and his brother Nick had certainly gotten into their share of scrapes.

"It's a wonder our Sunday school teacher didn't just kick us out-a class, the way we two delinquents acted," He'd told her. "Looking back on it now, I have to believe Mrs. Gillespie was some kinda saint to put up with us."

Marcie had laughed along with Dean, relishing the sound of his deep chuckle. Dean McRae was nothing like she'd imagined him to be when she'd agreed to come and write this piece about his business. He was actually nothing like any other man she'd ever known. And she was starting to like being around him—way too much.

As they left the main road and started climbing through the hills, the road twisting and narrowing as they went. When they came to an extremely sharp curve, she wasn't surprised to see a large round convex mirror installed up ahead on a fence post. Marcie knew why it had been placed there—

turned in such a way that allowed the traffic from both directions to see around the sharp corner so the drivers would know if another car was coming. She'd seen those mirrors often on these back roads, and it made her thankful that someone had finally come up with a way to avoid accidents—accidents that took people's lives.

After another half hour, up ahead, Dean finally slowed at a break in the trees and turned onto a small dirt lane that led through even more trees, and Marcie slowly followed him. Marcie couldn't imagine traveling these trails in the winter when there was snow on the ground. But then, this part of Tennessee didn't get a lot of snow—usually. And if it did snow, Marcie knew it would melt away in a matter of a day or two.

Finally, Marcie could see an opening in the trees up ahead. Then she saw the house. Nestled in a flat open area was a two-story white house with a porch running across the front of it. In some ways, it reminded Marcie of the Walton house on the old television show she used to watch as a child. Here, no children were running around, but Gordie's semi and flatbed were already parked off to one side of the house, so she knew the guys had arrived ahead of her and Dean. She pulled her car in and parked next to Dean's pickup truck.

When Marcie noticed a large Golden Retriever get up from where he'd been laying on the porch, she hesitated before opening her car door. The dog slowly made his way down the steps toward Dean's truck as if he'd been waiting for him.

She watched as Dean jumped out of his truck. He turned and looked toward where she was parked and shot a quick smile before turning back toward the dog, who ran and almost leapt into his arms in greeting. Marcie gulped and finally opened her car door and got out of her vehicle. She stood back and watched as Dean hunched down and accepted the animal's lavish attention—including multiple licks and loud whines.

Then Dean glanced over his shoulder as if finally noticing Marcie had been hanging back.

"Miz Marcie, I'd like you to meet Buster. Buster, this is a very sweet lady that you will need to be nice to. No jumping on her and tryin' to lick her face now, ya hear?"

The dog looked up at her as if assessing how sweet Marcie might actually be, then slowly walked over and sat down directly in front of her, looking up at her with the most sorrowful eyes Marcie had ever seen. As she stared down into the dog's face, it came to her that this was the closest she had been to a dog in years, and Marcie was surprised to discover she actually didn't feel the fear she had as a child. Perhaps she'd been wrong all those years for being afraid of the four-footed creatures.

"Well, Buster, it's a pleasure to meet you."

Marcie wasn't sure what else to do in greeting the animal, but leaned over a little and reached out her fisted hand for him to sniff, hoping he couldn't bite her fingers off in the process. His cold, wet nose nuzzled against her hand, then he pushed himself against the closed fist, almost forcing it against its will to open and pet him—which Marcie did.

"Well. It looks like you've found a friend, Marcie. Buster is a friendly sort but usually doesn't warm up to folks quite this fast. He must really like you."

Dean stood next to Marcie, both of them gazing down at the dog as he continued to gratefully accept Marcie's attention. Marcie couldn't help but notice how soft his fur was, and after a few moments, she realized how calming it could be to pet a dog. It was a shame she'd spent so many years in fear of the animals.

"How long has your mom had Buster?"

The man at her side chuckled, then shook his head, and Marcie wondered what he found so funny.

"Sorry. Buster's my dog. He stays here with Momma most of the time 'cause I'm gone so much. I didn't feel it would be fair to leave him alone at my house all the time. But he's *all* mine." He reached out with both hands and leaned over to ruffle the dog's fur around his neck.

Marcie nodded. That made sense, she guessed. Dogs needed companionship as much as people did.

"Besides," Dean added as he gave the animal one last pat on the head and stood back up. "Buster keeps Momma company. I don't worry so much about her being out here alone in the middle of nowhere as long as she's got Buster to keep an eye on things."

He nodded toward the truck, then back at the house. "We'll go in and say 'howdy-do,' then I'll come back out and get our things outa the vehicles later. That all right with you?"

"Sure."

Following Dean up the wooden steps, Marcie couldn't help but notice how neat and tidy everything was. The porch floor was painted a light gray and didn't appear to have a speck of dirt on it. White wooden rockers sat one on each side of a small wooden table at one end of the porch. The other end of the area was covered with large pots of a variety of colorful flowers. Evidently, in addition to being the world's best cook, Mrs. McRae also had a green thumb.

Before they reached it, the front door opened wide, and a petite woman Marcie assumed to be Dean's mother greeted them. Well, she welcomed Dean. The woman barely acknowledged Marcie as she opened her arms to hug her son, who immediately leaned down to give his mother a return hug.

"Y'all are finally here!"

Mrs. McRae's voice was muffled as she hugged her son, but Marcie could hear the tears of joy between those words. A twinge of longing swept over her, wondering what it would be like to be so loved by a mother—so missed.

Then Dean released his mother, and the two of them turned toward her.

"Momma, I'd like you to meet Marcie Starr. She's the one I told ya about—here from the city to write a magazine article about the business."

He gave Marcie a little wink, and she wondered if he had any idea how nervous she was about meeting his mother. She didn't know why. Marcie had met all kinds of people over the years she'd worked at the magazine—from all walks of life. But for some reason, it felt important to her that Dean's mother like her.

"Marcie, this is my momma, LizBeth McRae."

Before Marcie knew it, she was pulled into the older woman's arms. A sense of coming home swept over her as she inhaled the aroma of lilacs and what smelled like freshly baked bread.

"Miz Starr, welcome. Welcome."

Marcie stood there for a few seconds allowing the older woman's eyes to study her face—looking for what, Marcie didn't know. While under Dean's mother's scrutiny, it also gave Marcie a chance to get a good look at the other woman. It was easy to see where Dean had gotten his dark red hair and green eyes from. Although at her age, Mrs. McRae's hair was a faded version of Dean's and was now streaked with gray.

"Mrs. McRae, thank you for letting me stay here."

The other woman waved her hand through the air as if dismissing the notion that it was any bother and tugged open the door to the house.

"Come in, come in. I just took sweet rolls out of the oven." She chuckled as she went into the house. "Hopefully, the boys haven't eaten 'em all yet."

Marcie felt Dean's hand on her elbow as he led her into the house, then felt his breath on her cheek as he leaned down to whisper near her ear.

"I think Momma likes you."

She released a nervous little laugh and almost asked out loud what difference it made if Dean's mother liked her or not but caught herself. Her nerves were on edge enough without finding out what was going on in Dean's head.

"Why do you say that?"

"She made sweet rolls. They're saved for *very* special company and the big holidays—you know, Christmas and Easter."

He gave her a huge grin, then she felt him let go of her elbow as they reached the kitchen door. Everyone else was already sitting around a round oak table, and Marcie nodded at the three men who all stood as she and Dean's mother entered the kitchen. When they resumed their seats, Marcie noted they all had a cup of coffee in front of them, along with a plate with at least one massive roll on it.

Dean pulled out a chair next to Gordie and offered it to Marcie. She sat in the chair, clutching her hands in her lap and feeling self-conscious as all the eyes seemed to have landed on her. Then Dean pulled out a chair next to her and folded his long frame into it.

"So, did you characters leave any sweet rolls for Miz Marcie and me or did ya hog them all down already?"

Mrs. McRae chose that time to return to the table with a big flat aluminum pan covered with frosted sweet rolls. Marcie knew her eyes must have grown huge at the sight as Dean chuckled and nudged her in the shoulder.

"I told ya Momma liked you."

She finally gave in and released a chuckle as Dean handed her a plate with two rolls on it. Only seconds later, a cup of hot coffee appeared in front of her.

"Probably it's more like she's happy to have her son home again."

She glanced over long enough to see Dean lick some frosting off his lips. When she raised her eyes from his lips, Marcie felt her face grow warm at the look she saw in his eyes. Then he grinned at her, and the tension disappeared.

"Well, there's that too."

"Now there's plenty, y'all. Hopefully, this will tide ya over until lunchtime."

Marcie took another bite of the soft, warm roll and closed her eyes in ecstasy. Who needed lunch? She'd gain ten pounds just by eating these rolls.

But they *sure* were good.

12

Dean watched Marcie as she interacted with his mother and the three guys sitting around his momma's kitchen table. He couldn't help but wonder what the woman was thinking.

He'd been paying close attention to Marcie when they'd first arrived. When his mother had enveloped Marcie in her ample arms, there had been such a look of longing on Marcie's face, it had gone straight to Dean's heart. For just a few seconds, Dean had gotten a glimpse at the lost and forlorn little girl Marcie Starr hid most of the time, and he couldn't help but wonder at the story behind that look.

Marcie appeared to have recovered, though. Now she sat next to him at the table, her eyes darting around the room as if trying to soak it all in. Taking a sip of his coffee, Dean returned his cup to the table top and silently sent up a prayer to his Heavenly Father.

Lord, Marcie's hurting. I can see it in her eyes. If I'm supposed to be the one to help her find her way, lead me. If not, place her pain on another's heart so they can help her. She needs You, Lord—she needs Your love and forgiveness, just like the rest of us.

There was only one week left, and Marcie Starr would be going back to her life in the city. Dean didn't know why, but somewhere down in the depths of his soul, he knew Marcie didn't belong there any more than he did. She belonged in the hills of Tennessee.

She just didn't realize it yet.

MARCIE stared through the screen of the open window of the bedroom where she was staying at Miz LizBeth's house. She'd already been informed that she *wasn't* to call her Mrs. McRae by the woman herself.

"It's Miz LizBeth, dearie. Not Mrs. McRae."

Marcie had smiled, noting how everyone said the older woman's name—with the emphasis on the first part.

LIZBeth

"Yes, ma'am. But I thought your name was Elizabeth," Marcie had felt her face grow warm when she realized her mistake. At least she hadn't actually called the woman that.

But Dean's mother had just laughed and had shaken her head.

"Well, it was supposed to be. My momma wanted to name me after her granny, but one of her cousins beat her to it and named *her* first girl Elizabeth. They tell me my momma was so angry, she wouldn't even speak to that cousin for almost a year!"

Marcie had joined the older woman in her laughter, loving the sound of the Eastern Tennessee drawl as the other woman recounted the story.

"So, my momma decided she was *still* gonna name me after her great-granny, but gave me the name LizBeth instead." Her green eyes, so much like Dean's, had sparkled as she smiled over at Marcie. "Truth be known, I like LizBeth much better than Elizabeth. Elizabeth sounds so stuffy, don't ya think?"

Marcie had nodded and smiled at the older woman. "I agree, Miz LizBeth. Your name fits you perfectly."

And it did. Somehow, Marcie felt as if she had known LizBeth McRae forever. There was a wonderful wholesome goodness about the woman. Within seconds of entering her house, Marcie had felt at home. She wasn't sure how LizBeth did it, but it was indeed a gift. Love seemed to radiate from the woman.

Marcie sat in the chair she'd pushed over closer to the open window and continued to gaze out into the night, feeling the cool breeze drift in and listening to the crickets singing their chorus outside. The evenings she'd spent at Dean's house had been quiet, but here—in the depths of the mountains—it was not only quiet outside; it was also dark. The only lights she could see were the soft lights coming from the building Dean had called the Bunkhouse. He'd told her he'd built it for him and the boys to stay in when they used his momma's house for a headquarters whenever they worked in this part of the state.

Marcie sighed. She was well aware she should be in bed, getting some sleep. Dean had informed her they'd all get up and go to church the next morning right after breakfast and Marcie was tired. But Marcie wasn't sure she wanted to go with them. She hadn't been in a church since she'd left home. On the other hand, she certainly didn't want to start out the week by insulting Miz LizBeth, so she supposed she would have to go with the rest of them.

But she wasn't going to enjoy it.

TAKING another look in the mirror, Marcie sighed. She hoped she had dressed appropriately for Miss LizBeth's church. She'd chosen to wear a dark blue skirt with a white blouse and had slipped her feet into a pair of simple black flats. Fortunately, she'd brought the more dressier clothes along with her when she'd packed. Otherwise, she'd be going to church this morning in her jeans.

She'd left her hair hanging loose today and was pleased with how long it was getting. In the past, she'd tried to keep it trimmed, never allowing it to grow much past her shoulders. But she had been so busy these past few months, she hadn't had time to visit her friendly hairdresser, and now her hair hung halfway down her back.

Grabbing her purse, Marcie left her room and started down the steps. When she was about halfway down, she saw Dean turn and look up the stairs, his eyes brightening at the sight of her. Dutch released a soft whistle, and Mac nudged Gordie in his ribs as if to stop him from staring up at her. Marcie couldn't help but grin at the sight of the four guys, obviously appreciating the sight of her dressed up. Hopefully, she looked a little more feminine than she did in her old clothes and work boots.

They didn't look so bad themselves—especially Dean. Today he wore an honest-to-goodness suit—dark charcoal gray with a white shirt, which seemed to set off his bronze hair and green eyes. His shoulders looked even broader in the suit coat, and Marcie couldn't hold back her smile at the sight of him.

"Hey," Dean's deep voice sounded hushed in the small foyer as his eyes continued to rest on her face.

"Hey yourself. Y'all clean up real nice."

They all chuckled as Miz LizBeth breezed into the entry, purse and Bible clutched tightly in her hands.

"Are y'all ready to go then? Don't want to be late."

Marcie followed the rest of them out the door, wondering what the driving arrangements were going to be. There were six of them—far too many to fit in one vehicle. Her question was quickly answered when Dean touched her elbow and steered her in the direction of a dark blue four-door sedan parked at the end of the house.

"Thought we'd take Momma's car," he whispered near her ear. "The boys can ride in the other vehicle, but I thought this would be easier for you and Momma to get in and out of—seein' as how you're all dressed up."

Marcie gave Dean a smile as he held the door open first for his mother and then for her, placing his momma in the back seat and Marcie in the passenger side in the front.

"Wouldn't you rather ride up front, Miz LizBeth?" Marcie asked before fastening her seat belt.

"Land sakes no, girl. If I'm not the one doin' the drivin', I prefer to sit in the back where I can't see the road. Makes me dizzy-like to ride up front."

With Miz LizBeth settled in the back and Marcie in the front, Dean got in the driver's seat, fastened his seatbelt and started the car, following the others as they drove down the same narrow lane they'd come in on the day before. Marcie relaxed as the scenery passed by, listening to Dean's mother in the back seat, telling how Dean had moved her to this place after her sweet Mr. McRae had passed on.

"The old house wasn't much to look at when ya bought it, was it, boy?" Without even waiting for Dean to respond to her question, LizBeth continued. "He spent his first winter living here with me, hammering and patching and paintin' up a storm. Oh! So much work."

Marcie took a moment to glance over at Dean's profile, seemingly concentrating on driving the narrow roads, but she could see his lips soften in a small smile on his face and noticed the tips of his ears were turning pink. Apparently, this wasn't the first time he'd heard his momma share this story.

LizBeth chuckled. "My boy sure is good to me. What a blessing." Marcie glanced over her shoulder long enough to see the older woman nod her head as if in agreement with herself. "Yup. God's been good."

"Well, you certainly have a lovely home, Miss LizBeth. I would say Dean did a good job of re-doing it for you."

Seemingly satisfied that Marcie was in agreement with her observations about her son, LizBeth's chatter turned to the scenery out the window, recounting the names of the families that lived in the hollows they drove through and telling a bit about each one. Marcie smiled as she remembered what it was like living in these mountains, where you knew everyone, and everyone knew you. There was little anonymity here—unlike back in the city where she didn't know a thing about any of her neighbors.

A short time later, they arrived at a small frame church, its white steeple pointing toward the blue sky. The church building looked like it belonged there in the little hollow tucked between mountain ranges and Marcie couldn't help but smile. It looked exactly as she'd expected Miss LizBeth's church to look.

Marcie took a deep breath for courage and walked through the open wooden double doors of the church with Miz LizBeth on one side of her and Dean McRae on the other, his large hand lightly resting on her back as if to encourage her not to bolt. She glanced over at him once to see his green eyes looking at her intently, as if trying to gauge her reaction to attending his mother's church. She just smiled back at him, hoping he couldn't see how genuinely nervous she was.

Inside the church, it felt to Marcie as if Dean and his mother were greeted by everyone. She tried to shyly melt into the background, but Miz LizBeth was having none of it.

"This here is Miss Marcie Starr, come all the way from Washington D.C. to write a big magazine article about my boy Dean and his business. Ain't that excitin'?"

Marcie pasted a smile on her face and bravely shook hands with everyone she was introduced to. She was more than relieved when Dean took hold of her elbow, and they followed his mother down the aisle toward a pew near the front. Marcie sat down and released a deep breath of nervous energy as she tried to take in her surroundings. She glanced over her shoulder once and caught a glimpse of Mac, Dutch, and Gordie as they slid into their seats a few pews behind them. She hadn't seen them earlier and had even wondered if they'd decided not to attend after all. Somehow knowing they were there made her feel better—more like this was a group outing of the *McRae* crew and she wasn't being singled out.

As she settled into the pew and looked around, Marcie tried to relax. If she didn't know better, she could almost fool herself into thinking she was sitting in the church where she'd grown up. Wooden pews lined both sides of the sanctuary. Tall windows were pushed open slightly to allow some fresh air to come into the large high-ceilinged room. In the front was a raised area—up two steps to a spot where the choir members sat on the right, and the preacher's podium sat on the left. In the middle of the front wall, a plain wooden cross hung. A piano was tucked in the corner below where the choir would sit, and shortly after they took their seats, Marcie noticed a woman slide onto the piano bench as if getting ready for the service to start.

Marcie felt Dean's elbow nudge her lightly and turned her attention to him as he handed her what she assumed was a bulletin with the order of service inside. She knew the drill. There would also be a list of announcements and activities happening during the week, a prayer list of those who were ill or were shut-ins, and a list of people with birthdays or anniversaries in the upcoming week. Some things stayed the same, and she'd spent the years of her childhood in a church just like this one. She whispered her thanks to Dean and opened the bulletin not really seeing what it said, but it gave her something to do with her hands and something to look at. Having the large frame of Dean McRae sitting at such close quarters to her was doing odd things to her heart.

In an attempt to overcome those feelings, Marcie turned toward his mother, who sat on her other side.

"This is a lovely church, Miz LizBeth."

The older woman patted her on the knee and gave her a quick smile. "It's just a little country church, dear, but it's been my church home for many years now, and I love these people dearly." She nodded toward the front where an older gentleman in a dark blue suit moved in front of the microphone. "And Pastor Dave is a wonderful preacher. He's a good Bible-teachin' man."

Marcie smiled and nodded and then turned back to face the front as the service began.

Pastor Dave led the congregation in a couple of old hymns, the words and music in worn hymnbooks in the pews where they sat. There was no video up on a screen in the front as Marcie knew she would have found in the city churches. There was no praise and worship band with guitars and drums. There was just the little lady plunking away on the piano in the corner and the deep voice of the pastor leading the songs. It was a straight-forward service, but somehow or another just felt right as Marcie sang the words of the old familiar hymns along with everyone else. Dean's deep voice sang next to her, easily carrying the tune.

When it came time for the message, Marcie sat back and readied herself for what she was sure would be a fire and brimstone sermon. She'd sat through enough of those in her youth that she knew what to expect and was already preparing to tune it out.

Instead, Pastor Dave spoke steadily and firmly, preaching from the book of John on salvation. There was no pounding of the pulpit with his fist. There was no admonition to turn from your wicked ways or spend your eternity in hell—although Marcie knew that was the gist of the sermon. Instead, the tall, thin man quietly explained how God had a purpose for each and every life, and that He loved us enough that He had sent His Son to die on a cross for our sins. It was a sermon Marcie had heard for years, although the language and tone were different from those of her childhood. And it ended much quicker than Marcie would have expected. When they stood for the final song, she was surprised to find that she'd actually enjoyed hearing God's Word preached again. It had been a long time since she'd felt that way. Perhaps there was hope for her soul yet.

It was silent in the car on the drive back to Miz LizBeth's house—almost as if the three of them were privately digesting the words the pastor had shared from the pulpit that morning. Marcie didn't dwell on the message too much but did feel a sense of peace she hadn't felt in a long time. There was something rather comforting about sitting in a church and quietly reflecting on your life and purpose.

Back at the house, Dean helped his mother out of the car, then turned to help Marcie who had gotten out on her own. She quickly greeted Buster the dog with a pet to the head, then hurried after his mother, amazed as always that the older woman could move so fast. It was apparent that Miz LizBeth was on a mission to get the food on the table as quickly as possible.

By the time Marcie reached the kitchen to help out, Dean's mother had an apron swathed over her Sunday dress and was pulling an enormous tray of fried chicken out of the oven where she'd apparently been keeping it warm. She pulled off the aluminum foil covering, and the aroma of the meat hit Marcie full in the nose.

In a matter of fifteen minutes, the table was laden with more food than Marcie would have thought possible. The fried chicken was joined by mashed potatoes and gravy, buttered carrots, coleslaw, homemade rolls, applesauce, and peach dump cake for dessert. Sweet tea filled each glass, and as the six of them sat down to eat, a hush fell over those around the table.

"If you would, please," Miz LizBeth gave a little nod to Dean, who immediately stood from where he was sitting next to Marcie.

"Father, we thank You for another beautiful day here in the mountains. We thank You and praise You for the opportunity to worship You this morning in church, and for the freedom to do so. We thank You for the food laid before us on this table, and for the loving hands that prepared it. And we especially thank You for the sacrifice of Your Son, our Lord Jesus Christ on that cross all those years ago. In His name, we thank You, Amen."

A chorus of 'amens' followed, and as Dean retook his seat, the platters and bowls of food were quickly passed around. The four men seated at the table ate heartily while they chatted about hunting, and the weather, and the job they had coming up the next day. Marcie sat quietly and listened, eating the food on her plate, and feeling out of place, although she wasn't sure why. She hadn't felt that way when she'd eaten at Dean's table and wondered why she was feeling that way this time. Then she felt Dean's mother's eyes resting on her. There was something in the woman's green eyes so much like her son's that unsettled Marcie—caring, compassion, curiosity. Whatever it was, Marcie was reasonably sure that Miz LizBeth was a woman who wasn't going to let Marcie leave her house without knowing her whole life story.

And that wasn't something Marcie was willing to share.

13

Early the next morning, Marcie rolled out of bed and got dressed, then tucked all her usual work items into her backpack in preparation for a long day. Dean had warned the crew the night before that they were going to work until dark to get as much accomplished on disassembling the Potter cabin as possible. The sooner they got it moved to its new location, the sooner they could get to work putting it all back together again for Drew Marshall, who was anxious to start using it as his home office.

Chatter around the breakfast table was loud as everyone seemed to be in a boisterous mood. Miz LizBeth joined in the humorous banter, teasing the two younger men on Dean's crew until Marcie actually started to feel sorry for the guys. Mac and Dutch seemed to enjoy the attention, however, and each leaned over to give the older woman a hug and a quick peck on the cheek before they headed to the bunkhouse to grab the stuff they needed for the day. Before he left the house, Gordie also stopped at the kitchen door and turned to give Dean's mother a hug like the others had done.

"Thank you for another delicious meal, Miz LizBeth. Anytime you want to cook for us, you're more'n welcome."

"Yer welcome, Gordie. Y'all have a good day."

Marcie watched the interchange as she picked up a few dirty dishes and carried them to the counter next to the kitchen sink.

"Oh, don't worry about those, dear. I'll take care of 'em after y'all leave." She grinned at Marcie. "It will give me somethin' to do to pass the time. Although I'm already thinkin' about what I want to make for supper tonight." She chuckled. "I sure do love havin' y'all around to feed. Reminds me of when my boys were both still at home."

The older woman got a wistful look on her face, and Marcie felt a twinge of sympathy. She imagined Dean's mother was often lonely. She really did seem to love having someone to fuss over.

Before Marcie had time to say anything further to the older woman, though, Dean's broad shoulders filled the kitchen door as he peered around the corner, obviously looking for Marcie.

"You ready, Mars? Time to head out."

Marcie gave him a nod, feeling her face grow warm at the nickname he'd used. She'd never had anyone assign her a nickname before, but she kind of liked it. It made her feel like she somehow belonged. She turned to thank the older woman again for breakfast, but before she could get out a word, Miss LizBeth engulfed her in her arms, then pulled back and looked her full in the face.

"You have a good day, young lady. And take care. Sometimes my son isn't careful enough when he's doin' these jobs. At least, *I* don't think he's careful enough." Her voice increased in volume as if to make sure Dean heard her.

Then Miss LizBeth dropped the volume back to speak to Marcie. "I know I'm just his mother, and he would say I worry too much." She chuckled. "Anyway, you take care, and I'll see y'all tonight."

Feeling completely out of her comfort zone at the unexpected emotion sweeping over her, Marcie mumbled a quick thank you, then exited the kitchen and grabbed her backpack she'd left at the foot of the stairs. As she hurried out the front door toward Dean's truck, Marcie thought about how sometimes Miss LizBeth made her wish for things she couldn't have.

Like a mother who loved her.

MAC'S voice reached across the yard to Dean as he hollered over to Dutch, who worked near him on another ladder.

"Hand me that doohickey, Dutchman. Can't get this nail out."

In response, Dutch pulled a small tool out of his tool belt and tossed it over to his fellow worker, and both the men continued what they were doing. Dean stood with a smile on his face and watched his crew function like a well-oiled machine. Most of the time, he didn't even feel like their boss; they so well knew what to do, he didn't even have to give them much direction anymore. He was sure if he left right then, they'd just go ahead and finish the job without any trouble.

But, he wasn't going anywhere.

Mac and Dutch were up on ladders, carefully peeling off the metal roofing from the back side of the cabin. Down below, Gordie was pulling nails from window frames in preparation to remove the windows from their casements. He and Dean had already inspected them and knew some of the frames would have to be repaired, but all in all, the majority of them were in excellent shape considering their age. Oh sure, some cracked window panes would have to be replaced, but that was expected.

He turned around long enough to spot Marcie who stood back from the work area with her ever-present camera in her hands as she shot photos of the guys doing their jobs. Dean wondered how many pictures she actually needed for this article of hers. After all, he was reasonably confident the magazine wasn't going to publish all of them. But then, he didn't mind her taking the photos. And it *did* keep her busy and out of the way.

He was glad to see she was still wearing the yellow hard hat he'd given her that first day. Then he gave himself a mental shake at the thoughts running through his head. There was just no way anyone should look that darling in a hard hat. Today her jet black hair was pulled back in a long braid that reached halfway down her back. Even with the hard hat on her cute little head, she was a distraction.

At least to him.

And he didn't need to be distracted. That was when people got hurt.

Dean strolled back over to the side of the cabin and went to help Gordie as he struggled to get another window frame loose from the cabin wall. It was dirty work as there were years of grime and dirt collected on the wood. Dean didn't mind, though. This was a labor of love for him. It didn't matter how many times they took down an old cabin and rebuilt it, it felt like Christmas.

He turned at the sound of someone coming from behind him. Marcie was striding through the tall grass toward him, keeping her eyes on her feet, and Dean felt his lips turn up in a grin. He knew she was terrified of stepping on a snake, which was always a real possibility.

"What 'ya need, Miz Marcie?"

She looked up, flashing him a small smile—almost shy-like.

"Do you suppose I can get up on a ladder when the guys take the last few sheets of roofin' off the front? I'd really like to get a shot of them doin' it from up there."

Dean stood with his hands on his hips for a moment as he thought about her request. There wasn't really any reason she couldn't do what she'd asked. He'd just need to stay close by and make sure nothing happened. The last thing he wanted was a lawsuit by her employers for her getting hurt on one of his jobs.

"Sure. I think we can arrange that."

Leaving Gordie to work on removing the last window frame, Dean strode around to the front of the cabin with Marcie trailing behind him. An extra ladder was laying on the ground there, so he quickly propped it up at the back corner of the cabin on the opposite end of the cabin where the guys were working. The roofing was already off this end, so she should have a clear shot of them doing whatever they were doing up there.

All the time he was getting the ladder set, he could hear Marcie telling him how much she appreciated him doing this for her. She kept saying how she wanted to get a good shot of Mac and Dutch working on disassembling the roof, but couldn't seem to get the right angle from the ground. Well, she *was* here to help the business by writing a nice article, so Dean supposed it only fair that he do what he could to make her job easier.

Dean held the bottom of the ladder for her as Marcie scrambled up the rungs, surprisingly fast for someone he had been sure would be afraid of heights. Evidently, he'd been wrong about that. Maybe she was just scared of snakes. The woman continued to be a contradiction of everything he'd thought she would be.

Once near the top of the ladder, she started taking photos of the work going on. He glanced up a couple of times to check on her. Then Dean decided it might be best to keep his eyes on the ground in front of him as the sight of her long jean-encased legs along with the rest of her backside tended to distract him from what he was supposed to be doing.

Marcie had been up on the ladder only a few moments when Dean suddenly felt the ladder shake and start tipping. Marcie let out a little squeal, and Dean looked up to see her arms wind-milling in the air. He stepped closer to the ladder just as it tipped to the side. That's when he realized Marcie was falling. Instinctively, Dean reached out to grab her and felt the weight of her as she landed in his arms. The impact of her body knocked him flat on his back.

But thankfully, he never lost hold of her.

Dean heard a grunt and wasn't sure if it was her or him as the two of them came to rest in the tall grass, his arms still holding her tightly against his chest. His nose was buried in the ponytail of her hair. It smelled like flowers and fresh air. But for a few seconds, the only thing Dean was really aware of was the weight of Marcie in his arms.

When he finally got enough breath back to speak, Dean croaked out, "Are you all right?"

He continued to hold her tightly, almost afraid to let her go as he felt her shudder and tremble against him. Dean hoped him holding her would give her a little comfort until she was able to pull herself together emotionally. He didn't know if she realized how close she'd come to crashing to the ground in a heap instead of crashing into him.

After a few seconds, Dean thought about trying to get up. At that point, though, he still wasn't sure his own shaky legs would hold him upright. Seeing her fall had scared the daylights out of him.

She gave a little squeak and a nod, and Dean released a sigh of relief. Thank the Lord, she appeared unhurt.

Right then, three concerned men came running around the side of the cabin toward the two of them.

"What in tarnation happened?" Gordie roared.

Dean flinched at the sound. He couldn't remember Gordie ever raising his voice, but he knew the older man had probably been as scared by what had happened as Dean had been.

Feeling Marcie struggling to get up, Dean finally released her enough that Mac and Dutch could take hold of her arms and help her to her feet. Gordie reached out a firm hand and pulled Dean to his feet, and he took a couple of deep breaths as he tried to get his legs to stop shaking.

"I'm sorry," Marcie almost whimpered. "A bat came flying out of the corner of the cabin roofline and scared me."

Dean saw her visibly shudder and release a breath. She might not be afraid of heights, but it was clear to see that the poor girl was terrified of bats. He had a momentary temptation to laugh about it but decided that might not go over very well, so instead only grunted.

"Well, for cryin' out loud! You plumb scared twenty years off my hide, girl!" Gordie was still fuming, and his round face under his mustache was a bright shade of red. Dean reached out and lightly touched his arm as if to tell him to take it down a notch.

"I'm sure Miz Marcie didn't intend to scare anyone, Gordie. And thankfully, nobody's hurt, so let's just get back to work. Our little bit of drama is over for the day, fellas."

The three other men mumbled in agreement and left to return to their work spots, leaving Dean and Marcie standing at the end of the cabin near where they'd fallen. Marcie hadn't looked at Dean since they'd gotten up off the ground, and Dean couldn't help but wonder what was going through her pretty little head. He finally reached out and gently took hold of her arm.

"Are you sure you're okay, Mars? That was quite a fall."

She turned her red face to look at him, and it was all he could do to not grin at the look of embarrassment on her face.

"I'm afraid you bore the brunt of it, Dean. I mean, I know I'm no light-weight. I'm so sorry!"

He fisted his hands on his hips to keep from reaching out and pulling her into his arms. Her falling *had* terrified him, and having her land in his arms had totally unnerved him to the point he was still having trouble thinking straight. Even though the landing had been a little painful to his backside, it had felt really good laying there with his arms wrapped around her.

"I'm fine, Marcie. But what about your camera? Did it get damaged?"

As if suddenly remembering it, Marcie reached down toward the camera which still hung from a strap around her neck. "I don't think so. Thankfully, I keep it strapped around my neck." She shook her head. "If I'd dropped it, I might have damaged it beyond repair, and that wouldn't have been good. It belongs to the magazine."

Dean rubbed the palm of his hand across his chin in frustration. "I'm more worried about you getting hurt than that stupid camera."

He reined in his temper as he realized how harsh his voice must sound to her and reached out and touched her cheek where a smudge of dirt rested on her face.

"Are you positive you're all right?"

Marcie looked over at him with an expression he couldn't quite figure out, then she gave him a smile and a firm nod.

"I'm sure. How about you? Did I hurt your back?" She released a nervous little giggle. "I can't believe you caught me, Dean!"

He grinned back at her as relief swept over him. She was giggling now, so that was a good sign.

"Well, it was either catch you or be flattened by you, Miz Starr."

The two of them laughed again, and Dean felt the strain between them ease.

Dean made certain before he returned to help Gordie, however, that the ladder was removed and Marcie Starr was seated on the tailgate of his truck drinking from a bottle of water and as far from the action as Dean could get her.

There would be no more taking any chances with the magazine writer from the city. If anything happened to Marcie Starr while under his care, his mother would never let him hear the end of it.

14

Marcie carried a stack of dirty dishes to the kitchen and placed them on the counter next to the sink. Miss LizBeth had once again outdone herself. The evening meal had been delicious.

"Y'all don't have to help, Marcie."

She gave the older woman a smile. "That's okay. I'd hate for you to have to do all these dishes by yourself."

Dean's mother gave her a smile. "Oh, I don't mind really. It gives me some quiet time to reflect on my day, enjoy the view out the window, and pray."

"Pray? What do you pray for?"

As soon as Marcie said the words, she wished she could take them back. What Miss LizBeth prayed for or about was none of her business.

The other woman just smiled and started filling the sink with soapy hot water. "Well, I pray for people God brings into my life. Like you."

"Me?" Marcie stared at the woman in surprise. Why would Miss LizBeth waste her time praying for her? She didn't need anyone's prayers, did she?

"Yes. You, missy." LizBeth McRae gave Marcie a pointed stare. "I'm worried about you, dear. And besides, prayer is something we can all use. Don't you ever have a good old-fashioned talk with the Heavenly Father, young lady?"

Marcie flinched.

"I guess not lately. But I *am* a Christian," she muttered as she grabbed a dishtowel and started drying off the clean and rinsed dishes the other woman handed to her. "But, He probably doesn't want to hear about what's goin' on in my life."

"Hmmm. Well, I couldn't help but notice y'all didn't look particularly comfortable in church the other day. How long has it been since you've worshipped Him, read His Word, or taken your hopes and dreams to Him in prayer?"

Marcie hadn't expected this line of questioning from the sweet-looking lady, but then she remembered Miss LizBeth's eyes studying her over the breakfast table. She swallowed hard. She'd known this was coming sooner or later. LizBeth McRae didn't appear to be a woman who failed to speak her mind.

"Ten years."

Miss LizBeth gave a little nod. "Jist like I thought." The older woman frowned. "Ten years is a mighty long time to turn your back on God."

Releasing a sigh, Marcie concentrated for a moment or two on the dish she was drying. Miss LizBeth's mind was way too sharp. Weren't folk's brains supposed to dull with age? Evidently, Dean's mother hadn't received that memo.

"Oh, girl." The older woman's voice had taken on a sorrowful tone. "You can run from your past. You can run from your mistakes, but you can't outrun God. He's gonna keep on lovin' you no matter what."

She reached out and lightly patted Marcie's arm.

"So ya see, I'm just gonna keep on prayin' for you."

Fortunately, nothing further was said, and Marcie tried not to look at the other woman as they finished the dishes. The last thing she wanted was for Dean's mother to start trying to 'fix' Marcie's problems. Sometimes things just couldn't be fixed.

A short time later, Marcie put the last clean dish away in the cupboard, then hung the dishtowel she'd been using on the towel bar. Not much had been said by either of them after Dean's mother's gentle scolding. And for that, Marcie was thankful.

"Thank you again for helpin' with the cleanup, Marcie. It was nice to have a woman in the kitchen to keep me company."

She turned and gave the older woman a small smile. "I'm glad I could help."

Standing in front of Marcie, Dean's mother reached up and tucked a stray strand of Marcie's hair behind her ear—much in the way her mother used to when she was a child. At the memory, a small pain appeared in the region of Marcie's heart and caused her to release a little gasp as she quickly closed her eyes. When she opened them again, it was to find the other woman studying her intently.

"I would say yer momma raised you right."

"Humph." Marcie didn't bother to hold back the sound of disgust, then tried to gentle it with a sigh. "I guess she did. When I was younger."

Miss LizBeth pursed her lips and then motioned toward the kitchen table.

"Let's sit and rest a spell." She pulled out a chair and slowly lowered herself into it. "Ah. My feet get weary after a while of standin' at the sink."

Marcie frowned while she pulled out a chair for herself. "You should have let me and the guys take care of the cleanup then, Miz LizBeth. You could have rested."

The other woman waved her hand in the air and shook her head. "No way am I lettin' them boys into my kitchen. Why I wouldn't be able to find a thing by the time they finished."

The two of them shared a chuckle over the vision of the four men stumbling their way around Miss LizBeth's spotless kitchen.

"Besides, I don't have a-hankerin' to have all my dishes broken, you know?"

Marcie grinned and nodded, thankful that the two of them had moved on from their earlier somber moment. There was something about Dean's mother that touched a part of Marcie's heart—a portion she'd closed off a long time ago—ever since she'd walked out of her momma's house for the last time.

Miss LizBeth released a weary sigh as she leaned back in her chair and looked across the table at Marcie. Somehow Marcie knew what was coming next was going to be a test of some sort. She just didn't know what she needed to do to pass it—or even why it mattered so much to her that she do so.

"Dean tells me you live in Washington, D.C."

She nodded. "Yes, ma'am. I work in D.C., but I have a nice little apartment just outside the city."

The older woman nodded as she continued to look at Marcie. "But, of course, yer not from there originally."

Marcie kept the smile on her face as she nodded. "Correct. I moved there about six years ago—right after I graduated from college."

"So, where y'all really from?"

She'd known this question was coming. Marcie had known it from the first moment she'd met LizBeth McRae. The woman's eyes and ears saw and heard everything, and those bright green eyes—so much like her son's—gazed at you as if they could see directly into your heart.

"I'm originally from Tennessee."

"I knew it." The older woman grinned. "I could tell you were from the mountains someplace, and I tol' Dean I was sure you were from these parts." She chuckled. "Every now and again you let a little somethin' slip, and your mountain heritage shows through."

Marcie flinched. If only Miss LizBeth only knew how many hours and days she'd spent getting rid of that 'mountain heritage,' as the other woman called it.

It was quiet between the two of them for a few seconds, but Marcie knew the questions weren't over yet, and she steeled herself—all the time trying to figure out how she was going to answer the woman. She didn't want to lie to Mrs. McRae. Even in the short time she'd known her, Marcie had already taken a liking to the woman.

"Yer folks still around the area?"

Again, Marcie flinched inwardly. She never should have sat down with Dean's mother. She'd known LizBeth McRae was going to want to know more about her.

"My father's dead." She hesitated a few seconds before adding, "I'm not sure about my mother."

LizBeth's head came up, and those green eyes locked onto Marcie's.

Here it comes.

"Jist what does that mean?"

Marcie swallowed hard, trying to stem back the emotions threatening to tear open old wounds. It was ridiculous, really. It had been ten years ago. Why couldn't she get over it and move on with her life?

"I haven't seen nor talked to my momma since I walked out of her house ten years ago to go to college."

There. She'd said the words out loud, so now Miss LizBeth knew the truth about Marcie Starr. She could judge her for being a terrible daughter, an awful ungrateful child; it didn't matter to Marcie what the woman thought. Did it? After all, no one knew what her life had been like back in those days but Marcie herself. And she was leaving the mountains in a week to go back to her comfortable life in the city anyway and what she said to Dean's mother wouldn't mean a thing. It would just be a forgotten memory in no time at all.

Surprisingly, Miss LizBeth didn't say anything in response. She merely sat there in her chair at the table, her weatherworn fingers playing with the edge of the cloth placemat on the table in front of her. Marcie wasn't sure if the woman was trying to figure out what question to ask next, or praying. After a bit, however, the silence became somewhat uncomfortable to Marcie. Perhaps she needed to tell Dean's mother all of it. Maybe that was the only thing that would satisfy the other woman's curiosity, and then perhaps the questions would stop.

Marcie's voice sounded hollow to her own ears as she began to talk. It had been a long time since she'd spoken to anyone about her father's death.

"My daddy died in a car accident the summer before I turned sixteen."

She saw the sympathy appear in Dean's mother's eyes but turned away from the sadness she saw there. If she wasn't careful, Marcie knew she'd fall apart in the telling. And she'd cried enough about her losses over the years.

"My mother didn't handle his death very well. She took up drinking as a way to drown her sorrow and numb the pain."

Marcie released a weary sigh. Even now, Marcie couldn't believe how her mother—a woman who professed to be a good Christian—could have turned to alcohol the way her mother had.

And because of it, her mother hadn't been there for Marcie after losing her daddy—right when Marcie had needed her mother's love and support more than ever. Instead, Lois Starr had turned inside herself and become a selfish, self-centered alcoholic. The only good thing was about her drinking was that she'd never been violent toward Marcie. She just hadn't cared about her anymore—or anything else for that matter. Her mother had simply sat around the house like a parasite, leaving everything up to her teenage daughter to take care of.

"Even though Daddy had a life insurance policy, we struggled to make ends meet for a while until momma got the hardware store sold."

Marcie glanced over at LizBeth's face long enough to register the fact that the older woman was still listening. "Fortunately, Daddy had set aside enough money for me to go to college—money that couldn't be spent for anything else. Thank God." She swallowed hard. It had been a good thing, or her mother would have probably drunk away that money too.

"I worked at the hardware store for the new owner until I graduated high school. Then I packed my bags and left for college. And I've never been back."

She heard the sigh from across the table and steeled herself for a lecture. Marcie had heard it all before—she wasn't fair to her mother; she'd suffered a loss too; it was time to forgive and forget. Marcie had heard all the excuses and platitudes from a variety of people over the years. But they didn't *know*—they didn't understand what it had been like for her back then. Marcie had just been a teenager and had not only lost her father, but she'd also lost her mother.

"I'm so sorry, Marcie. That must have been a terrible time in your life. And you were so young to go through all that by yerself."

Gulping back her tears, Marcie nodded and raised her eyes. LizBeth McRae's green eyes were also filled with tears, and it took everything in Marcie to not sob out her grief. She'd been brave and strong for so long, and somehow it felt good to be able to talk about it—with someone. Someone who didn't judge. Someone who just listened.

It was silent between them again for a short time before LizBeth spoke again, her voice quiet in the room.

"When I lost my Douglas, I thought my life was over too." She gazed at Marcie for a moment. "Has Dean talked to you any about his Daddy?"

Marcie shook her head, wondering why the other woman would think she and Dean had discussed their personal lives. It wasn't like they were good friends or anything. Then she remembered the pain they'd shared over the betrayals made by people who were supposed to love them. Perhaps they had shared more than she'd thought, but his mother certainly couldn't know that.

"My Douglas, he was a good man—and such a hard worker. When my boys were just little tykes, we lived in West Virginia—coal mine country. And Douglas worked in the mines. It was an awful job—even if it did pay well. We scrimped and saved every penny we could, and eventually, we moved to Tennessee, and he got a job working in a factory—making parts for cars."

She grimaced and then chuckled. "I don't know much about what he did there—just knew it was some tool and die place. Douglas worked hard and earned a good wage." She sighed. "He didn't love the job, but it sure was a sight better than workin' under the ground all day every day in that mine. And I didn't have to worry about him dyin' down there one day.

"Although that didn't stop him from dyin' anyway. He was at work one day when he collapsed—they told me it was a heart attack."

Marcie saw the woman swallow, and it was silent in the room for a few moments. Marcie could tell the other woman was struggling to collect herself.

"I've never felt so lost in my life, Marcie. The only man I'd ever loved was gone."

LizBeth shook her head. "I was mad as a hornet for quite a while. Mad at God, mad at my kids, mad at myself. I had no idea how to be alone and go on without him. Honestly, I didn't want to live either."

She sniffed and pulled a hankie out of her apron pocket and blew her nose before continuing.

"Thankfully, I pulled out of it." She glared across the table at Marcie. "But I'm tellin' ya, young lady, it wasn't easy. And I certainly don't judge any woman who loses her man and falls apart. Until you've loved someone that way, y'all don't know what it's like. I felt like half of me was jist...gone. I can still feel that pain—even today."

Marcie didn't know what to say in answer to the woman, so she didn't say anything. LizBeth could defend her mother if she wanted, but it didn't change Marcie's opinion of her. Her mother hadn't been there when Marcie had needed her, and Marcie wasn't about to forget that. Or forgive.

"I was at my lowest 'bout that time, and then Dean came back from California. Of course, he'd had his share of troubles too, but I think he saw what a mess I was in and decided to move me here so I'd be closer to him."

She smiled a little at this point. "I was born and raised not too far from here, ya see. So it was a-comin' home thing for me. Anyway, Dean's taken good care of me, and I've recovered. I do what I can for those around me—especially when God brings someone into my path that's suffered some sort of grief themselves."

She looked pointedly at Marcie. "Like you."

Marcie shook her head. "I'm sorry you went through all that, Miss LizBeth. But that doesn't excuse what my mother did—and didn't do."

LizBeth slowly nodded her head.

"You're right, Marcie. But you *do* still have a momma out there someplace. Remember that, girl. People die, and it's a sorrowful thing when the ones we've loved die without ever knowin' how much we love them. I don't think that's the way the Good Lord intends for families to be."

She sighed. "Family is all we got on this earth that means anythin', Marcie girl. For your sake, if not your momma's, go and find her before you leave these hills. Or I'm tellin' ya if somethin' happens and she's gone, you'll never be able to forgive yerself."

Marcie didn't respond. How could she do what Miss LizBeth asked? For one thing, she didn't even know if her momma was still alive.

And if she was living, could Marcie go through the pain of seeing her again and remembering everything she'd lost that rainy and stormy night almost thirteen years earlier?

15

Dean watched Gordie run the forklift as he carefully moved the top log off the Potter Cabin and swung it around and loaded it on the flatbed trailer. Dutch and Mac stood ready on ladders—one at each end of the cabin—to aid in the removal of the next log.

Once they got to the lower logs, the guys would muscle them off, and Gordie would load them. It was a slow operation, the dismantling of a cabin. If they were just tearing it down for parts, it wouldn't have been so important to take it slow. But this one needed to be taken down as carefully as possible, so as not to do any more damage to it then had already been done by time and nature.

Leaning on a shovel he'd used earlier to remove the sod from around the lowest course of logs, Dean's eyes swung over to where Marcie Starr stood and watched the proceedings. Today, Marcie wore her usual jeans and work boots, topped with an orange Tennessee Volunteer T-shirt. Her black hair was pulled back into a perky ponytail, and even though she wore the required yellow hard hat, he could see the sleek raven-colored hair hanging over her shoulder. Her ever-present camera was up to her eyes, and she was snapping photos of the guys working. And for some reason Dean couldn't get a finger on, he just couldn't keep his eyes off of her.

She'd been unusually quiet this morning on the ride to the work site. Thinking back on it, he'd hardly heard her speak two words during breakfast either as they'd sat around his momma's table. He'd noticed a shadow of sadness lurking in her brown eyes that hadn't been there before. Something was bothering her, and Dean didn't know why, but it felt important to him to find out what that something was.

Then there had been the somewhat cryptic remark his mother had whispered to him when she'd given him a quick hug before he left the house that morning.

"Take good care of that girl, Dean. She's hurting a lot more than she lets on."

Dean leaned harder on the shovel and bit back a groan. Leave it to his momma to dump a guilt trip on him. Like he didn't have enough on his shoulders without needing to treat this magazine writer from the city with kid gloves. Besides, Marcie didn't look like she was some delicate flower that would wilt and simper and cry over the least little thing. Well, she wasn't tiny, for sure. She was built reasonably solid. That was something he had personally experienced.

His lips turned up in a little smile at the remembrance of holding Miss Marcie Starr in his arms—all of her weight on him as they tumbled into the tall grass. He might have enjoyed the experience a little more if it hadn't been for the fact that his breath had been pushed out of him at the impact and he'd been terrified that he'd drop her on the way down and she'd be injured. But as they had sat there on the ground and attempted to recover from the fall, he had held onto her just as tight as he could, as if his arms unknowingly hadn't wanted to let her go. She'd smelled good, and had felt soft, and her hair brushing against his cheek had felt like satin and smelled so good.

Dean stood up straighter and gulped a deep breath of fresh air and released it. See what his momma's little suggestion had caused? Now all Dean could think of was Marcie Starr.

Not good. Not good at all.

AFTER eating a quick bite of lunch—this one cooked and packed by his momma and consisting of cold fried chicken and potato salad with apple crunch for dessert—Dean wandered across the open area around the cabin where Marcie sat perched on a fallen log. Her ever-present sketch pad was in her lap, and her head was bent low over her work.

Dean cleared his throat to give her warning he was coming up behind her. She seemed somewhat skittish since the fall she'd taken the day before, so he didn't want to scare her. At the sound, her head swiveled around and saw him, and his heart gave a little lurch at the sight of a shy smile appearing on her face. Then she turned her head back to her sketch pad.

He took a seat next to her on the log, his eyes studying the pad of paper in front of her. At least this time she hadn't closed the sketchbook and hidden what she was working on as soon as he'd appeared.

Today she was drawing the forest, with a deer standing at the edge of the clearing. Her sketch looked so real, Dean actually turned and looked in that direction to make sure the deer wasn't actually standing there.

"You get enough to eat?"

She turned her head just enough to shoot him a quick grin. "Of course. Your momma sure does know how to put on a feed, doesn't she?"

Dean chuckled at the country expression coming out of this very city-fied lady sitting beside him. Every now and then, she let down her guard, and he loved hearing her drawl.

You can take the girl out of the country, but you can't take the country out of the girl.

"I told ya. Momma will never send anyone away from her table hungry."

It was quiet between the two of them for a bit, then Marcie flipped the cover closed on her pad and placed it and the box of pencils back in her backpack. Then she leaned back as if to stretch her shoulders.

"You're kinda quiet today, Marcie. Everything okay?"

She lifted her head and pushed a strand of loose hair back behind her ear. Dean couldn't help but stare as the sunlight caught the back of her head and set it on fire—the sleek black strands looking almost silver in the sunshine. Where in the world had she come by such gorgeous hair? It wasn't dark brown. It was actually black. Maybe she colored it with dye to get it that color, but he didn't think so. It looked too...real...too natural.

Marcie sighed again and then nodded.

"I guess." She looked over at him and gave him a lopsided smile. "Your momma got ahold of me last night, and we had quite a talk."

Dean almost groaned as he leaned back a little on the log. No wonder his mother had whispered those words to him this morning.

"I'm sorry, Marcie. Momma does have a habit of pushin' herself into other people's private lives—uninvited, I'm sorry to say."

She shook her head. "It's all right, Dean. Really."

He heard her sigh. "She said a lot of good things to me— things that made me think differently about stuff in my past and people I've pushed into the back of my mind for a long time."

Marcie turned and looked him in the eyes, hers dark and intense as they locked on his.

"She told me some of what she went through when your daddy died."

He swallowed as his own memories returned to that time. What a terrible period that had been—for all of them. Dean had never seen his mother so lost, or her faith so shaken.

"Did she tell you she actually quit goin' to church for a time? It wasn't until I got her moved back here to the mountains that Momma got right with God again. I think she blamed Him for taking Daddy."

She shook her head. "No, she didn't tell me she quit going to church."

The only sounds around them for a while were the birds chirping in the trees and the quiet murmurs and laughter of the guys' voices drifting across from the other side of the clearing.

"I can't imagine what it must be like to love someone that much. I mean, I was hurt when David cheated on me, but I think I was madder at him than anything. And angry with myself for thinking he actually cared about me."

Marcie's voice was hushed, and Dean had to turn toward her to catch her words. His own mind repeated the words she's just spoken. He'd thought he'd loved his wife that much, but the pain he'd felt when she'd left him had been more of a prideful thing than the actual loss of his wife. At the time, Dean had come to the conclusion that he'd never really known her, and had possibly been more in love with the idea of being in love than actually caring for her the way he should have.

"I know what you mean." He sighed. "I always thought my parents acted more like best friends than a married couple, but perhaps that's what makes the difference in a relationship. Passion may lessen over the years, but if you're friends first…"

She nodded. "Yeah. 'Cause friends don't hurt each other, and my record with boyfriends hurting me is relatively long."

A little chuckle came from her, and Dean watched as her lips turn up into a half smile. "So I guess that's my new goal. To find a friend. Nothing more than friendship is required."

He chuckled as he tilted his head and looked over at her. "A purely platonic relationship, huh? Do you think that's possible between a man and a woman?"

Marcie gave him another one of her shy smiles. "I don't know. But friendship is a good place to start—and it's a whole lot safer on the heart."

MARCIE pulled on her robe and slippers and padded down the stairs. She couldn't sleep and had paced around her room long enough she was afraid she was going to wake up LizBeth sleeping in her room down the hall. Perhaps she'd go downstairs and pace the floors for a while. At least down there, she wouldn't bother anybody.

'Cause she sure wasn't gonna sleep anytime soon.

All day Marcie hadn't been able to get Miss LizBeth's words out of her mind.

People die, and it's a sorrowful thing when the ones we've loved die without ever knowing how much we love them.

Thoughts of her mother kept racing through Marcie's brain. After Marcie had left home, she'd received letters and cards from her mother—not often, but always around her birthday and holidays, she had received mail. Marcie had placed the envelopes in the trash unopened, but at least she'd known when they arrived that her mother hadn't totally forgotten her.

But now, Marcie hadn't heard from her mother in almost two years. Was Lois Starr even alive anymore?

Though she didn't want it to, the thought that her mother might have died tore at Marcie's heart. She wasn't sure she wanted to actually see and talk to her mother, but it had always given her a small measure of comfort to know she was still out there...somewhere.

For a time Marcie had hoped there would come a day when she would feel her mother's love again, but over the years she'd given up on that idea and had allowed her mind to forget her mother even existed. Now though...she worried that it was too late to see and talk to her mother again.

Marcie tiptoed down the hallway leading to the kitchen, and when she reached that room, flipped on the light. Buster stood up from his bed in the corner of the kitchen and trotted over to her and gave a whine as if he sensed her unease. Marcie took the time to scratch the dog behind his ears and murmured to him as if to assure him she was okay. Once Buster seemed comfortable with her appearing in the kitchen in the middle of the night, he returned to his bed where he settled back down with a sigh.

She watched the dog curl up in his bed, and then Marcie took a seat at the kitchen table, glancing around the comfortable room. It didn't feel the same way tonight. Without people in it—especially Miss LizBeth—it was just another room. The people in a room were what made the difference to Marcie. When they weren't there anymore, there was only loneliness. And truth be known, she was tired of being alone.

Her eyes fell on a book sitting at the end of the table and pulled it closer. It was a Bible, the well-worn cover showing many years of use. It was Miss LizBeth's, proven by the small gold lettering in the bottom right-hand corner.

LizBeth Ann Montgomery McRae

For a moment, Marcie hesitated to open it. Then she thought about the woman herself and knew Dean's mother wouldn't have an issue with Marcie reading her Bible. She'd probably jump up and down in joy at the notion and shout 'praise the Lord!'

Marcie gently opened the book, pausing when she noticed notes written in the side margins in various places. This Bible wasn't just read, it was studied and absorbed. She finally turned to the center and paused in the book of Psalms as words on the page jumped out at her.

Remember, O LORD, thy tender mercies and thy lovingkindnesses; for they have been ever of old. Remember not the sins of my youth, nor my transgressions: according to thy mercy remember thou me for thy goodness' sake, O LORD.

Did God still remember Marcie Starr?

'The sins of my youth.'

Marcie had told Miss LizBeth the truth when she'd told her she was a Christian. The summer Marcie was eleven she'd given her heart to the Lord and been baptized. And she'd meant it when she'd done it—it wasn't just something she'd done because she thought it was what her parents wanted her to do.

But that had been in the past.

She'd run from God and from her faith and beliefs for so long that now it was almost second nature to push all thoughts of what had been before behind her. And she'd always felt that along with her mother not caring about her, that maybe God didn't want her anymore either.

She flipped over a few more pages, and her eyes fell on another verse in Psalms.

I called upon the LORD in distress: the LORD answered me, and set me in a large place.

Well, the mountains of Tennessee certainly qualified as a large place, and if God had indeed sent her here, perhaps there was a reason for it.

So, why am I here?

As Marcie sat and stared at the words on the page in front her, her thoughts raced. Maybe she'd been wrong for refusing to contact her mother all this time. But now, Marcie was here—now far from her hometown. It wouldn't be difficult at all to make the drive there before she headed home to D.C. And as Miss LizBeth had so clearly stated, if Marcie left the area and found out later that something had happened to her mother and she'd never be able to talk to her or see her again, Marcie would be sorry the rest of her life. Wouldn't she?

Perhaps it was time.

She closed the book on the table in front of her and closed her eyes. There was only one way to begin the journey ahead of her. She'd run from God for too long. It was time to quit running.

Lord God, I need You. I need You in my heart and in my life. I can't go through life anymore without You. I'm so sorry I pushed you away when I needed you most. But now I want to start over—if You'll take me back.

Please help me know what to do about my mother. I pray it's not too late to find her and to somehow find the strength to forgive her—even if it doesn't matter to her. I know it matters to You and I feel like I'll never be free of my past until I do.

But I'm going to need your help, Lord. Because I can't do it on my own.

16

The next day things moved smoothly at the work site. As a matter of fact, Dean couldn't believe how quickly the Potter cabin was dismantling— and without any hitches. Gordie had already taken one load of material over to the new location and unloaded it. It looked like the crew had two more days of work here, and then they'd spend all their time at the cabin's new home putting it all back together again—plus do the upgrades the client had requested. Then it would be ready for the electrician to come in and finish it.

Dean chuckled when he caught the tail end of one of Mac's jokes as he told it to Dutch and Marcie. It was a silly one—one he'd heard Mac tell a hundred times, but Dean couldn't hold back a smile as he heard Marcie's sweet laughter drift across the clearing.

It was good to hear her laugh.

There was something different about her today. Dean couldn't put a finger on it, but it was as if a light had gone on behind those gorgeous dark brown eyes of hers. She appeared more at peace and much more carefree than she'd been since her arrival. He didn't know what had happened between

.yesterday and this morning, but whatever it was he was thankful for it.

Marcie had even surprised his mother this morning with a gift of one of her sketches. Dean had watched in awe as Marcie had engulfed his momma in a hug—of her own volition. In the past, he'd noticed Marcie hadn't been the one to hug but had stood stiffly as his mother had offered her physical comfort. His momma was a hugger—no doubt about it. And it appeared some of that was starting to rub off on their guest.

Dean felt himself grinning at the thought of someday possibly being the recipient of one of those hugs from Miss Marcie Starr. He wouldn't be against that. Nope. Not at all.

As he remembered the sketch Marcie had given his mother, he sighed in contentment. The drawing was of Dean's dog Buster, stretched out in front of the fireplace in Momma's living room with his eyes closed and sleeping away like he didn't have a worry in the world—which he probably didn't. He was a dog, after all. It was a good drawing—really good. And even though it was just a pencil sketch, it looked so real Dean could almost see the dog's chest going up and down as he dozed.

Marcie Starr had a God-given gift—and it wasn't just writing for a magazine and taking photos. He couldn't help but wonder why she wasn't doing anything with her artistic abilities. Maybe one of these days he'd be brave enough to ask her.

Dean looked over at Gordie, who was removing another layer of logs from the cabin. When he turned back to look in Marcie's direction, the topic of his thoughts was headed his way, a big smile on her face.

"Y'all are makin' excellent progress, aren't you?"

She came and stood next to him, close enough he caught the scent of the flowery-smelling shampoo she used. Just a whiff of it took him back to the day he'd held her in his arms.

"Yeah, it's going a lot faster than I thought it would."

Marcie stood there with him and watched Gordie work for a bit, then turned toward Dean, her hand up in front of her face to help shade her eyes from the sunshine as she looked over at him.

"I'm sorry to say I'll have to leave before you get the cabin rebuilt at its new home. Do you think you can email me a couple of shots of y'all chinking the logs and then more of the final product? If you get them to me soon enough, I'll be able to include them in the article. I think the readers would really like to see what happened to this cabin after you took it down."

Dean nodded and continued to gaze into her face as his brain replayed the words she'd just said.

"Sure. I think I can manage that," he finally mumbled.

Suddenly there was a heaviness in his chest, and he struggled to breathe. Three days. She was leaving in three days. He'd been trying not to think about that and take things a day at a time. Now suddenly, the fact that she was leaving so soon hit him like a log to the chest. He needed to do something— anything to spend a little more time with her.

"You wanna ride into town this evening with me? I'll even buy you dinner."

Marcie's eyebrows shot up as she turned to look him full in the face. He couldn't read what he saw in her eyes, but finally, her lips turned up in a smile.

"Sure. Why not?" She chuckled. "Should I dress up in my fanciest duds, Mr. McRae?"

He tried to keep things light-hearted too. He supposed he should take her someplace nice and let her dress up, but she could do that in the city—although the thought of her going to a fancy restaurant with some other guy made him more uncomfortable than he cared to think about.

"What you've got on will do. It's not a fancy place—just good food." He added as she turned her eyes from his. "And it will give us a chance to talk without a bunch of other ears around listenin' to every word we say to each other."

She turned back toward him with a questioning look on her face, then gave him a small smile and a nod.

"Sure. I'd be happy to tag along with you, boss man—especially if you promise to feed me."

Dean grinned. Let her think this dinner invite was to talk business. But if he had his way, it would be anything but.

AS she rode in the truck with Dean later that evening on their way into town, Marcie thought about Dean asking her to dinner. She felt funny thinking about this outing as a date, but didn't know what else to call it—and that wasn't acceptable. After all, the man was a client—someone she was writing an article about for her job at the magazine.

So it was entirely wrong for her to feel thrilled at the prospect of spending some time alone with him away from the rest of his crew—and his mother. But Marcie couldn't help the way she felt. The thought of spending the evening alone with the man brought Marcie much more happiness than she could have believed.

Ever since they'd left his mother's house, Dean hadn't had much to say. The two of them had been sent out the door by his mother with a caution to be safe on the roads. Miss LizBeth had given them both hugs, Dean assuring his mother they wouldn't be late. They were just in need of a few minutes away from the rest of the guys so they could talk business, he'd explained.

But something told Marcie that Dean's mother wasn't buying that story. For that matter, Marcie wasn't either.

Marcie had seen the way Dean's eyes had lit up at the sight of her after she'd changed into her best pair of blue jeans and a teal-colored blouse covered by a worn denim jacket. He'd told her not to dress up, but she had spent more time in front of the mirror before coming downstairs than she had in the almost two weeks she'd been there. And she'd brushed her long hair until it practically snapped with electricity. It wasn't often she wore it down, but tonight it felt good to let it hang straight. And the appreciation she'd seen in Dean's green eyes had made her happy she'd spent a little more time primping than usual.

They reached the main street of the small nearby town, and Dean turned left at the first of two stoplights and drove another block before turning into a paved parking lot. Marcie looked out the window at the restaurant that appeared to be housed in an older one-story brick building off the road. By the looks of the number of cars in the parking lot, it was a favorite place. After finally finding a parking spot for his truck, Marcie saw Dean's frown as he turned off the engine.

"I didn't think they'd be this busy in the middle of the week. Sure hope we don't have to wait." He chuckled. "I'm starving. I don't like havin' to wait when I'm *not* hungry. But when I *am* hungry, I get grumpy if I have to wait."

Marcie laughed. "I'll remember that. If you come across as a little ornery, I'll try not to hold it against you."

The two of them got out of the truck and headed across the lot toward the glass doors of the restaurant. Marcie glanced back at the sign near the road that announced the place as "The Char House." She hoped the food was good because she *was* hungry.

Dean reached over and took hold of her elbow as they made their way to the door. His touch sent an instant spark through Marcie, and she hoped he couldn't tell she was blushing.

"I know it might not look like much from the outside, but this place has the best ribs in East Tennessee."

She chuckled. "I'll have to take your word for it until I can find out for myself."

As the two of them went through the doorway, they were greeted by a cute college-aged gal wearing black pants, a red polo shirt, and a white apron.

"Welcome to The Char House. How many will it be tonight, folks?"

Dean grinned. "Just two of us." He glanced around. "Do you actually have a free table? The place looks packed."

The gal laughed. "It's your lucky day, mister. We have one booth that just opened up. If y'all follow me, please."

Marcie smiled back at Dean when he grinned over at her as if he appreciated the fact that they weren't going to have to wait. With the pleasant smells that had hit Marcie's nose as soon as they'd entered, she was going to have a difficult time waiting for their food to come too. Her stomach gave a rumble as if in agreement.

The waitress took their orders for drinks—iced tea for both of them—handed them each a laminated menu and said she'd be right back for their orders. Marcie looked at the choices on the menu, feeling a moment of panic as she tried to figure out what to order. Dean barely glanced at his before folding it closed and placing it back on the table top.

"You already know what you're ordering? That was fast."

Dean chuckled. "An order of ribs, some of their seasoned steak fries, and a side order of coleslaw. It's been delicious every time I've had it."

Marcie smiled and closed her menu and placed it on top of his.

"Sounds good to me."

The waitress returned with their tea, took their orders, grabbed the menus, and left the table. She was only gone for about a minute when she came back with two small plates and a basket of hot rolls and a little dish of butter packets.

"Enjoy," she said with a smile. "Your meals will be out in a jiffy."

Dean chuckled after she left and picked up a roll and put it on his plate. "You ever run across someone who makes you feel like you're a hundred years old?"

Marcie grinned. "She *does* have a lot of energy, doesn't she?" She laughed. "But she should. She's young. I suppose I had a lot of enthusiasm and energy when I was her age, although I really can't remember."

The two of them bowed their heads briefly while Dean asked the blessing on their food. Marcie felt comforted by the fact that something that had felt so foreign to her when she'd first arrived now felt like the norm. If nothing else, this trip back to the mountains had accomplished her return to her faith and trust in God.

Marcie reached out and took one of the rolls from the basket, the waft of garlic butter hitting her nose. She took a bite of the warm goodness and all but melted into her side of the booth.

"Oh, that's good," she mumbled around her mouthful, then frowned. "Sorry." She covered her mouth with her free hand and glanced across the table where Dean sat with a big smile on his face, looking as if he were trying not to laugh at her. Then he waved his hand a little in her direction.

"Don't apologize. I love a woman who appreciates good food and isn't afraid to show it."

She felt her face warm at his use of the word 'love,' then finished chewing and swallowing her bite of roll.

"Well, that's good to know, but I don't need to be rude about it."

He chuckled as he took a bite of his own roll and it was quiet again between the two of them as they each enjoyed their food.

"So, Miss Starr, are you getting everything you're gonna need to do justice to this article you're writing?"

Dean's deep voice brought Marcie back in focus. Perhaps this really was going to be just a business dinner. Maybe that *was* the only reason Dean had asked her to come with him. A tug of disappointment swept through her at that realization, then she straightened her shoulders and lifted her chin. No worries. That was fine with her. She could keep it strictly business too.

"I think so. I've already written a portion of it and emailed it to my boss. He seems to like what I've given him so far. I've got some great photos too, although it's going to be tough to decide which ones we'll use in the spread."

She took her knife and spread a little butter on a corner of her dinner roll. "Of course, Mr. Avery will make the final decision as to what goes in and what doesn't—which is probably a good thing. I'd have a hard time choosing."

She raised her eyes to find Dean's green eyes steadily watching her and felt her face grow warm again under his scrutiny. A part of her almost wanted to ask him what he saw when he looked at her—but then, maybe she didn't want to know. He probably just saw her as a career-minded city gal, and she supposed that was what she was. But that wasn't who she really was deep down. She knew that now.

"Well," his deep voice continued. "I hope you've enjoyed your trip here to the mountains—at least a little bit."

Marcie nodded. "Oh, I have."

She stopped talking for a moment as it suddenly hit her that she *had* enjoyed being back in the hills of Tennessee— much more than she would have thought. The sight of the smoky blue ranges in the distance still brought the same thrill to her that it had as a child. It had also been enjoyable to relax and slow down and not feel as rushed as she did in the city. And surprisingly, even the sound of the locals' speech patterns and drawl was somehow comforting to her.

She saw Dean's dark eyebrows go up as if he didn't believe her, and she shrugged. Let Dean McRae think whatever he wanted about her. It didn't really matter. She was going home in a few days, and after that, she'd probably never see or talk to the man again.

Somehow, that thought didn't give Marcie any comfort. In the week and a half she'd spent with Dean McRae, she'd come to think of him as a friend and had enjoyed their time together much more than she would have thought.

It was quiet for a moment or two as the waitress brought their orders, and they both dug into the food on their plates. Marcie tried not to groan in enjoyment as the taste of the BBQ sauce on the ribs hit her taste buds. Once again, Dean had been right. The ribs were so tender they almost melted in her mouth.

"Well, maybe you can come back for a little visit again sometime then," Dean added. "Maybe do a follow-up article?"

Marcie chuckled. "Maybe. Who knows?"

Dean leaned back a little in his seat. "What it's like for you, back in D.C.? I mean, what's your life like there?"

She brought her eyes up to meet his green ones, studying her again in that intense way he had of doing that totally unnerved her—a way that made her feel like he could see right into her soul.

"Well, I keep busy. Work takes up most of my time, but I go places with friends—my co-workers mostly. We go to the movies, or out to eat. There are some great places to eat in the area."

He gave her one of his toothy grins.

"With food as good as these ribs?"

She laughed. "Well, you've got me there. I don't think there's any food on the face of the earth as good as these ribs."

17

That evening Marcie was awakened by the booming sound of thunder and the flash of lightning outside her bedroom window. She rolled out of bed and padded barefoot to the window and pushed the curtains out of the way so she could better see the storm moving in. As a child, Marcie had always loved watching thunderstorms move across the hills. Strangely, she'd felt it comforting to know she was safe inside while nature put on a tremendous light show outside.

Tonight's storm wasn't any different. The sound of the thunder echoing across the mountains sounded like music to her ears. A thunderstorm in the city didn't seem anywhere near as intense and powerful as it did out here in the hills. Even with the rain splashing in torrents against the windowpane, Marcie was able to see the jagged forks of brilliant lightning as it slashed through the darkened skies above them. One particular flash looked exceptionally bright, and the crash of thunder that followed cemented the knowledge that the specific strike had been close. Hopefully, the lightning had struck a tree in the woods someplace and not someone's house or barn.

While Marcie kneeled on the floor in front of the window and watched the storm putting on a light-show outside, her mind replayed her evening with Dean. She had really enjoyed their time together. He was such a gentleman and genuinely fun to be around. His teasing ways and sharp mind kept her on her toes, and she appreciated that about Dean.

The man was almost too good to be true. She'd never known another man like him.

Then her lips turned down into a frown. Was it wrong that she was going to miss him when she returned home? After all, she'd only known him for two weeks. Surely she couldn't be attracted to someone in that short period of time, could she? And to what purpose? You only needed to spend a few hours with him to realize that Dean McRae was a man of the mountains—pure and simple. And Marcie lived and worked in D.C. Their two worlds were miles and miles apart, so there was no sense in her even thinking along the lines of having anything more of a relationship than the working one they had now.

No, Dean McRae was a nice guy, but he certainly wasn't the guy for her.

DEAN threw the last of his tools he needed for the day in the back of his truck and slammed the tailgate closed, then stood and took a deep breath of the fresh air. There was something special about a morning following a good thunderstorm. The air felt cleaner, purer, and he couldn't seem to get enough of it into his lungs.

It was difficult to believe the storm had been so strong the night before as this morning, the sun shone brightly through the treetops above him. The remaining raindrops from last night's deluge dripped off the green leaves of the trees and almost shimmered in the sunshine like little glass diamonds. God sure had made this world He'd given them to live in a beautiful one.

His head came up at the sound of the front door squeaking, and Dean found himself mesmerized as he watched Marcie Starr stride onto the porch, pulling her backpack over one shoulder as she went. Today she was back in what he thought of as her work clothes—worn jeans tucked into work boots, dark blue T-shirt covered by a blue and white plaid flannel shirt, her beautiful black hair pulled back into a ponytail. Just the sight of her took his breath away.

Get a grip, McRae. What are you? A high school student?

Marcie shot him a sunny smile as she opened the passenger side of his truck and threw her backpack behind the seat.

"Good morning, kind sir. I'm ready when you're ready, boss."

Dean mumbled a gruff 'good morning' as he got in the truck and started it, all the while feeling Marcie's dark eyes studying him as if he'd done something wrong. What had he done now to upset the woman? Although he was well aware he'd been a bear to the guys—and even his mother—during breakfast.

"Didn't sleep well, Dean?"

He took his eyes off the road long enough to glance over at the lovely woman on the other side of the truck, noting the sunshine pouring in the truck's back window and how it made her black hair almost glow. What would it feel like to drag his fingers through that black satin?

Dean looked away, blinked a couple of times and focused his eyes back on the road in front of him while he attempted to get his bearings.

"I slept all right."

Her only response was a "hmmm," and Dean let it go. He hadn't slept well at all, but he wasn't about to tell Marcie Starr that—nor admit to the reasons why. Of course, the storm that rolled through the mountains in the middle of the night hadn't helped much, waking him when he had finally dozed off. But the primary reason he'd struggled to sleep was the vision of Marcie that was determined to come to him every time he tried to close his eyes.

Lord, what are you doin' to me? This woman is trouble, Lord. She's a city gal, and I said I was never going to have anything to do with a city gal again. Remember?

Dean released a sad sigh, not even caring if Marcie heard him. Whether because of a lack of sleep or just his all-around frustration at life, it was lookin' to be a very long day.

LATER that evening, well after the supper dishes had been cleaned and put away and the guys had left the house, Marcie sat on the back steps of Miss LizBeth's porch. Her sketch pad was in her lap, and a pencil was in her hand.

Knowing this was her last night here in the mountains, Marcie wanted to soak up as much of them as she could. For a person who hadn't wanted to come, God was really making her glad she had.

Marcie watched the sun hanging low in the west. It was just beginning its decline toward the earth, and the light was perfect. It was that magical time of night Marcie loved the most. The birds had stopped their chirping, the crickets hadn't started in on their songs yet, and the breeze had stilled so that not even a leaf seemed to be moving on any of the trees.

Her eyes scanned the mountain ranges through the opening in the trees and watched as the world around her turned a rosy pink, then slowly darkened as the sun continued to fall. It was what the old-timers here in the mountains called 'the gloaming,' that mystic time of twilight that had been Marcie's favorite as a child.

She'd tried to sketch earlier—attempting to catch the light fading from the countryside—but she knew there was no way a simple sketch could match the real thing. Listening and watching the world prepare to go to sleep had always left Marcie with a funny feeling in her heart—a yearning of sorts. Although for what, she was never sure.

Tonight's sunset left her with the same feeling.

The squeaky sound of the back door opening and closing drifted to where Marie sat in the gloom, and shortly, a tall, dark form sat down next to her. She didn't have to look to know it was Dean. She could feel it was him even before he'd taken a seat.

"This is my favorite time of day—or night, I guess I should say," his deep voice almost whispered in the silence.

She nodded, then realized he probably couldn't see her very well—even though there was a little light drifting out through the kitchen windows.

"Mine too."

Marcie heard him sigh and recalled his sigh that morning when they'd been driving to the work site. He didn't sound as sad or upset tonight though—just tired. He and the guys had worked hard today, but Dean had told them they'd made good progress. The next day they were going to start working at the new location of the Potter cabin. She felt terrible that she wouldn't be around to see it when it was finished. The work these guys did amazed her. They were real artists in their line of work.

Dean's voice interrupted her musing.

I'm sorry I was such a bear today, Mars."

She smiled at the sound of the nickname. Hearing him saying it did funny things to her heart.

"That's okay. I know you were tired."

It was silent between them for a few moments before Dean's deep voice spoke again in the darkness.

"So, did you find what you were looking for when you came here, Marcie?"

She glanced over at Dean's silhouette, wondering at his question. What was he really asking her?

"I guess so. I think I have enough solid information about your business that I should be able to write an article to accurately inform people of what you do, which will hopefully result in much more business for you."

She chuckled. "And I've got some great photos to go with it. Hundreds more than I'll ever use!"

"That's not exactly what I was talking about, Mars. Although I'm glad you were able to get what you needed for the article."

She felt him shift a little on the step, his left shoulder brushing her arm as he moved and turned to face her. Even though she knew in the dark he couldn't clearly see her face, Marcie felt herself pull inward as if to hide from him. There was a subtle change in the air between them, and Marcie didn't know what to think about it. It was almost as if Dean had come to a decision about something.

"What are you talking about, Dean?"

It was silent for a second or two before he finally answered.

"You can't disagree that God sent you here for a purpose."

"I suppose He might have had something to do with me being assigned for the article. I have to say, I was surprised Mr. Avery gave me the job."

She frowned. "Although at first, when I found out it was here in Tennessee, I didn't want to come. I thought it would be a huge mistake to come back here. Too many bad memories."

His quiet sigh unnerved her. "Do you still feel it was a mistake?"

She clamped her lips shut, not trusting herself to say anything further. Marcie was glad she'd come but was afraid her heart was never going to be the same after meeting Dean. Regardless of whether she ever saw her mother again, Marcie had changed by coming here. Out of the whole experience, the most awesome thing was she'd resumed her relationship with God. Knowing she'd never be alone again…that God still loved her. No, it hadn't been a mistake. But she couldn't tell all that to Dean.

Dean sighed again. "I think God brought you back here to the mountains to deal with something from your past, Marcie—something you've been running from." She heard his quiet sigh again in the darkness before he continued, his deep voice hushed.

"These mountains are ancient, and my daddy used to say that if you just listen to them, you can hear God's voice. He'll give you the wisdom to get through the tough times—the hard times when you don't know what to do."

It was quiet for a few seconds before Dean continued. "I hate to think what my life would have been like if I hadn't come back to these mountains—and God. *Please* remember, Marcie, whatever happened to you here before—*whatever* it was, God can help you deal with it. And you'll never be ready to move forward in the future God has planned for you until you *have* dealt with your past. That's something my divorce taught me."

Before Marcie realized his intention, her right hand was caught up in both of Dean's, held tightly in his grasp. The warmth of his rough hand shot through her, causing her heart to jump and she almost lost track of what they'd been discussing.

"Whatever you've been running from, Marcie—whether your failed relationship with David the Jerk or something else—God brought you back here for a purpose—and I don't think it was just to do an article about my business. Before you head back to D.C., I'm praying you come to terms with whatever happened to you here."

She felt him give her hand a gentle squeeze. "I'm here if you want to talk. If not, that's okay too. God already knows what it is you're goin' through, and He's more important than I am. But I want you to know, I'm prayin' for you, Mars. And even after you leave, I'm gonna keep right on prayin'."

His voice thickened with emotion, and Marcie swallowed hard at the sound. "And I for one am *so* thankful God brought you here, Mars. 'Cause I wouldn't have given up the chance to get to know you for anything in the world."

With that, Dean surprised Marcie even further by leaning toward her and kissing her lightly on the lips, the shock of it reaching to her toes. Then he released her hand and stood up and clumped back up the steps and into the house, leaving her sitting alone in the dark, feeling much more confused than she had been when he'd first joined her on the steps.

Dean McRae had just kissed her.

And she wasn't sure how she felt about that—other than she'd liked it. A lot.

18

The next morning arrived bright and warm. It was the day Marcie was leaving to start her trip home. With mixed feelings, Marcie tucked the last of her clothes into her suitcase before zipping it closed. Then she allowed her eyes to drift around the comfortable room where she'd stayed in Miss LizBeth's house, making one last check to see if there were any items she'd overlooked. She'd spent a week in this cozy room. Like the previous week when she'd stayed at Dean's home, Marcie had slept better here than she had in years. With the quiet of the night air drifting in through her open window—much different than her closed windows back in the city—Marcie had found peace. She was actually going to miss this place.

And the people. Especially the people.

Sitting on the edge of the bed, Marcie couldn't stop the frown from forming on her face. Somehow in the two weeks she'd been back in Tennessee, the bad memories that had driven her from this part of the world so many years ago had been overridden by good memories—including those made with Dean, his crew, and his mother. They had touched her life and her heart in indelible ways that would never be forgotten.

Dean.

The memory of his lips on hers swept over her and Marcie blinked as she tried to stop the tears that came to her eyes as she thought about how much the man had come to mean to her. She knew the kiss had significantly affected her, but what had it meant to Dean—and why had he kissed her anyway? He knew she was leaving to return to her life—her real life. And Marcie had thought they were just friends. Friends didn't kiss each other like that. And furthermore, a friend's kiss wouldn't have rocked her world the way Dean's had.

I want you to know, I'm prayin' for you, Mars; and even after you leave, I'm gonna keep right on prayin'.

Some people might take those words as weak promises, but Marcie knew Dean McRae well enough after two weeks to realize he wasn't a man to make promises he didn't plan to keep. Marcie was positive that Dean *was* praying for her and intended to do so until…until what?

I think He brought you back here to the mountains to deal with something from your past—something you've been running from.

Dean's words reverberated through her mind until she knew exactly what he was talking about. How he'd known, she didn't know. But somehow, he knew.

Okay, God, I'm here. What do You want me to do about it? What do I do about my mother?

Marcie quietly whispered the words into the empty room, reaching out to the Father in heaven. Since the night she'd found Miss LizBeth's Bible on the kitchen table, Marcie talked to God more than she had in years. And He had made His presence known in her life again. There were no spoken words from Him, but whenever she turned to prayer, Marcie was always given a measure of peace she had never experienced before.

Today was no different. There was no instant answer from the heavens, and Marcie couldn't help but release a little laugh at that thought. But as she sat there, an idea came to her mind and continued to grow stronger the more she thought about it.

The question was, though, was Marcie strong enough and brave enough to do what God was telling her to do?

DEAN leaned against the railing on the front porch of the house along with his momma, Mac, Gordie, and Dutch—waiting. Even Buster sat in front of the door as if he had picked up on his humans' tension.

They'd all discussed Marcie's leaving at breakfast that morning before she'd joined them. Even though they needed to get to work, none of them wanted to miss the opportunity to say goodbye to the lovely woman that had so enchanted them during the brief time she'd been there.

It was a somber bunch—not even Dutch was cracking any jokes this morning, and it hadn't missed Dean's notice that his momma had been quieter than usual at the breakfast table. She'd outdone herself; in addition to the standard breakfast of grits, bacon and sausage, fried potatoes, and scrambled eggs, LizBeth McRae had baked a batch of her famous cinnamon rolls. But no one seemed to have their normal appetite—including Dean, who had forced himself to stuff the food in his mouth even though it all tasted like sawdust.

He'd silently scolded himself half the night for allowing his emotions to override his common sense. Marcie Starr was just a writer from a magazine in Washington, D.C. They'd only known each other for the sum total of two weeks—surely not long enough to build any sort of a relationship. But they *had* become friends, and Dean felt more for her than he had any woman since his divorce. If he were honest with himself, though, he probably felt more for Marcie than he ever had for his ex, Patty. He and Patty had certainly never been best friends.

And then, of course, there was the kiss. Ever since Dean had placed his lips on Marcie's, he hadn't been able to get the feel and taste of her out of his mind. And the knowledge that was the first and last time he'd ever be able to kiss her was tearing him up inside.

Because she was leaving.

Today.

At the sound of the screened door squeaking open, everyone came to their feet, and the object of Dean's thoughts walked out the front door, rolling her suitcase with her laptop case and purse hanging from her shoulder. As she came through the doorway, Marcie's head was down, and her black hair hung loose and partially hid her face so Dean couldn't get a good look at her.

Suddenly everyone jumped into action.

Mac stepped forward and took her suitcase from her.

"I'll just put this in your car for you, Miz Marcie," he said quietly.

Dutch stood next to him. "I can take your laptop for you, ma'am."

Marcie looked up and gave both the young men a gentle-looking smile before relinquishing her luggage to them. Then Gordie moved in front of her, his large hand outstretched for a handshake. But to his and everyone else's surprise, Marcie put her arms around the big man and pulled him into a hug, then stood on her tiptoes to kiss his whiskered cheek.

"Please thank Sally for being so nice to me, Gordie. You never know, I may appear at your back door someday, lookin' for a hot meal."

Gordie's face turned red at her kiss, but then he grinned like a schoolboy. "You are welcome at our house any time, little lady. Y'all remember that."

By this time, Mac and Dutch had returned from stashing her luggage in her car and stood at the bottom of the steps. Dean's mother reached out for Marcie, enfolding the taller woman into her ample arms. Dean swallowed back his own emotions at the tears he saw in his momma's eyes. Evidently, he wasn't the only one who had become rather attached to the young woman.

After pulling apart, LizBeth reached up with both hands to hold onto Marcie's face and pulled it down where she could gaze into her eyes for a moment as if wanting to memorize what she looked like.

"I'll miss you, young lady. Y'all take care, and you come back some time to visit, ya hear?"

She handed Marcie a paper bag. "There's some cinnamon rolls in there for you to take with you. Can't send you away without those."

Marcie gave a little laugh, but it sounded forced to Dean's ears.

"I can't believe you had any left, Miss LizBeth." Marcie glanced around, briefly letting her eyes come to rest on each of the four men. "Sounds like the boys are slipping."

Dutch kicked at a small stone near the base of the steps. "Reckon we weren't real hungry this mornin', Miz Marcie," he mumbled.

Then it was time for Marcie to leave, and Dean stepped off the porch to walk her to her car. This was the moment he'd been dreading all morning. The pain in the region of his heart made him wonder if he were having a heart attack. And he couldn't seem to get enough breath into his lungs.

How did he say goodbye to her? After the brief kiss they'd shared on the back porch a few nights earlier, Dean wanted nothing more than to pull her into his arms and attempt a repeat—kissing her in such a way that she'd forget everything but him. Maybe then she'd change her mind about leaving.

But he knew he couldn't do that.

God had sent her here to the mountains for a reason. But Dean knew *he* wasn't that reason.

Marcie put her purse and the sack of rolls on the car seat, then turned around to face him. Her eyes locked onto his, and he struggled to keep the smile on his face. Her eyes looked like dark pools of sorrow—even though there was a smile on her face.

"Well, time for me to hit the road, boss man."

He forced his lips up into a grin. "Looks like it."

Dean reached out his hand for a shake, but she shocked him when she wrapped her arms around him in a hug, then stepped back so quickly he almost could have believed he'd imagined it. But no, the feel of her arms around him still warmed him to his toes.

"Thanks for sharing your passion for your business with me, Dean McRae. You are a good man and a brilliant businessman. And I promise I will do the best job I can on your article."

She lifted her chin a little. "I'll try and do ya proud."

He nodded as he continued to gaze at her, trying to memorize everything about her face. From her dark brown eyes, high cheekbones, full red lips, and black satin-like hair, Marcie McRae was the most beautiful woman he'd ever known.

Dean cleared his throat, trying to get rid of the lump residing there.

"I have no doubt that you will do an excellent job on the article, Marcie. I truly believe you can accomplish whatever you set your mind to."

He took hold of her hand one last time, not yet ready to relinquish the touch of her. "And I meant what I said to you last night. I'm gonna keep praying for you—that you allow

God to lead you wherever you're supposed to be. I'll also pray for safe travels for you as you drive back home."

Her eyes filled with tears, and then she blinked a couple of times as she continued to gaze at him. Then she gave him a little nod and slowly tugged her hand from his, leaving Dean feeling bereft at not touching her anymore.

"Thanks, Dean. I appreciate the prayers."

She turned around and got in her car, looking up at him just one more time and adding, "Well, time to hit the road."

He watched as Marcie put on her seatbelt and closed the door with the window rolled down. As she started the car, Dean took a step back out of the way, then gave her a return wave as she lifted her hand toward him and drove down the drive toward the main road.

And out of his life.

Goodbye, Marcie Starr. God go with you and protect you—today and every day.

19

I t took Marcie a full ten miles down the road before she finally got her emotions under control. She had known it was going to be difficult to say goodbye to all of them, but it had ended up being much harder—especially with Dean looking at her like he couldn't let her go. Which begged the question, did he feel the same pull toward her that she did toward him?

Well, even if he had, Marcie guessed she'd never know now. There would be no reason for her to return to this area in the future—unless Bob Avery *did* decide to send Marcie back to Tennessee to do a follow-up article on *McRae's*. And Marcie had never known the magazine to do that. But she could always hope and dream.

Driving the winding country roads on the way back to the main highway, Marcie decided at the last minute to take a detour. It had been years since she'd driven the Foothills Parkway outside of Townsend, and before she headed back, she needed a good dose of mountain views. If Marcie had more time, she would have also driven through Cades Cove, but she couldn't do it this trip. Several times as a child, Marcie had ridden in the car with her parents as they drove the eleven-mile loop, and she had always found it fascinating. Marcie had absolutely adored the small authentic cabins in the woods that had been saved and restored after the Cove had been made into a part of the Great Smoky Mountains National Park. And now that she'd watched Dean and his crew work at saving cabins just like those, it would mean even more to her to see the Oliver, Lawson, and Shields cabins. But that would have to wait until another time.

Traffic was light on the Parkway, and whenever she chose to pull over at a lookout and get out of the car, there were no other cars or people around to disturb her. At the final lookout, Marcie stood for about ten minutes and soaked in the view of the multiple green mountain ranges in the distance as they flowed one into the other. It was a clear day, so she could see for miles. She could even tell that the leaves on the trees in the higher elevation in the mountains had started to change. Marcie knew from past experience that in another month the view would look totally different, and instead of the smoky green colors, the mountain ranges would appear more like a multi-colored patchwork quilt.

Too bad she wouldn't be around to enjoy it.

Heaving a sigh filled with sadness at that thought, Marcie took one last look at the view and got back into her car and drove the roads down the mountain. Before heading to the main highway, however, her car turned almost on its own toward the small town she'd been avoiding since she'd hit the Tennessee state line.

Her hometown.

As she entered the small community, Marcie's eyes darted around as she attempted to take it all in. She'd been there with Dean almost two weeks earlier, but this time she wasn't afraid to look—or be seen. It was unnerving to be back driving the streets she had left behind, and it didn't feel real to her.

The downtown looked much the same as it had her entire life—a few more empty storefronts than she remembered, but Marcie was happy to see that her daddy's old hardware store was still in business and wondered if Mr. Feeney still owned it.

Once she left the main downtown area, Marcie turned down a side street and drove slowly past her childhood home. Did her mother still live there? Was her mother still alive? On a whim, Marcie pulled her car over and stopped, parking across the street from the small white frame house. Her old home actually looked pretty good. Someone had taken the time to paint it a crisp white and even installed light green shutters at all the windows.

As Marcie stared out the car window at the house where she'd grown up, a young boy—who looked to be about nine years old—ran out the front door of the house to the front sidewalk. Seeing Marcie parked in front of the house and staring, he paused for a second and looked in her direction. Before Marcie had a chance to react and put the car in gear to drive away, the boy ran over to her open window.

"Are y'all lost lady?" His high-pitched voice was thick with the eastern Tennessee drawl she remembered so well from her own childhood.

Marcie shook her head.

"Not really. Do you live in that house?" She nodded her head toward the front door of the home he'd just exited.

"Yeah. Me and my momma and daddy live there. Why y'all askin', lady?"

She chuckled. There was nothing quite like the brutally honest questions of a child.

"Just curious. Believe it or not, that used to be my house when I was your age."

The little guy's brown eyes grew wide. "Really? Cool!"

Then the towheaded young man gave her a quick grin and was off and running before Marcie had time to ask any more questions. But he'd answered her most significant question. Her mother didn't live there anymore. Marcie didn't know where she was living—or if she was still alive—but she wasn't here.

She took one last long look at the house before putting her car into gear and leaving. As she drove back to the main part of town, Marcie pondered where to go next. Maybe she'd stop into the hardware store long enough to say hello to Mr. Feeney before she left town. It would be silly not to while she was in the area. Who knew when she'd be coming back? And maybe he would tell her where her mother was living—hopefully without her having to actually come out and ask him.

Marcie drove to the main downtown block and found a parking spot in front of the old brick building she remembered so well. Just looking at the storefront brought back fond memories of her dad and if she tried really hard, she could almost see him standing out front wearing his black pants, white shirt, covered with the green apron he always wore at the store. He'd be sweeping the sidewalk with that ratty old broom as he had every morning she could remember.

Then Marcie blinked her eyes a couple of times and released a sigh and got out of the car. Her daddy wasn't there anymore and never would be again. She needed to remind herself of that fact and prepare herself before walking through that glass door into the building, just as she had every day when she'd worked for Mr. Feeney after her father's death.

When Marcie pushed the glass-paned heavy wooden door open to enter the building, the ringing sound of the old familiar bells above the door brought a smile to her face. It surprised her how the smell of the place brought back even more memories. The aromas of old wood and paint and metal hardware hit her nose, along with the lemon smell of the cleaner she remembered Mr. Feeney had always used to keep the old hardwood floor shining. And Mr. Feeney had demanded Marcie also use it to dust the shelves when she'd worked for him. Boy, did that smell take her back.

She strolled down the center aisle, glancing to her right and left at the shelves of screws, paint brushes, doorknobs, and other various hardware items as she walked by. It didn't look like Mr. Feeney had changed a thing since she'd left.

Why I'd be able to step right in and start stocking shelves again without any trouble.

Somehow, that thought tickled her.

When she reached the main counter near the rear of the store, Marcie stood back and waited as Mr. Feeney finished waiting on a customer who was purchasing what looked like several pounds of six-penny nails. While she waited, Marcie took a few minutes to study her old employer. She wasn't surprised to see his once thick dark brown hair had thinned and now had smatterings of grey running through it. Marcie did some figuring in her head and came to the realization that since she knew Mr. Feeney was several years older than her dad had been, that meant he must be in his late fifties. He still looked fit for his age, but she supposed the physical labor involved in running the store probably helped keep him in shape. Unloading the weekly delivery truck bringing inventory to the store had always been a real workout; she remembered well.

The customer finished his purchase and left the store with his paper sack of nails, and Mr. Feeney turned his glass-rimmed eyes on her. After a few seconds, Marcie saw them narrow and knew the instant he recognized her.

"Well, I'll be! Marcella Starr. If you ain't-a sight for sore eyes!"

Before she knew what had happened, Mr. Feeney had come from behind the counter and engulfed her in a breath-smothering bear hug. He still smelled like tobacco, which meant he still smoked his pipe. When she'd been young, Marcie had always thought it was an awful smell that hung on him, but now…it was a comforting aroma.

Just when she thought she was never going to breathe again, he finally released her, then took a couple of steps back. As his eyes carefully studied her face, Marcie was left feeling like a child again.

"Why, you've turned into a beautiful young woman, missy!" His deep chuckle warmed Marcie to her toes.

"Hi, Mr. Feeney. It's good to see you too."

He continued to stare at her, his fists clenched at his hips. "Heard you moved to the big city. What y'all doing now?"

Marcie grinned. When she'd worked for Mr. Feeney, she'd only dreamed about having a job doing what she did now. There was a certain amount of pride in her voice as she answered his question.

"I work for an architectural history magazine in Washington, D.C. I've been down here collecting information for an article I'm writing for the magazine."

Mr. Feeney's eyes about bugged out of his head, and it was all Marcie could do not to laugh. She was sure he'd never thought she would amount to anything.

"Well, I'll be! So, what's ya doin' here in town, girl? You here to see your momma? I bet she's real proud of you."

Marcie's heart raced. Well, that answered one question. At least by what Mr. Feeney had just asked her, Marcie now knew her mother was still alive.

"Maybe. But I drove by the old house and some other family is living there."

Mr. Feeney waved his hand through the air. "Oh, yer momma sold that old house several years ago. She's livin' next to the Union Church at the end of town now." He gave her a grin. "She'll be so tickled to see y'all."

"Well then, I suppose I'd better go, Mr. Feeney. I just stopped in to check on you and see how you're doing. The store looks great, by the way."

The man nodded his head as he looked around at his domain.

"I've left everything pretty much the same. I figure if it ain't broke, it don't need fixin'."

Marcie chuckled, told him good-bye, and gave him a little wave as she turned to make her exit. She didn't want to answer a bunch of questions and knew if Mr. Freeney got started, he'd want to know her whole life story before she could get away.

She returned to her car, then headed out of town toward the church Mr. Feeney had mentioned. She remembered it well as it was the church she and her parents had attended her entire childhood—until her daddy's death. Then her mother had quit going and so had Marcie.

Somehow Marcie found it ironic that now her momma lived right next door to their old church and wondered how that had happened. Based on the shape her mother had been the last time she'd seen her, Marcie couldn't imagine her mother having anything to do with a church.

It didn't take her long to reach the location, and Marcie pulled her car over to the curb and parked while she stared at the building. The church was still as she remembered it—a brick structure with a white steeple that looked as if it recently received a new coat of paint. As a matter of fact, the old building actually looked much better than Marcie remembered.

A small one-story white house sat next to it, but there was also a big brick building on the opposite side that looked like it might be an apartment building. So, where did her mother live then?

Marcie was sitting in her car looking out the window and trying to decide which one might be where her mother was living when a tall, lanky-looking man dressed in dark pants and a long-sleeved plaid shirt came out of the church. He looked her way for a moment and then headed toward her car. Seeing him headed in her direction, Marcie leaned out her window and called out to him. After all, Pastors usually knew everyone in town. He'd probably know where her mother was living.

"Excuse me, sir. Can you help me? I'm trying to find someone."

The man, who had graying hair and looked to be about the age of Mr. Feeney back at the hardware store stepped to the side of her car and leaned over to peer in the window. His eyebrows went up when he got a look at her, and a broad smile swept over his face.

"Marcella Starr, is that really you?"

Marcie stared at him as she struggled through her memory, trying to figure out who he was. And failed. He wasn't the pastor she remembered from her childhood. Pastor Neilson had been old when he'd been the pastor of the church. By this time, he had to be in his eighties and retired.

"I'm sorry. Do I know you?"

He laughed and shook his head. "Naw. I apologize, young lady. We've never met, but your momma has a photo of you sittin' on the dresser. You haven't changed that much, so it was easy to tell it was you.

"Does she know you're here yet? Your momma's gonna be fit to be tied."

Marcie stared at the man while he rambled and attempted to decipher everything he'd just said. One thing he said stood out, however. Why would this man know a photograph of her was sitting on her momma's dresser?

"So, *who* are you exactly?"

The man had the grace to blush. "I'm so sorry. I haven't properly introduced myself."

He held out a hand for her to shake, which she awkwardly did through the open car window.

"I'm Pastor Ethan Carter. I'm the pastor of this church, and as of about four years ago, your momma's husband. Which I suppose makes me your step-daddy."

20

Marcie stared at the man standing next to her car in shock. Her momma had remarried—a preacher man? How was that even possible?

"Hey, what are we doin' talkin' out here? Come on into the house. Lois is gonna be so surprised to see ya."

Feeling numb, Marcie exited the car, thinking to grab her keys and her purse at the last moment before she hit the key fob and locked it. Unless things had changed drastically, chances were slim anyone would bother her car in this small town—especially parked in front of a church. But after living in the city for as long as Marcie had, locking her car had become second nature.

She hesitantly followed the man as he crossed the street and walked up to a sidewalk that led to the front door of the house. Marcie could feel her fingers shaking as she opened her purse and dropped her keys inside.

What was she doing? This hadn't been what she'd planned at all. She wasn't ready to see her mother again.

Not now. Maybe never.

I should just turn around and get back in my car and drive away. This is such a bad idea.

Yet, she continued to follow the man. Once he reached the front door, he turned and gave her a friendly smile as if he was able to hear the thoughts jumbling around in her brain.

"Don't be nervous, girl. I promise, your momma is not the woman she used to be. And regardless of what you may think, she loves you dearly."

Marcie gulped as he opened the front door and led her into a small foyer. She didn't take the time to look around as the preacher called out as soon as they entered the house.

"Lois! Where you at? There's someone here to see you."

As the two of them walked a little further into what was apparently the main living area of the house, Marcie heard footsteps coming from another room and turned to face in that direction—not knowing what to expect. She kept gulping air and felt as if she was having difficulty breathing as a sense of panic swept through her.

A few seconds later, her mother walked through the door, wiping her hands on a towel. Marcie's eyes looked at the apron tied around her middle and felt as if she'd stepped back in time. How many times had she seen her mother walk through the kitchen door in that very way?

As Marcie raised her eyes to study the woman's face though, it was easy to see this woman was older and heavier than Marcie remembered. Her once blond hair was now streaked with gray. It was cut in a cute style that came down to her chin, and even though Marcie could see the lines and wrinkles of her mother's face from where she was standing, she could also tell that her mother looked much healthier and more at peace than Marcie remembered from the last time she'd seen her.

But it was the expression on the woman's face when she saw Marcie standing in front of her that took Marcie's breath away.

"Marcella!"

Her mother stopped in her tracks, her face turned pale, and a look of shock swept over her that quickly turned to joy. Before Marcie realized the woman had moved closer, Marcie was pulled into a warm hug. At first, Marcie held herself stiffly and tried to resist her mother's affection, but the smell of lilacs she'd always associated with her mother softened her heart and she unconsciously wrapped her arms around the older woman. It felt strange, and yet it felt like she remembered.

Home.

The woman in her arms trembled, and after a few seconds, Marcie finally realized why. Her mother was sobbing, and Marcie looked over her shoulder in desperation at the man as she struggled to know what to do. Her mother's husband moved closer and finally reached out and patted Marcie's mom on her shoulders.

"It's okay, Lois. Your girl's here, and she's just fine. You got no need to worry and fuss anymore, honey. She's okay."

Marcie felt her mother's arms finally release her and Marcie took a step back, swallowing hard and blinking her eyes. She needed to remove herself from this awkwardness. If she didn't get hold of her own emotions quickly, she'd be sobbing herself.

Her mother continued to stand in front of Marcie and gaze up into her face as if still unbelieving that she was really there.

"You are so beautiful, girl!" Her momma laughed, and somehow, the sound warmed Marcie's heart. It had been a long time since she'd heard her mother's laughter.

"I still can't believe you're here!"

Her mother motioned toward the other room. "Come into the kitchen and set a spell. I'm in the middle of stirrin' up some cinnamon muffins and jist need to finish 'em and get them in the oven."

Marcie shook her head. "I don't know....I really need to get going."

Her mother's husband cleared his throat and gave her a pleading look. "Now, you can spare a few moments to visit with your momma, can't you?"

He chuckled, the sound filled with joy, and hearing it brought emotion to Marcie's heart she hadn't felt in years. It was the feeling of being wanted.

"Surely you didn't come all this way to leave right away."

She finally gave him a small nod and trailed after her mother to the kitchen. It looked much like the kitchen of her childhood, and Marcie thought she actually recognized a few of the items sitting on the kitchen counters—the old ceramic flour and sugar canisters that her mother had always used, along with a square cookie jar. The kitchen table was oak, with four spindled oak chairs sitting around it. The table wasn't a piece of furniture she could ever remember seeing before so must be new—although it looked well used.

"Go ahead and have a seat, Marcella. Finishin' these will only take a minute."

Sitting in the offered chair, Marcie watched her mother as she deftly poured the batter into muffin tins and then put them in the oven and set the timer. Running water from the faucet into the bowl in the sink, her mom wiped her hands on the same towel she'd been using earlier before she pulled out a chair next to Marcie and sat down.

"I still can't believe you're really here. I have prayed so long for the chance to see you again..."

When Marcie saw the tears in her mother's eyes, she dropped her own. There had been a time ten years ago when seeing a look of concern from her mother would have meant so much to her. Now...Marcie didn't know what to think.

"But what are you doin' in Tennessee?"

She raised her eyes, expecting to find anger or judgment on her momma's face, but instead, there was only confusion and genuine interest.

"Not that I'm upset, sweetie. I just thought you still lived in Washington, D.C."

Marcie flinched as she allowed her mother's words to sink in.

"You knew where I was living?"

Her mother slowly nodded. "I did—for a time. I used to send birthday cards and Christmas cards and letters to you, sweetheart." She frowned. "But I never heard back from you. Then a few years ago—shortly after Ethan and I got married, everything I mailed to you came back as undeliverable. I didn't know where you'd gone to."

She sniffed. "I've prayed for you every day, Marcella. Prayed that God would bring you back to me." Her mother reached out and lightly touched Marcie's hand for a second, as if making sure she was real. "And He has."

Marcie looked down at the worn hand resting on her own, the older woman's fingers lined with age and pursed her lips together, more to keep herself from saying what she really wanted to say than for any other reason. She had to keep reminding herself that a lot of time had passed since she'd last talked to or seen her mother. The woman sitting before her wasn't the mother of her childhood, but neither was she the drunken woman who had made Marcie want to leave home. At least, she hoped she wasn't.

"I moved around a couple of times, and I guess the post office had a hard time keeping up."

"But you got my earlier cards and letters then?"

Marcie nodded. She'd received them, but of course, she'd never opened any of them. But there was no way she was going to tell her mother that—at least not yet. Maybe never. She felt a shudder go through her and started to stand.

What am I doing here?

Her mother instantly reached out and lightly touched her arm.

"No. Please, Marcella. Please don't go. I have some things I need to say to you."

A shadow passed over her mother's eyes. "Once I'm done, if you still want to leave, I won't stop you. I promise."

Marcie chewed on her lower lip, finally gave a nod, and resumed her seat.

"I go by Marcie now. Not Marcella."

Her mother gave her a gentle smile. "Marcie. I like that. It's real pretty.

"Did you know you were named after your great-grandma Starr?" Marcie heard her mother's soft sigh. "I wanted to name you Susanna, but your Daddy put his foot down and said you didn't look like a Susanna." She chuckled a little, then gave Marcie a small smile as her eyes seemed to reach out to Marcie, asking for something. Forgiveness?

"Oh, honey. I can't say 'I'm sorry' enough times to make up for the wrong I did ya all those years ago."

Marcie finally had to turn her eyes from her mother's face. What she'd seen there seemed sincere, but Marcie also well remembered the days she'd come home from school after her father's death to find her mother sitting in the kitchen with an empty bottle of booze in front of her. How was she supposed to just forget that? How was she supposed to forgive her for the pain she'd caused her—her own daughter?

"I know I wasn't much of a momma to you after your daddy died." Her mother sighed again. "Truth be known, I wanted to die too," she added, her voice no more than a whisper.

Turning her eyes back to her mother's face and really taking the time to look at her, Marcie flinched. She'd always wondered if the depression her mother went through after her husband's death had driven her to drink, but had thought sooner or later Lois Starr would pull herself out of it for the sake of her daughter. Well, that hadn't happened.

"I'm not makin' excuses, mind you," her mother continued. "I know you were more of a parent to me than I was to you back then."

She gave Marcie a gentle smile. "You were such a good girl, and I was so proud of you—getting that full scholarship to college."

Then her face dropped. "But I didn't know how to tell you. I felt like such a failure."

"You were."

The words were out of Marcie's mouth before she could stop them, and when she saw the hurt pass over her mother's face, she felt like a heel. But she was only being honest. After her dad had died, her mother hadn't been a real mother to her.

Marcie had been the adult in the household. Marcie had done the grocery shopping, and the cooking, and the cleaning, and the laundry. And after they'd sold the hardware store to Mr. Feeney, Marcie had even gotten a part-time job there. Her mother had just sat in the house and drank herself into a stupor every day. Marcie had felt like an orphan after her daddy's death. And she'd only been sixteen at the time—way too young to have all those responsibilities on her small shoulders.

"I know I can't change what happened between us back then, Marcella—Marcie. But if you can find it in your heart to forgive me, I do want to be a better mother to you now. I'll spend the rest of my life asking for your forgiveness if that's what it takes."

Marcie sat quietly, wondering what to do. She should have left when she had the chance. Or never come in the first place.

Now her mother was sitting there, looking at her with those sad eyes, and wanting—begging for forgiveness. But what if Marcie didn't have it in her to forgive her? What if she felt her mother didn't deserve to be forgiven?

"I don't know, Momma. I'm not sure I can ever forgive you."

She saw her mother blink a couple of times, swallow, and then Marcie saw her drop her eyes and look at the floor as if she was too ashamed to look Marcie in the eye again.

"I don't blame you, dear. If I were in your shoes, I'm not sure I could either." Her mother's voice felt strangled as if she struggled to hold back her tears.

"But can we at least be civil to each other?" Her mother looked up and gave her another nervous smile. "I really would like to hear about your job and your life in the city."

Her mother nodded and then her eyes brightened as she sat up straighter in her chair. "Will you stay for supper? We have an extra room, and you're welcome to stay overnight."

Marcie shook her head. "I can't stay. I need to get back home."

When she saw the disappointment on her momma's face, however, Marcie caved. The story LizBeth McRae had told her about her own actions when Dean's father had passed away came back to Marcie. LizBeth had told her she'd felt like her life had ended the day her husband had died, and she hadn't wanted to go on living without him.

Marcie swallowed hard. Her mother had evidently felt the same way about the loss of her husband. The only difference was, Miss LizBeth hadn't turned to alcohol to take away the pain of her loss. But how could Marcie judge her mother for her weakness? Did Marcie know how she would have reacted if it had been *her* husband who had died? The memory of the pain she'd felt just that morning when she'd left Dean behind her returned. And she'd only known Dean McRae for a couple of weeks. Her parents had been married for almost eighteen years.

Besides, who was she to refuse to forgive her mother? Hadn't God forgiven Marcie Starr again not that long ago for all her mistakes? Marcie knew if her decision to turn back to God had been real, she couldn't reject her mother's attempt at reconciliation.

"Well, I guess I could stay one night. It *is* Labor Day weekend, so I don't have to be back in the office until Tuesday."

Her mother's face lit up like it was Christmas morning.

"Wonderful!"

Marcie gave her a weak smile and sighed. She didn't know how wonderful it was, but she guessed she was committed to staying one night. But that was it. And she wasn't going to enjoy it. After that, she was going home—knowing she'd found her mother like Miss LizBeth had told her she should and had buried the hatchet once and for all.

Forgiveness? That was going to take a little longer.

21

Marcie opened her eyes the next morning and stretched out her long frame. The guest room her mother had shown her to the previous evening was small. There was only space in the room for a twin bed, a dresser, a small desk, and a chair, but it was spotless and somehow reminded Marcie of her old bedroom back in the old house.

Surprisingly, following a delicious evening meal, Marcie had talked to her mother and new step-father for hours, telling them about her years at college and her job at the magazine. It had been emotionally freeing to discuss her life with her mother. And Marcie had felt as if telling her mother everything that had happened to her since she'd left home might make her mother realize even more all she'd missed out on in Marcie's life by her actions of the past.

And it had somehow released Marcie from some of the hate held toward her mother. The more she chatted with this woman who was so much the mother of her childhood, the more Marcie wanted to know her better.

There was no question about it, Lois Starr Carter had changed.

Marcie wasn't sure what had happened to change her—whether meeting and marrying Ethan Carter had been the instigator of the transformation, or if it had been something else. It didn't really matter. She just knew that the woman her mother had become was everything Marcie had wished and prayed for right after her father had been killed in the car accident. The woman her mother had never been.

Lord, I don't know why You brought me here—other than to reconcile with my mother. I'm not sure I can ever forgive her completely, but if You can work it out so that we can at least have some sort of relationship, I would be forever grateful.

Marcie grabbed her Bible from the nightstand and opened it to read some scripture before she started her day. Today's verse was from Matthew, chapter 6, and verse 14:

For, if ye forgive not men their trespasses, neither will your Father forgive your trespasses.

She had to smile upon reading those words. God couldn't make it any clearer to her what He expected of her.

Well, she was going to keep working on it—that was all she could promise God right then. And He was going to have to help her because she surely couldn't do it under her own power.

Once she was out of bed, Marcie took a quick shower in the small bathroom attached to her bedroom, then dressed and repacked all her luggage. Marcie had told her mother she could only stay the one night, and that had been true. Even though she'd like to spend more time with her mom and her newly-discovered stepfather, Marcie had a life and a job to return to. There was still a lot of work to be done on her article on *McRae's* before she'd be finished with it. Marcie needed to make it as perfect as possible before she turned in the final piece to her boss Tuesday morning.

After breakfast, tearful goodbyes were made. Marcie hugged her mother one last time and got in her car to leave, looking back out her car window at her mother and Ethan, standing there—both of them looking at her, their faces filled with love.

"You have my phone number, right?"

"We do," Ethan's deep voice replied. "And you have your momma's phone number too, right? Please feel free to call us anytime, Marcie. I mean it."

Her mother sniffed, and Marcie felt her own eyes fill with unshed tears.

"Oh, yes, dear. Please keep in touch. Call anytime. I'd love nothing more than to hear from you—at least once a month."

Marcie smiled. Would her mother be shocked to find out she actually wanted to talk to her more than once a month? Who would have believed it?"

"I'll try and call once a week, Momma." Marcie loved being able to call her mother that precious name again.

She gave the two of them a final wave. "Thanks again."

When she glanced in her rear-view mirror a few seconds later, she couldn't help but smile at the vision of her mother and Ethan standing at the curb in front of their house, still waving.

On the way out of town, Marcie knew there was one more stop she wanted to make. No. One she *needed* to make.

Just outside of town and down a narrow curving road, Marcie found the village cemetery. It appeared much larger than she remembered, but then she supposed more souls had been added to it in the years she'd been absent. Surprisingly, Marcie was able to find the spot where her dad's grave was located without any problem, though. Kneeling next to the grave, Marcie brushed some dried grass from the most recent lawn mowing off the face of the stone and sighed.

I miss you, Daddy. I'm trying to make things right with Momma, 'cause I know you wouldn't want me to treat her poorly. I hope you're proud of your little girl, Daddy. I've tried to be the kind of daughter you would have been proud of. I still miss you so much.

She sat there a little longer, then brushed the tears off her cheeks and stood. She knew her father wasn't on earth. His soul had long ago gone to be with his Savior in Heaven. But it was comforting in some ways to have this earthly place to still come and talk to him.

Thank you, Lord, for giving me the years I had with my father. He was a good Daddy.

With that, Marcie got back in her car and pointed it northeast. It was time to go home.

She knew without a doubt that she would call her mother and keep in touch. Their relationship was far from perfect, but it felt good to actually *have* a relationship with her mother again. Who knew where it would go.

But at least it was a start.

And Dean McRae had been correct when he'd told Marcie God had brought her back to Tennessee for a reason. Maybe someday Marcie would have an opportunity to tell Dean he'd been right all along.

UPON her return to D.C., Marcie's life settled into a measure of normalcy. Her article on Dean McRae's business was well-received by her editor, and she waited patiently for February to arrive and the release of the March issue in which her piece on *McRae's* would be the prime cover article. After years of hard work, she was finally going to be granted a solo by-line. She couldn't be more excited.

Marcie made sure to make time in her busy life to make the promised weekly phone calls to her hometown—spending hours on the phone with her mother as they caught up on each other's lives. Marcie still had times when feelings of resentment would sneak up on her, and she struggled with re-forgiving her mother each time. She knew it was going to take a long time to make those feelings go away. After all, they'd been a huge part of her life for ten years, but she was attending church services again and faithfully reading her Bible. Hopefully, getting back into the Word would give her the strength to do the right thing. And every time she was tempted to return to the feelings of doubt and unforgiveness, Marcie would once again turn it all over to her Heavenly Father through prayer.

Her evenings were quiet—usually spent reading or watching the latest movie on DVD. There were several occasions when she joined her fellow magazine employees and went out on the town to a favorite restaurant, or took in a movie. But for the most part, Marcie was still the loner she'd always been.

Marcie never dated. Every now and then one of the guys from work would ask her out for dinner, but she always declined—the thought of Dean McRae making her think that no other man would ever meet her expectations. The men she knew all seemed so shallow in comparison. She knew her impressions of Dean were probably overblown—based on only knowing him for two weeks. She was sure that even Dean McRae wasn't perfect. But, at least in her mind, he was much more of an example of what a good Christian man should be than most of the guys she knew.

SHORTLY after Christmas—a somewhat disappointing holiday for Marcie as she hadn't been able to go to see her mother and Ethan as she'd initially planned—Marcie placed a phone call to LizBeth McRae. She was long overdue for a 'thank you' call for the gracious hospitality she'd shown Marcie when she'd been in Tennessee. The two of them chatted for almost half an hour as Marcie told LizBeth about her reconciliation with her mother.

"Oh, girl! That's such wonderful news. I've been prayin' somethin' fierce that would happen. I'm so happy for you."

Marcie chuckled as she heard the love and happiness in the sound of the familiar voice coming through the phone.

"Well, we still have a long way to go, but it does feel good to get rid of the resentment and hate I've held in my heart for so long. And I have you to thank for that, Miss LizBeth. If you hadn't talked me into it, I don't think I ever would have been brave enough to make an effort to stop and see her."

She heard the other woman's chuckle on the other end of the phone. "That wasn't me, honey. That was the Lord workin' in your heart. And I'm prayin' He's still workin' on you."

"Oh, He is. I'm back to going to church and reading the Bible too. Even then, the Lord still has a lot of work to do on me. I've got a long ways to go yet."

Miss LizBeth chuckled again. "He has lots of work to do on all of us, Marcie girl."

Their conversation eventually drifted to Dean and the boys, as Marcie had been sure it would. LizBeth informed Marcie that she was concerned about her son—that every time they talked on the phone lately, Dean seemed to be in a cantankerous mood.

"He's like a bear that's been woke up early from his winter sleep. Can't say as I envy his crew havin' to work with him every day like that. Hope he works out whatever's got in his craw."

Marcie couldn't help but wonder what was causing the man she'd known to only be gentle and kind, to be such a grump, but decided it really wasn't any of her business. She just hoped it didn't have anything to do with his business not doing well. Marcie knew wintertime was tough on Dean's type of business.

But her magazine article was due to come out in a few months, and hopefully, it would bring in lots of new clients for *McRae's*.

VALENTINE'S Day was the official release date for the March issue of the magazine, but Marcie picked up several extra copies ahead of time to mail to Dean and the crew. She also put one in the mail to LizBeth and one to her mother and Ethan—hoping they would enjoy reading the article that had brought her back into their lives.

Marcie was more than a little proud of how the article had turned out. Her boss had told her several times that she'd done an excellent job on it. They did have a tough time choosing which photos to include in the spread, though, as there had been so many good ones. But Marcie had been delighted with the finished product. The photo they'd picked for the cover was one of her favorites; Dean, Gordie, Mac, and Dutch standing in front of the Potter Cabin, tools belts strapped around their hips and hard hats on their heads, they looked ready to go to work.

She still had all the photos stored in a file on her own computer, and every now and then spent a few minutes scrolling through them one by one, remembering what a fun experience the assignment had been. Just seeing the photos of

Dean and the guys at work made her feel warm inside—and more than a little homesick.

Marcie hoped and prayed that article wasn't going to be her last big assignment, but since her return, she was back to covering more local historical societies and museums. Marcie had assumed that by successfully completing a big job, it would lead to future ones. So far, that hadn't happened. But she knew how things worked in the office and was trying to be patient.

The morning of February 14th arrived just like every other day in Marcie's life—other than she knew it was the day the March issue with her article in it would hit the store shelves.

As for it being Valentine's day—with no boyfriend— Marcie knew the chances of her receiving a cheesy card and a box of tasty chocolates were non-existent but tried not to let it bother her. As if to show the world she was doing just fine as a single woman, that morning Marcie chose her brightest, cheeriest red blouse to wear, along with a dressy pair of black slacks. As there was no snow on the ground in D.C., she slipped her feet into a pair of short fashionable black boots and called it good.

When she arrived at work and stepped off the elevator onto their floor, she was surprised by how quiet it was in the office. Everyone was working away at their desks—intent on whatever their assignments were. But there was an overriding sense of…Marcie couldn't put her finger on what it was. But something was going on.

She said good morning to Cindy, the young receptionist at the front desk. At least *she* still had a smile on her face.

"Good morning, Marcie. You have a *special* delivery sitting on your desk."

She gave Marcie a secretive smile and a wink, causing Marcie to almost trip as she hurried down the hall toward her small cubicle. Cindy had been right. There in the center of her desk sat a huge bouquet of the most beautiful pink long-stemmed roses she'd ever seen. Marcie dropped her purse and laptop on the floor in her hurry to get to the card.

It looks great! Congratulations and Thank You! Dean and the boys

Marcie smiled and leaned over to breathe in a deep breath of the intoxicating smell of the flowers. Apparently, Dean had received the large envelope holding the advance copies of the magazine with her article in it. She'd sent him enough copies so all four of them could have their own copy. How sweet it had been for Dean to send her flowers. She certainly hadn't expected such a gesture, yet somehow it seemed like something he would do.

She'd just taken off her jacket and draped it across the back of her chair when Harvey Jones, the Human Resources Manager of the magazine, stuck his head in the door.

"Got a minute, Marcie?"

Marcie looked up, surprised by the somber look on his face.

"Sure. What's up?"

"If you would just come with me, please?"

Feeling unsettled by the formal way Harvey was speaking, Marcie followed the man back the way she'd entered, catching her breath in a gasp when he led her to Bob Avery's office door. What was going on?

"Go on in, Marcie. Bob's waiting for you."

Marcie gave a little knock on the door, then went ahead and opened the door and entered, noting Bob Avery was alone. By the frown on his face, he evidently didn't feel any happier than anyone else in the office did this morning. Again, Marcie wondered what was going on.

"Have a seat, Marcie," his gruff voice sounded even hoarser than usual, and Marcie couldn't help but wonder how long it was going to be before his constant smoking caught up with the man. Even though no one was allowed to smoke in the office, you could smell the smoke on the man's clothes, so she knew he hadn't given up the nasty habit yet.

"What's going on, Bob?"

His answer was a heavy sigh as he gazed across his messy desk at her.

"First of all, I want to commend you again on the superb job you did on the McRae piece. You surprised me, Ms. Starr. The article was good. Really good."

Marcie relaxed a little in her chair as she allowed the words of approval to drift over her. Praise from her boss was rare, so she was going to enjoy it.

"Thank you. I really enjoyed doing the article, and I'm hopeful I'll have the opportunity to write many more like it in the future."

The man's mouth moved into a larger frown, and Marcie heard him clear his throat. Her heart dropped by his actions. They did not bode well for future assignments like the McRae article, and she instantly started worrying about what she'd done wrong.

"Yes, well. I'm sorry to have to tell you that I don't have good news for you this morning, Miss Starr." He reached up and ran his hand across his face, as if frustrated.

The feeling of unease came back, and Marcie tensed up, her hands clenched on the arms of the chair she was sitting in. She got the impression that her beautiful morning was about to end.

"We've been informed by the owner—I should say former owner—that the magazine has been sold to a conglomerate out of New York City."

Marcie frowned. "I assume that's not good."

Bob shook his head. "Not for some of us it isn't. The new owner's first order of business was to eliminate several members of our staff in order to 'better their bottom line.'" Bob held up his hands and made air quotes in front of him—

a move which Marcie had never seen him do before. Then he finished his announcement.

"Unfortunately, you are one of the people we're letting go."

Letting go.

They were firing her. Marcie felt as if the air had suddenly left her lungs.

"I don't understand, Bob. You just told me how good the McRae piece was, and now you're firing me?"

The man on the other side of the desk shook his head. "Not firing, Marcie. Letting you go. There *is* a difference. I'll be happy to give you a letter of recommendation. You've done good work here, and I'm sure you'll have no trouble finding another position."

He cleared his throat again and acted as if he needed to look down at a paper on his desk—as if he couldn't stand to face her any longer.

"You'll receive three weeks' severance pay, plus whatever pay you have coming to you for any unused vacation time you may have. And you'll be eligible to draw unemployment, of course. That should keep you going until you can find another position. I'm sure you'll be fine."

Marcie just sat there and stared at the man, not wanting to believe what he was telling her.

She had lost her job, the job she'd taken such pride in. The job she'd worked at so diligently. The job she'd poured her heart and soul into—even though it had never been her passion. And she'd been good at it. And they were firing her— just like that.

"I'll have Harvey go with you to your desk so you can collect your personal belongings before leaving the building."

He stood and reached out his hand, which she automatically took and shook, not even realizing what she was doing. She tried to think of what to do—what to say. But it felt as if her brain had quit working.

Harvey waited right outside the door, and as Bob Avery had told her he would, he led Marcie back to her desk where he stood by nervously and observed her as she went about collecting her personal items out of the office. There wasn't much to clean out of her desk as Marcie had never been one to cover her desktop with personal memorabilia. It was a work area, after all—not her home.

A short time later, with the vase holding the lovely flowers from Dean and the crew at McRae's, Marcie was walked to the doorway of the magazine office and sent on her way. Harvey did have the grace to tell her once again how sorry he was before he closed the door behind her.

Marcie stood on the sidewalk a few seconds later as the shock continued to roll through her. Then releasing a weary sigh, she stiffened her back and made her way to where she'd parked her car.

It appeared she had nothing on her schedule for the rest of the day.

Perhaps she'd go home, have a good cry, and then take a nap. She deserved it.

22

D ean stretched his arm across his desk to reach the ringing phone, wondering who was calling him at nine o'clock at night on the office phone. *McRae's* phone had been ringing like crazy the past two weeks—even since Marcie Starr's magazine article had hit the newsstands. They already had jobs lined up for the next four months.

Now that it was the middle of March and the weather was warming up some, they were going to be even busier. Marcie had done a great thing for *McRae's Recycled Logs and Materials* by writing that article. Business was booming.

"McRae's Recycled Logs, Dean McRae speakin'."

"It's always so good to hear your voice, son."

He automatically sat straighter in his chair. Dean hadn't heard from his momma in over two weeks and frowned at the thought that he hadn't taken the time to call her either. And now she was calling him—at nine o'clock at night. This couldn't be good.

"Momma. Everything okay?"

"Just fine, son. I just thought I oughta give you a call and make sure you're still alive since I haven't heard anything from you in a coon's age."

Dean closed his eyes and dropped his chin.

"I'm sorry, Momma. We've been swamped with new jobs comin' in. Ever since the magazine article came out, my phone won't stop ringin'."

His mother's chuckle on the other end of the phone helped Dean relax a little, and he leaned back again.

"And that's a good thing, right?"

He joined her chuckle. "Very good. So, is everything all right with you, Momma?"

"Yup. I just wondered if you've heard anything from that magazine gal lately?"

Dean sat up straighter again.

"Marcie? Why are you askin' about Marcie?"

"Well…"

Dean recognized his momma's voice was changing into her 'I've-got-a-story-to-tell-you' mode and almost sighed but then caught himself at the last minute. His momma would have even more to say to him if she ever thought he didn't take her advice seriously.

"You know she sent me a copy of that magazine article, so I called her to thank her for it. I had her number since she'd already called to thank me for takin' such good care of her when she was here doing that article for y'all—like I'd do it any other way. Anyway, I thought I should thank her for takin' the time to send me a copy. It was so kind of her. She didn't have to do that."

He closed his eyes and pushed his hand through his thick hair as a familiar frustration swept over him. Why his Momma took so long to tell a story, Dean had never figured out.

"And?" Hopefully, he could prod her into getting on with the crux of the story before his patience ran out.

"Well anyway, we got to talkin', and you'll never guess what that magazine did to her, Dean. I'm so mad at them! I'm half tempted to drive to D.C. myself and march into their office and give them a piece of my mind. And after all she's done for them.

"Anyway, they got bought out by some other company. And that new owner decided he didn't want her anymore. They fired our Marcie. Can you believe it? After that nice article she wrote and everything? Why I'm just sick about it."

Dean heard the words his mother was saying, but it took a moment for them to sink in. Marcie had lost her job? The poor girl. That was an awful thing to have to go through. And he knew she really enjoyed her job—well, as Dean replayed their conversations about their respective professions, he thought she liked what she did well enough.

Suddenly Dean had a momentary thought of her moving back here and getting a job locally but quickly threw that idea out the window. Marcie Starr was a city gal, and she'd stay there. Knowing what little he knew about her, she'd find another job without any problem. She was smart, and she had a lot of talent. She'd be fine.

"That's terrible, Momma, but I'm sure Marcie will be okay. She's a smart gal. She'll find another job."

"I know she's smart. That what makes me so mad. I guess it's the principle of the thing. I mean, that's the problem with them big city businesses. They don't appreciate their employees. Thank the Lord, it's not that way around these parts."

Dean nodded his head in agreement. He could remember clearly how distant the relationships had been in the architectural firm he'd worked for in California. He'd just been an employee—no one cared about who he really was or what he thought. And he was discard-able—easily replaced.

Here, Dean's employees were like family, and even though it had been a tough winter with fewer jobs, Dean had scrimped on his own pay so that he could still pay his employees what they were counting on to survive. That's what a good employer did. At least, that's the way Dean McRae did business.

"Well, I jist wanted to make sure you knew about Marcie's job situation so you could be prayin' for her." His mother's voice turned serious. "I'm sure she's havin' a tough time with all this, but I also know the Lord has a reason for it happenin'. God don't make mistakes."

Dean's lips lifted as he heard his momma's words—a mantra he'd heard from her over the years. God certainly didn't make mistakes.

"I'll be sure to pray for her and her job situation, Momma. Thanks for letting me know about it."

They said their goodbyes and Dean hung up the phone, then stared unseeing at the paperwork on his desk for a few moments. Finally, he closed his eyes and sent up a prayer about the news he'd just received from his mother.

Somewhere out there, Marcie Starr was struggling, and even though Dean couldn't do anything to help her through her trials, at least he could pray for her. He'd promised her when she'd left Tennessee that he would pray for her. And he had been—and would continue to do so.

MARCIE hit 'send' on another email application to another job opening. She'd sent out what seemed like hundreds of resumes in the past two months, but so far had only been called for one interview—and that had ended up being a part-time receptionist job that only paid minimum wage. Fortunately, they'd never called her back on that one.

In the two months since she'd lost her job, Marcie had been angry, sorrowful, furious, defiant, and finally, accepting of her situation. She didn't know why she'd lost her job, but she'd deal with it.

Her mother, during one of their weekly phone conversations, had suggested that the Good Lord obviously had other plans for Marcie. Her mother had encouraged her by telling her that perhaps because Marcie wouldn't move to the next thing in her life on her own, so maybe God was using this situation to *encourage* her to move onto something else.

Well, that was all well and good, but that didn't help to pay the bills. So far, Marcie was okay financially. But, if something didn't happen soon, things were going to start getting tight. And then tighter.

Her cell phone sat on the desk next to her, and when it started to ring, she gleefully grabbed it. Maybe this was the job offer she'd been waiting for.

Seeing the caller ID, however, Marcie frowned. It was her mother calling—which was unusual. She never called during the day, stating she didn't want to bother Marcie when she was working to find a new job.

"Hello, Momma."

But it wasn't her mother's cheery voice on the other end of the phone.

"Marcella—Marcie. It's Ethan."

Marcie's heart lurched. Ethan wouldn't be calling unless something terrible had happened.

"Ethan? What's wrong?"

"Sweetheart, your Momma's in the hospital. They think she's had a stroke."

"Noooo."

Marcie felt the breath leave her body and was a little light-headed for a few seconds until she remembered to breathe.

"I'm not sure she's gonna make it, Marcie." Ethan's voice sounded so sad and weak. It was easy to tell he was shaken.

"I'll be there as quickly as I can get there, Ethan."

A sigh was his response. "Oh, thank you, dear. I'm at my wit's end. I don't know what to think or do, Marcie. The doctor says she might recover, and then again, she might not." Marcie heard the catch in his voice. "I'm prayin' she does, 'cause I don't know what I'll do if she doesn't."

"Just hold on, Ethan, and keep praying. I'm on my way."

23

Four weeks had passed since the phone call that changed Marcie's world. After a couple of weeks, her mother's health had steadily improved to the point she had eventually been transferred to a rehab facility where she was undergoing physical and occupational therapy. It was going to take some doing to get Lois Carter back to where she'd been before the stroke, but Marcie was thankful that at least she was alive. It had been touch and go for the first few days.

Marcie had stayed with Ethan at the house until she was sure her mother was settled into the rehabilitation facility all right, then she'd made the trip back to D.C. That was after giving Ethan a promise that once she had everything taken care of back in the city, she was going to return to help take care of her momma.

"Are you sure you wanna do that, girl? I mean, you wanna give up everything you've worked so hard for all these years? Your momma isn't gonna be very happy about you leavin' your dreams behind for her."

Pastor Ethan's face had been sincere as he'd questioned Marcie's decision.

"I'm sure, Ethan. And just for the record, I'm not giving up my dreams. In reality, since I lost my job at the magazine, there's nothing for me anymore in D.C."

She'd sighed as she struggled to come up with the words to explain a decision she'd been contemplating for months—even before her mother's stroke.

"I can't explain it, but I feel like I'm supposed to come back home, Ethan. At least for a time."

The older man had patted the back of her hand and nodded. "Sounds like the Lord is leading you in another direction from that which you had originally planned." He gave her a little grin as if he was privy to information she wasn't. "He has a way of doin' that with His children. When we least expect it." He chuckled. "Keeps us on our toes."

Back in the city, it didn't take Marcie long to get rid of the trappings of her former life. She didn't have much in the way of furniture, and what didn't sell to neighbors and friends, she gave to a local homeless shelter. She packed what little was left and shoved it into the back of her SUV, closed her bank accounts, forwarded her mail, and left her past behind—much like she had ten years earlier.

Only this time, she was going home.

ANOTHER month passed, and Marcie, along with Ethan and all the doctors and nurses, were in awe at the progress Lois Carter was making. Marcie's mother was apparently a fighter, and even though she still had to use a walker, and her stride was more of a shuffle, she was back on her feet. She still had trouble forming words—sometimes getting frustrated with herself as she searched her mind for the word she wanted—but was able to communicate.

And the day the doctor released her to finally go home, Lois Carter's face was one huge smile. Sitting in her wheelchair as they readied to leave her room in the nursing facility, she reached out with her hands to clasp Ethan's on one side of her and Marcie on the other.

"Home."

Standing there, looking down into her mother's radiant face and feeling her warm hand clasped in hers, Marcie said a prayer of thanks. There had been days when her mother had first taken ill that Marcie had feared she would soon be losing her. But it appeared she was going to get a second chance to get to know her mother better after all.

And for that, she was more than thankful.

ON a Saturday three weeks later, Marcie was standing at the kitchen sink, rinsing off the breakfast dishes and putting them in the dishwasher when she heard the doorbell. Grabbing a hand towel, she hurried down the hall toward the front door, wondering who it might be. Ever since her mother's stroke, the ladies of Ethan's and her mother's church had visited often and had been more than generous with casseroles and desserts. Perhaps it was someone from the church visiting again.

Tugging open the door, Marcie couldn't hold back her grin when she saw who was standing there. Holding a huge bouquet of daisies and roses in front of him stood none other than Dean McRae.

"Good morning, Miz Starr. I'm here to see Mrs. Carter. Is she feeling up to havin' visitors this morning?" He gave Marcie a gentle smile, then the smile turned to a frown. "Or am I too early?"

Marcie finally pulled herself together enough to answer him, feeling her lips widen in a huge smile at the sight of the man.

"No, it's not too early." She held the door open the rest of the way and motioned for him to enter, catching a whiff of Dean's aftershave as he walked by. She'd forgotten how good the man always smelled—and how good he looked. Marcie struggled to breathe as she took in the sight of him.

Dean scuffed his boots on the front door mat and shot her a shy smile. Feeling suddenly awkward, Marcie pushed a loose strand of hair back behind her ear as she struggled to get control of her emotions. Just seeing the man was making her face heat up. For goodness sake, she felt like a moonstruck teenager.

Then footsteps came from the back of the house where Ethan's study was, and Marcie turned to make the introductions.

"Dean, this is my step-father, Pastor Ethan Carter. Ethan, this is Dean McRae—you remember, the man whose business I did that article on for the magazine?"

"Sure, I remember." Ethan smiled widely and reached out to grasp Dean's free hand with his own large one. Marcie watched as the two men seemed to size each other up, and she couldn't help but smile a little at the picture they presented.

They were both tall, with Ethan the slimmer of the two. Dean was a few inches taller than the older man, and his shoulders were much broader and muscular. Marcie had forgotten just how big a man Dean McRae was, but seeing him again after all this time, it came back to her. And the fact that she still found herself attracted to Dean McRae was more than a little disconcerting.

"Well, come on in, Mr. McRae."

"Please, call me Dean." Dean gave her a wink as he brushed past her and followed her step-father down the hallway to the room they'd created into a sitting room for her mother to use. Lois Carter was already dressed for the day and was seated in an overstuffed chair reading. Her walker was close at hand, although she rarely used it anymore and had recently taken to just using a cane—even though Marcie kept telling her she needed to be careful.

It appeared mother was just as stubborn as daughter.

After her mother had 'oohed and aahed' over the beautiful flowers, Marcie took them to the kitchen to find a vase large enough to put them in. She took a whiff of the beautiful yellow roses amid the lovely daisies, all the time in awe that Dean had taken time out of his busy day to bring them to her mother.

And just how had he known about her mother's stroke anyway?

Miss LizBeth.

That *had* to be how Dean had known about her momma. Marcie had continued to keep in touch with Dean's mother over the past few months. At first, it had been because LizBeth McRae had requested she be kept up-to-date on Marcie's mother's progress. She'd cited the reason being that her church's prayer warriors were praying for Lois, but now Marcie couldn't help but wonder if Dean's mother had an ulterior motive.

It *was* nice that Dean had made an effort to come to visit her mother though—and the flowers were gorgeous. And, of course, Marcie was happy to see him again.

Marcie carried the vase of flowers back to her mother's room to find the other three deep in discussion about a Bible verse. It was actually a verse she and her mother and Ethan had just read in that morning's devotions, so Marcie was very familiar with what they were discussing. They were verses from John, Chapter 14.

And I will pray the Father, and he shall give you another Comforter, that he may abide with you for ever; Even the Spirit of truth; whom the world cannot receive, because it seeth him not, neither knoweth him: but ye know him; for he dwelleth with you, and shall be in you. I will not leave you comfortless: I will come to you.

She listened to Ethan and Dean interact as they discussed the verses and couldn't help but smile. In the short time she'd known her step-father, Marcie had come to care for him a great deal—mostly because of the obvious love between him and her mother. But Ethan Carter was also a good man—a man obviously called by God to be a pastor and a shepherd, and he took his job seriously. He was interested in everyone and everything and saw each meeting with an individual as an opportunity placed there by God for him to make sure the other person was aware of the knowledge of Jesus's saving grace and how much God loved them.

"I have to agree with you, young man. There are some things written in the Bible that we just aren't gonna understand 'til we see Jesus. I think we aren't supposed to comprehend everything. Some things we just have to take on faith and believe."

Marcie saw Dean nod his head.

"I couldn't agree more, sir."

Marcie felt her lips turn up in a smile, then turned her head away, hoping Dean hadn't seen her face. She didn't want him to think she was making fun of him. Quite the contrary.

Mr. Dean McRae continued to amaze her.

AN hour later, Marcie walked Dean to the door.

"Thanks for coming to see Momma, Dean. It was a nice surprise." She gave him a shy smile before she added, "For both of us."

He stepped through the door onto the front porch, and she followed him, feeling the need to have a few moments to talk to him privately as they hadn't had a moment alone ever since he'd arrived.

"I take it Miss LizBeth was the one who told you I was back."

Dean's green eyes locked on her face.

"She told me about your mother's stroke and that she was home and feeling better. I thought I'd try and bring a little sunshine to her life."

Marcie chuckled. "Are you callin' yourself a little ray of sunshine, Dean McRae?"

He laughed loudly, and she noticed with affection that the tips of his ears were turning pink as they always did when he was embarrassed.

"Not exactly."

Giving a little nod, Marcie took a step closer to him, loving the feeling of being able to tease him again. She sure had missed him.

"Well, in this case, you were, Dean. You were just what Momma needed. She's had plenty of people stop in from church and from the neighborhood, but I'm sure it was refreshing to see a new face. Although, she talks like she knows you—because of the magazine article, of course."

He chuckled and gave her one of his winks. "Of course."

Then his face sobered and he reached out and took hold of her hand, his green eyes looking into hers.

"I was real sorry to hear you lost your job, Mars. It doesn't seem fair after you worked so hard."

She shrugged, enjoying the opportunity to look deep into Dean's eyes. Intense green eyes she'd dreamed about for months.

There had been a time when the pain of losing her job would have overshadowed everything else in her life. But now, it just didn't seem to matter anymore.

"No worries." She grinned. "And Ethan seems to believe that it was God's way of getting me back to the mountains. And who am I to argue with that logic when that's exactly what happened?"

Dean continued to gaze into her eyes, then reached up and lightly touched her right cheek with the back of his left hand, his knuckles running from her ear down to her chin—almost a caress that made Marcie's knees feel weak.

She saw him swallow hard before he got a surprised look in his eyes, then dropped his hand and looked away from her as if he suddenly realized what he'd done. When he looked back up at her, she could still read the emotion in his eyes.

"Well, I for one am glad He did."

Even though he released her hand, he continued to stare at her a few more seconds, before he took a step or two down the steps. Once he reached the sideway, though, he turned back to look up at her.

"Do you think it would be all right if I come back—you know, to visit your mother again?"

Marcie grinned. "I think she'd like that, Dean."

His answering grin warmed her heart.

"See ya later, Marcie Starr."

"Drive safe, Dean McRae. And tell your momma I said howdy next time you talk to her."

He chuckled as he started toward the drive where he'd parked his truck. "Tell her yourself. Somethin' tells me you talk to my momma far more than I do."

Dean gave her a wave as he backed out of the drive and left, and Marcie lifted her hand in response. It had been great to see Dean again. Really great.

But she wasn't going to try and make more of his visit than what it was—just a nice gesture from a man who did things like that. He was just being a good friend.

Surely it was nothing more.

24

Dean hoped he wasn't making a nuisance of himself, but another part of him didn't care. After his first visit to the Carter home, he started stopping over every Sunday afternoon to visit Lois Carter and play chess with her husband Ethan. Dean discovered he really liked Ethan Carter, and over the chessboard, they often got into in-depth discussions about Biblical truths. He hadn't had anyone he felt comfortable talking with about such personal things since his father had passed away.

Of course, there was another reason for his Sunday afternoon visits to the Carter home.

Those visits also allowed him to spend a little time with Marcie, although she usually sat quietly in another part of the room and just listened to the men's discussion. Knowing she was there somehow comforted Dean, even though she rarely had much to say to him. But she always invited Dean to stay for Sunday night supper, and he never turned her down. Between his Sunday noon dinners after church with his crew and his suppers at Carter's, Dean was eating well.

Today he'd awakened to the sound of rain on the roof, so while the boys worked in the pole barn in the Wood Lot, Dean was in his office in The Barn working on the never-ending paperwork involved with running a business. The guys were cleaning up items they'd used on their last job, sharpening chainsaw chains, and preparing their tools for the upcoming job. Dean just hoped the rain currently coming down in torrents would let up soon, or they'd be working in mud for the next week.

While he struggled to make sense of the stacks of paperwork on his desk, Dean's thoughts returned to a conversation he'd recently had with Ethan Carter. Dean didn't know what Marcie's real father had been like, but the Reverend seemed to be a good man. And Dean could tell he genuinely cared about Marcie—or Marcella as he occasionally called her.

"That was Marcie's great-grandmother's name," her mother had told him the first time Dean had asked her about it. Marcie had been out in the back yard watering flowers at the time, so Dean had felt free to inquire when Mrs. Carter had inadvertently called Marcie by the other name.

"The first Marcella married Jack Starr—Marcie's great-grandfather. Jack was a full-blooded Cherokee. I got pictures around here somewhere of them when they were both young. What a handsome man he was with his jet black hair and dark eyes."

Then Lois Carter had frowned for a minute as she'd added, "Guess when she left the mountains, Marcie didn't want to use the name Marcella anymore."

Personally, Dean thought the name Marcella was lovely— almost as beautiful as the woman herself. But in the time he'd known her, Dean had gotten used to thinking of her as Marcie.

He and Ethan spent hours most Sunday afternoons playing chess, and Dean had even gone fishing with the man a couple of times. It was the most recent fishing trip that Dean had on his mind today. Well, not so much the fishing—since neither of them had caught anything—as the conversation they'd had that day.

"I've meant to talk to you 'bout somethin', young man. As Marcie's stepfather, I have to ask; what are your intentions regarding my step-daughter?"

Dean had almost fallen out of the boat at those words. The serious look on the man's face worried him even more. And he had suddenly wondered if Pastor Carter owned a shotgun. Memories of his mother's stories of backwoods men from the mountains taking off after strange men who had compromised their daughters' innocence had come to mind and Dean had quickly gulped. He had to clear his throat a couple of times before he'd been able to swallow the huge lump that had suddenly appeared with the older man's question.

"I like Marcie a lot, sir. But at this point in our relationship, I would say we're just friends. Good friends, I think. I hope."

Dean had felt the warmth rushing up his neck and knew his face must be turning red. It hadn't been a discussion he'd been ready to have with Marcie's step-father—or anyone, for that matter. Dean knew his feelings for Marcie were growing every week, but he had absolutely no notion of how she felt about him.

"Hmmm." The other man had stared out over the blue water of the river back of his house a few seconds before turning his blue eyes back on Dean.

"Do you want to be more than just friends?"

Dean had swallowed hard again as he had stared over at the older man and wondered how he was supposed to answer that question? Of course, he wanted to be more than friends with Marcie. He found himself thinking about her all the time anymore. Seeing her smiling face each Sunday was the highlight of his week. He'd never known anyone else like her, and he was seriously becoming infatuated with the young woman. But that wasn't the kind of thing you said to a woman's step-father.

"I believe I *do* want to be more than friends with her, sir. But I also feel it's a might early in our friendship to go down that road."

The other man had given a little nod as if he approved of Dean's answer.

"I agree. Just wanted to make sure you weren't getting ahead of yourself. Learn to know the girl first before getting too serious, son. I happen to feel she's pretty special. Guess what I'm tryin' to say is, I would take it personally if anyone were to hurt her."

Dean had nodded as he heard the steel behind the last statement. Ethan Carter might be a pastor, but something told him he was not a man to cross and would do whatever it took to protect his loved ones.

"I totally understand, sir. And I totally agree."

Sitting in his office and thinking back on that conversation, Dean *still* agreed with Ethan Carter. The feelings Dean currently had toward Marcie Starr were far from that of a friend. But he needed to proceed with caution. They'd both been hurt in the past by bad relationships, and Dean didn't want to be hurt again any more than he wanted to hurt Marcie.

One time of having your heart broken into a million pieces was more than enough.

MARCIE looked up from the kitchen table where she sat working on another pencil sketch—this time a drawing of the most recent bouquet of flowers Dean had brought her mother. He didn't bring flowers every week, but when he did, they were gorgeous.

She heard footsteps coming through the door behind her but didn't look up, not wanting to lose where she was in the sketch. It was only when she realized her step-father stood next to her peering over her shoulder, that Marcie lifted the pencil from the paper.

"You're really good at that, Marcie."

"Thanks." She glanced up at Ethan and gave him a small smile. It didn't matter how many times someone praised her drawings, she still felt funny about it—like she was wasting her time on them. After all, it was just a hobby, and they never amounted to anything.

"Have you ever tried your hand at oil painting?"

Marcie glanced back up at her step-father who had pulled out a chair and taken a seat across the table from her.

She shook her head. "I've thought about it, but I've always been afraid to try it." She frowned. "Plus, I haven't wanted to spend the money on all the paints and supplies I would need."

Her frown deepened. "I *really* need to find a job."

He gave a little nod. "Not to worry. The Lord will provide you with the right one at the right time. No need to fuss about it."

Marcie frowned and released a little sigh. It was easy to say that, but it didn't make her feel any better.

"I know. But my unemployment has run out, and I feel like I'm just sponging off you guys by still living here."

Ethan waved his right hand in the air as if to dismiss her words. "That's nonsense, and you know it. Your momma and me, we want you here. This is your home."

His face turned serious. "And besides, I feel better leaving the house during the day knowing your momma isn't here alone, Marcie." He leaned back in his chair. "So, you're more help to us than we are to you. We should be paying you."

She gave her head a firm shake. "You are *not* going to pay me to help out, Ethan. You feed me and give me a place to live. That's more than enough."

Marcie frowned again. "No. I need to find something useful to do with myself. Now that Momma is feeling so much better, I'm kinda lost—like I'm not really contributing anything to the world."

Neither of them said anything for a few moments. Marcie had meant what she'd told Ethan about how she felt, though. It was as if since she'd lost her job, she had no identity anymore.

When her mother had first come home from rehab, Marcie hadn't felt that way as she had been too busy taking care of her and doing all the things for the household. But now...now that her mom was almost back to normal, Marcie wasn't sure what she was supposed to do next with her life.

She jumped as Ethan's large hand came down on the table with a thump.

"I just remembered something!"

He stood and motioned for her to follow. "Come with me, young lady. I just thought of somethin' I want to give you."

Marcie's curiosity got the better of her, and she trailed after Ethan as he crossed to a door she knew led to the basement. She'd gone down those same stairs many times over the past few months as that was where the washer and dryer were located. As to why Ethan was taking her to the basement now, though, Marcie didn't have a clue.

He led her past the laundry area of the basement to a door she hadn't noticed before that led into another small room. It was apparently used as a storage room as it held plastic totes and boxes of all shapes and sizes. Ethan pulled a box or two off the shelves and opened one after another, then closed them back up. Finally, he opened one large plastic tote.

"Aha! I knew I still had this stuff someplace."

Marcie moved closer to see what all the fuss was about and gasped in surprise. Nestled in the tote were a variety of paint brushes and tubes of oil paints. The tote also held some rolled up canvas and what Marcie recognized as painter's palettes.

"I don't know how good the paint will be, but the tubes that haven't been opened yet will probably still be useable."

He glanced over at her. "My first wife Carolyn loved to paint. These were her things." Ethan stared down into the items in the tote. "I forgot they were even here until I started talking to you about painting. Should 've thought about all this stuff being down here earlier."

Ethan walked over to a folded wooden easel standing in the corner and pulled it closer to where the tote sat. "You're welcome to any of these things you want, Marcie." He pointed to another shelf. "There are also a couple of cans of linseed oil and some turpentine."

He stared at her as if waiting to find out what her response would be. She wasn't sure how to respond. Here Ethan was offering his first wife's painting supplies to her to use. How did she react to that?

"Thank you, Ethan. I don't know what to say."

He finally smiled at her, the familiar twinkle returning to his eyes. "Say you'll use it, Marcie girl. My Carolyn would have loved to know her painting things were going to good use."

Ethan looked down at the tote again before raising his blue eyes back to hers. "We never had children of our own, but she sure would have gotten along with you just fine. She loved to draw and paint too, and I know she'd love the idea that her belongings were gonna be used by you."

Between the two of them, they hauled the tote and other items up the basement steps to Marcie's bedroom, although she knew she'd need to find someplace else to paint if she was actually going to do it. She didn't want the fumes in the house where it might be harmful to her mother's health.

Now that she'd seen the painting supplies, Marcie's hands almost itched to try out everything Ethan had given her. And for the first time in months, Marcie felt a sense of excitement sweep through her.

She didn't know where God was leading her, but wherever it was, she was going to follow.

25

D ean reached out to grab the phone from the desk as it rang for the third time. He'd tried to ignore it as he dug through the unremitting paperwork on his desk, but knew that wasn't wise. After all, it could be a potential client.

It was fantastic that the business was doing so well. He just couldn't keep up with the administrative end of the business anymore, and Dean didn't know what he was going to do about it.

"Hello."

It was silent for a couple of seconds until his mother's voice responded.

"Dean? Are you okay?"

He took a deep breath and released it, then leaned back in his desk chair and stared at the ceiling. He knew that 'hello' had been a little terse, and he hadn't even taken the time to answer the phone as he usually did—announcing that the caller had reached McRae's Recycled Logs and that Dean McRae was speaking. That just showed how stressed out he was becoming. Something had to change—and soon.

"Sorry, Momma. Guess my mind was elsewhere."

"Hmm. Sounds like it. What's goin' on, son?"

Dean smiled at the concern in his mother's voice. There was no hiding anything from LizBeth McRae. He pushed his hand through his thick wavy hair, mentally adding the fact that he needed a haircut to his 'to-do' list. With three days' worth of whiskers on his face and his longish hair, he probably looked like the mountain man he was.

"I'm all right, Momma. Just a little overwhelmed at being so behind in my bookkeeping. We've been so swamped with work lately, I've had trouble finding any time to get the paperwork done."

"Humph. I keep tellin' ya, y'all need to hire someone, Dean. I mean it. You can't do it all yourself."

He released a little chuckle. "Yeah, well that's apparent since I'm *not* gettin' it all done." He released another sigh. "I just don't know how to go about findin' somebody. It would only be a part-time job, and it has to be the right person. I don't want to hire a stranger to come in here and mess with all my financial stuff."

There was a pause on the other end of the phone for a second or two before he heard his mother's voice.

"Well, I jist may know somebody who fits the bill."

Dean groaned inwardly and closed his eyes, visions of one of his momma's old friends from church coming to mind. She probably knew some gray and grizzled retired CPA who wanted something to do with his spare time. He'd come into his business and criticize Dean for the way he ran it, and then call some morning at the last minute to tell Dean he wouldn't be in as he'd rather go fishin'. No, that wasn't what Dean needed at all. Before he was able to respond to his mother's cryptic remark, however, she had started talking again.

"I was talkin' to Lois Carter on the phone the other day, and she mentioned Marcie's lookin' for a job. Why don't you call Marcie and see if she's interested? I seem to remember her mentioning she had a college degree that included accountin'—or am I just dreamin' about that part?"

His mind raced. Marcie *had* told him once upon a time that she had a degree that included accounting. And was she really looking for a job? If she was, did that mean she was staying in Tennessee?

Even though he'd been spending his Sunday afternoons at her parents' house, Dean had been careful not to get too friendly with Marcie for fear she'd be leaving Tennessee as soon as her momma was back on her feet. And the warning he'd received from her stepfather had taken root—no matter how strongly Dean felt about her.

"I remember her mentionin' something about it." He frowned as he tapped his pen on the desktop, his mind racing.

"Really? Marcie's looking for a job? Why didn't I know that?"

His mother's laughter on the other end of the phone caused him to feel further embarrassment. Fortunately, his mother couldn't see his red face through the phone.

"Well, that could be because you don't spend enough time *talkin'* to her, son. I mean, it's all right that you go over there and visit her momma and play chess with her step-daddy. But if you are interested in the *girl*, you need to spend more time with *her*."

Dean groaned. "Momma, I don't need you tellin' me how to court a woman."

It was quiet for a split second before he realized what he'd said. Then he heard his momma chuckle again, and Dean felt the heat flowing into his face and was more thankful than ever that his momma wasn't there to see it.

"So, you *are* interested." There was a little grunt of satisfaction from the other end of the phone before she added, "Well son, you best get a move on and do somethin' about it then. And the first thing you need to do is find out if she'll come to work for you. 'Cause by the sounds of things you need someone to straighten out your bookwork. And the girl needs a job."

Dean nodded to himself. He couldn't disagree with his mother on that.

MARCIE sat in one of the overstuffed upholstered chairs in her mother's living room and attempted to read a mystery she'd borrowed at the local library. Her mother was sitting in another chair nearby, knitting away at a sweater she'd started before her stroke. Her manual dexterity was returning, but everything took her longer than it had previously. But Marcie knew she was a determined woman and that sooner or later, her momma would be able to do all the things she could do before her illness. It was just a matter of time and patience.

As they had a dozen times or more since she'd sat down, Marcie's eyes drifted up from the written page in the book in her lap and wandered across the room to the table where Dean and her step-father sat playing chess. Again. The two of them spent hours playing that silly game and talking about everything under the sun in between moves. Marcie was happy that Dean got along so well with her mother and step-father, but found herself feeling a little jealous at all the time he spent with Ethan. For some reason, she had hoped his weekly visits had something to do with the fact that she was living there.

Evidently, she'd been wrong.

Right then Dean lifted his head, and his green eyes locked on hers, a slow, gentle smile creeping across his handsome face. Marcie couldn't help but answer with a smile of her own, her eyes drifting over his nose and strong square chin, taking in the look of the man with enjoyment. His face was freshly shaven, and it looked as if he'd finally gotten a haircut—although, Marcie had thought he had looked somewhat rugged with the long hair he'd been sporting. Either way, she didn't think she'd ever get tired of looking at him.

"Well," Ethan's deep voice rang out in the quiet room. "Looks like you're getting ready to check-mate me again, young man." He released a deep sigh and pushed the chair back from the table. "Good game, Dean."

Dean smiled and pushed back his own chair, then stood. Marcie felt his green eyes resting on her from across the room, even though she'd turned her eyes back to look blankly at the pages of the book in front of her. She couldn't remember the last time she'd turned the page, and didn't have any idea what was happening in the story.

"Want to go for a walk, Marcie?"

She instantly closed the book with a snap and placed it on the end table next to the chair, not even taking the time to mark the page she'd been reading. Then wondering if she appeared too anxious, Marcie rubbed her hands down the legs of her jeans as her hands felt sweaty. Mentally scolding herself, Marcie smiled at Dean and hoped he couldn't tell how nervous she was.

"Sure."

The two of them left the living room, Marcie glancing back long enough to see her mother and Ethan exchange smiles as if they were privy to something she wasn't. Well, it was nice that Dean finally wanted to spend some time alone with her, so Marcie decided she wasn't going to worry about what their shared looks might or might not mean.

She trailed after Dean as he went through the kitchen and out the back door and down the steps where he stood waiting for her. As she reached the bottom of the steps, Dean's large hand came out and reached for her, and she automatically placed hers in his, relishing the feeling of his strong one holding hers. Dean McRae's hand was that of a working man— strong and warm and covered with callouses. At the feel of it, a sense of safety and contentment swept over her.

They strolled past her mother's rose bed and Ethan's vegetable garden and across the green expanse of the back yard that gently sloped downhill from the house toward the river that flowed through the back of the property.

As they walked, Marcie had thought Dean might start to talk to her, but since he hadn't, she was hesitant to break the silence. She's waited a long time for the chance to be alone with him, so she didn't care if they talked or not—as long as she was with him.

When they reached the river's side, Dean motioned toward the wooden bench Ethan had placed there sometime in the past. Marcie reluctantly let go of Dean's hand and sat, her hands in her lap as she waited expectantly for Dean to sit next to her. Surely he didn't bring her out her to just sit on the bench and watch the river go by, did he?

She heard Dean release what sounded like a nervous breath and allowed herself to smile. It did her heart good to find out the big man sitting beside her might be as unsure about their relationship as she was.

"I wanted to talk to you about something, Marcie."

Marcie looked over at him and found his green eyes studying her face. She nodded and waited for him to continue. He finally broke eye contact and turned as if to gaze out over the river. Dean didn't say anything more for a moment, and Marcie felt the silence on her shoulders like a cloak. Whatever it was Dean wanted to talk about, it evidently wasn't something he felt comfortable telling her.

"I guess the first thing I need to ask is if you intend to stay here."

Marcie raised her eyes back at him, staring at the profile of firm chin and sharp nose while her mind raced. What exactly was Dean asking?

"You mean here at my mother's house?"

He swiveled his head toward her, the intensity of his eyes almost unnerving.

"Yes. No. I mean here. In Tennessee. Or do you intend to eventually return to D.C.?"

She smiled a little and dropped her eyes from his. So that was what this was all about.

"I'm not going back to D.C., Dean. Ever."

She paused a second and rubbed her right hand across the jean material of her leg. She'd initially planned to look for another job back in the city someplace, but since she'd returned to her hometown, she'd discovered she didn't want to return to D.C.—or any big city. This was home, and somehow, Marcie knew this was where God wanted her to be. She didn't know what she was supposed to do now that she was here, but she was praying God would lead her in the direction she was to go when the time was right.

"I hope to find a job doing something here. I don't want to leave." She gave a nervous chuckle as her feelings of inadequacy returned. "Although I don't know what I'm supposed to do to earn a living. I feel like I'm just sponging off Momma and Ethan right now, and I don't much like it."

Dean nodded as he turned his eyes on her, then grabbed hold of her left hand, surprising Marcie.

"Well, I may have a solution for that—if you're willing."

Marcie stared over at him, wondering what he was talking about and braced herself for whatever it was. Goodness! Dean had such a serious look on his face. The man wasn't going to propose, was he?

"I want you to come and work for me."

"What?"

Her eyes widened at that thought. Dean wanted her to come and work for him? Doing what?

She released another nervous chuckle. "As much as I appreciate the offer, Dean, I'm not sure I'm cut out for running chainsaws and climbing ladders. If you remember, I didn't do so well in that department the last time I was up on a ladder."

She noticed Dean's lips turn up in a crooked smile, and his green eyes sparkled with humor. Suddenly Marcie was remembering falling off a ladder and into the strength and warmth of Dean's arms. And she recalled all too clearly what it had felt like to have those strong arms holding her tightly against his chest as if he'd never let her go.

Marcie felt her face grow warm, and she dropped her eyes from his, but not before noticing the tips of his ears were turning pink. Evidently, Dean remembered that same incident just as well as she did.

Dean chuckled. "Yeah. Well, I was thinking more along the line of office work."

Then he released what sounded like a frustrated sigh. "You've seen my office, Mars. I have this nice computer with an expensive accounting software program on it, and I don't even have the time to figure out how to use it. I'm still trying to do everything the old way—by hand. And I'm afraid I'm not doin' a very good job of that either. With all our new business, I just don't have the time, and it's too important to just let it slide."

He paused a second or two before continuing. "Would you at least be willin' to drive over and look at the setup and see if you'd be interested in doing it, Marcie? I can't afford to give you a full-time job, but at least it would be a little income for you."

Marcie had to smile at the almost pleading tone in Dean's deep voice. It was easy to tell he wasn't just creating a job for her. It sounded as if he really needed her help, which gave her a warm feeling in the region of her heart.

"Sure. Why not?"

The responding smile on Dean's face on hearing her words grabbed hold of Marcie's heart and almost made her second-guess her decision. She was beginning to feel much more for this man than she probably should. And working near him all the time probably wasn't going to help her get over those feelings. But it sounded as if he truly needed her help. So, unless the Lord told her otherwise, she'd at least go over to Dean's place and check out what he needed to have done.

"Fantastic! Do you think you could come over tomorrow morning? I planned on working in the office in the morning and then I'm gonna check out a couple of possible jobs in the afternoon while the crew finishes up a cabin teardown over by Sneedville."

She nodded. "I can do that. What time?"

Dean still wore that big smile. "It takes about half an hour to get to my house from here. Maybe 8:30? Will that be okay?"

Marcie gave him a smile and a nod.

"I'll be there, Mr. McRae. Ready to work."

26

After feeding his three employees a hearty breakfast, Dean sent them on the job near Sneedville. After they left, he spent fifteen minutes cleaning up the kitchen, continually glancing at the clock hanging on the wall above the stove to find out how long he had before Marcie's arrival.

He couldn't believe she was coming to his place.

Dean also couldn't believe she'd actually agreed to work for him. Maybe. It would depend on what she thought of the idea after she saw the magnitude of the mess his paperwork was in. Perhaps she'd just throw up her hands, tell him 'good luck, mister,' and walk away.

But somehow he couldn't see Marcie Starr giving up on anything.

Dean was already standing on the front porch of his house waiting when Marcie's SUV drove down the drive from the main road. A shot of adrenaline swept through him at the sight of her long legs climbing out of the vehicle, and he took a deep breath and slowly released it to steady himself. If this was going to work, Dean had to watch how he acted around her. The last thing he wanted to do was scare her off before she'd even started.

But he couldn't help but admire how beautiful she looked—as always. Today she wore a pair of jeans with a short-sleeved white cotton blouse. And he had to smile at the sight of her feet encased in the old work boots she'd worn when she'd been here working on the magazine article. Somehow seeing her dressed the way she was today looked more like what he felt to be the real Marcie Starr.

"Good morning!" she called out to him as she walked toward the porch.

He gave her what he was sure looked like a silly grin. "Good morning. You want a cup of coffee to take with you over to The Barn?"

"Sure."

Dean felt her presence more than heard her following him through the house to the kitchen where he pulled a mug out of the cupboard and filled it with a hot cup of the fresh coffee he'd made a little earlier. He topped off his own mug, and then the two of them headed back out the door and across the yard to The Barn.

"I'm interested to see what software program you're using," Marcie said as they headed up the staircase inside the barn that led to his office on the upper level.

He frowned. "I know very little about it other than it was highly recommended by a friend of mine who has his own business and really likes it. He said it was easy to learn and did everything he needed."

Dean gave her a quick glance as he pushed the office door open and motioned for her to enter first. "It's installed on the computer, and that's about as far as I got with it. I've never done accounting on a computer before, so I can't tell you whether it's easy to use or not."

Dean took a seat behind his desk, feeling nervousness flow through him as he felt Marcie's presence next to him. He wasn't sure what there was about this woman that totally unnerved him, but there was something. It wasn't a bad thing, but it sure made it difficult for him to keep his concentration.

When his computer finally booted up, they switched places, and he stood next to her shoulder, pointing out the icon that would take her to the accounting software. Dean was amazed at how quickly she clicked through screens and found her way around the program. He had been lost when he'd tried to use it, but Marcie appeared to be picking up on it in only a matter of minutes.

"This looks like great software," she finally said after a few minutes of studying the screen. She glanced up at him. "I think it was a good buy, Dean."

He relaxed as some of his anxiety left him. "I'm glad to hear it. I was afraid I wasted good money on something I'd never be able to use."

Marcie leaned back in his desk chair and continued to look up at him as he leaned against the corner of his desk. He looked back, noticing how comfortable she looked sitting there in his chair. Way too comfortable for Dean's own comfort.

"So, where is this old-fashioned bookwork you keep telling me about that needs to be transferred into the computer program?"

Dean spent the next twenty minutes going over his checkbook, General Ledger, Accounts Receivable and Accounts Payable, Payroll, and Disbursements Journal with Marcie, all the time wondering if she was going to back out of their agreement once she saw the whole scope of the mess he was leaving her. When he finished showing her everything he had, along with the stack of bills that needed to be paid, he released a frustrated sigh.

"I don't think we'll ever be caught up."

Marcie's light laughter rang through the high-ceilinged room, and he couldn't help but smile a little at the sound. He was glad she thought it was funny.

"It's really not that bad, Dean. I promise"

She narrowed her eyes a little as she gazed at the ledgers and books spread over his desk. "Although, I think the best thing for me to do is catch up on all the paper bookwork first. Then I'll start transferring everything over into the computer."

She nodded as if in agreement with that plan of action, gave him another smile, and reached out to give his arm a little pat as if offering him comfort.

"Relax, boss man. It's totally doable."

With those words, Dean felt as if a huge load lifted off his shoulders. She had no idea what hearing that meant to him. He wanted to do nothing more than to lift the beautiful woman in front of him out of his desk chair and give her a hug. However, he also realized that it would be totally inappropriate. So instead, he gave her a big smile.

"I can't tell you how happy you've made me, Marcie Starr. I love my business, and I love the work we do out on a job, but I absolutely *detest* the paperwork that comes with it."

Marcie laughed again.

"Well, as long as you give me a week or so to get things straightened out, I think I can soon have the bookkeeping end of *McRae's* running just as smoothly as the rest of the operation. So quit worrying about it. I've got this."

They spent a little more time talking about the logistics of her working for him—what hours she could work as she wanted to spend the mornings at home with her mother who was still in need of some help around the house.

Before they left the office, Dean reached down and tugged open a bottom desk drawer, dug around and found a set of keys and handed them to her, then went through them one at a time.

"This one is for the outside Barn door, and this one will let you into my office. I keep it locked when I'm not here."

He motioned to a safe in the corner. "I'll get you the combination for the safe too as I'd like you to take any money or checks that have come in and go to the bank with a weekly deposit." He frowned. "Having time to get to the bank has always been a struggle for me. There's plenty of working capital for the business right now, thank the Lord—ever since your article." He grinned at her. "But sometimes I don't get the chance to do the banking as often as I should. So if you can take care of that for me too, it will be a huge help."

She nodded and pointed to the third key on the ring. "Sure, that's no problem. But what's that key for?"

"It's to the house."

He felt his face grow warm and hoped his ears weren't turning red as they had a tendency to do when he was embarrassed. Sometimes being a red-head was a pain.

"Just in case you ever need to go over there for anything, and we aren't around, I thought it might be a good idea for you to have a key to the house too."

Fortunately, she didn't seem to think there was anything unusual about him giving her a key to his house and stood up from the desk chair to accept the keys from him before slipping them into her pants pocket. Dean stood in front of her near the corner of the desk and shuffled his feet as he tried to think of anything else he needed to tell her. He supposed he could always give her a call if he thought of something else.

"So what do ya think, Marcie Starr? Are you up to the challenge?"

Her musical chuckle warmed his heart. He sure could get used to that sound.

"I do believe I am, Dean McRae." She gave him a wink. "I'm just not sure *McRae's* is ready for me."

THE next day Marcie arrived at Dean's house a little after noon, excited and ready to get to work. There were no other vehicles in the driveway as she pulled in, but that didn't surprise her as Dean had told her the day before that they were starting a new job the other side of Marysville.

She dug out the set of keys Dean had given her and let herself into The Barn. Without the guys there and the television blaring, the big building seemed empty and forlorn to Marcie, and she quickly went up the wooden steps to Dean's office. It was just as they'd left it the previous day with books and ledgers spread all over the desktop. Marcie took a look around and decided the first thing she needed to do was clean up the mess they'd made.

Then it was time to sit in Dean's comfortable desk chair and get down to business. Since Dean had told her he hadn't had time to reconcile the past two months' bank statements, she started with that task. Once that was done, and she felt comfortable with how much money was actually in the checking account, Marcie sat down and wrote checks for the invoices and bills that Dean had left for her to pay, then set the checks aside for Dean to sign later and then she could mail them.

She worked all afternoon, only taking time out to visit the bathroom down the hall. Time passed quickly for Marcie, and it made her feel good when she thought about the progress she was making, considering it was only the first day.

Marcie had just finished filing a stack of paperwork and sat back down when she heard the sound of heavy boots coming up the steps toward Dean's open office door. When she lifted her head to see who it was, her heart gave a little skip when she saw Dean's tall form standing in the open door of the office, his dark red hair windblown and unruly as usual. His ruddy face was wearing a big smile, although his eyebrows were cocked in question as if he wasn't sure it was safe to enter.

"So, how ya doin', Marcie? Ready to quit on me yet?"

She chuckled, wondering if he were really that worried about her quitting. He probably was. The poor man didn't have a clue about how to run an office. Dean hadn't just created the job to make her feel better about herself. A warm feeling swept through her at the thought that he actually needed her.

"Not yet. Although you were entirely correct in your assessment of your bookkeeping skills, Mr. McRae. You best stick to the crowbar and hammer and leave the bookwork to someone else. Like me."

He playfully stuck his tongue out at her before giving her a grin. Then he walked the rest of the way into the office and dropped into one of the worn leather chairs in front of the desk. She watched in concern as Dean gave a little groan and leaned back in the chair and stuck his long legs out in front of him, and then released what sounded like a weary sigh. His eyelids drifted down, his long light-colored lashes brushing his cheeks.

"I will be more than happy to oblige, Miss Starr. Bookwork is my nemesis. You can have at it all you want."

Marcie smiled, feeling an unexpected tenderness as she looked across the desk at Dean. The poor man looked exhausted. The guys must have had a long day of hard physical labor.

"So, how did the job go?"

Dean opened his eyes a little and gazed across the desk at her, his eyes shadowed by his partially lowered lids.

"Not done yet, although we did get most of the logs down today. This one's been a real challenge. It was one of those days when anything that could go wrong did. But we managed."

It was silent between them for a time, and Marcie had begun to wonder if Dean had gone to sleep. Then she heard his groan as he sat back up in the chair.

"Well, time to call it a day, Mars. You'd best head home, and I'm gonna go find me a hot shower and a bowl of soup or something."

He stood stiffly and started toward the door, then turned and gave her one of his dimple-popping grins and a wink.

"Y'all are comin' back tomorrow, right?"

Marcie laughed. Despite his size, sometimes he looked like such a small unruly boy.

"Yes. I'm coming back tomorrow." She chuckled and added, "Somebody has to keep y'all out of trouble, McRae."

27

everal weeks passed, and Marcie comfortably settled into her new routine. Mornings were spent at home, helping her mother with cleaning, laundry, and other jobs around the house. After lunch, she made the drive to Dean's house and worked there.

Marcie was extremely pleased with the way things were shaping up in the office and had even begun to enter information about vendors and clients into the computer program. Marcie was rather excited at the prospect of having the program updated as she could see it would make the job even easier when everything was entered. The payroll especially would be much more efficient on the computer.

Back at her mother's house in the evenings, she spent her free time sketching and painting and had even finished a couple of small oil paintings. At her step-father's insistence, she'd taken them to a small gift shop in Gatlinburg that Ethan had told her sold artisan items on commission. The store's manager had appeared impressed with her work and offered to take in not only those three paintings, but also several sketches and told her he'd be interested in anything she brought in the future. So, Marcie was in the hopes that sometime soon she'd actually make a sale or two to supplement her income. But even more important, a sale would give her work a sense of worth.

No matter how much she loved to sketch and paint, until someone else felt it was worth buying, Marcie couldn't think of it as anything more than a hobby.

So far, Marcie hadn't been brave enough to show Dean any of her paintings. He'd seen several of her sketches, of course, and she'd even given the one of Dean's dog to his mother. But she felt nervous about letting him see any of her more recent work. As much as her passion grew for her paintings, she still felt there was so much more for her to learn about it.

Then one Sunday evening after supper, Dean wandered onto the porch on the back of the house where Marcie had been keeping her most recent piece. When he first headed that way, Marcie tried to come up with some way of stopping him, but then decided to follow him and see what happened. A part of her hoped he wouldn't even notice the easel sitting there.

The smell of the pine-scented breeze wafting through the screens of the porch hit Marcie as soon as she crossed the threshold. This room had quickly become one of her favorite spots in Ethan's house, and she spent most of her free time there working on her art.

She watched as Dean stopped in front of the covered canvas sitting on the easel and turned toward her, his bushy red eyebrows going up.

"Hey, what's this?"

She shrugged, trying to look nonchalant. Marcie couldn't believe how nervous she was to have Dean see her work. She hadn't felt that way with Ethan or her mother—or even the gift shop owner. But if Dean didn't think her paintings were any good, perhaps the people shopping at the gift shop wouldn't either.

"Just something I'm working on."

Marcie took of a sip of the glass of iced tea she'd carried onto the porch with her, then sat the glass down on a small nearby table and rubbed her wet hands on the legs of her jeans.

"So...can I see it?"

She frowned. For some reason, Dean's opinion meant more to her than anyone else's did. What if he thought her paintings were terrible? She chewed on the corner of her lower lip for a few seconds before she finally gave in. Dean was a friend, and even if he hated it, he probably wouldn't tell her. He was too much of a gentleman to do or say anything to hurt her feelings.

"Okay."

Marcie carefully removed the cloth covering the canvas and stepped back, almost afraid to look at Dean and fearful of what his reaction would be. She'd been working on the piece for over two weeks, but she knew it still needed a lot of work.

"That is so cool. It's the Potter Cabin."

His deep voice was quiet and almost sounded reverent as he continued to gaze at the painting. Marcie finally braved a look at his face and was touched to see a wistful smile resting there. She knew the painting wasn't close to being finished, but there was enough of the cabin and the surrounding meadow with the background of trees that he'd evidently been able to recognize the place. Marcie had painted it from a couple of the photos she'd taken the day they'd first checked out the place. Seeing the photos of the cabin had quickly returned her to that day, and what it had felt to be with Dean when they'd first seen the place. So, she had decided right then that she had to try and paint it. She didn't know if she were going to be able to transfer what her mind saw onto the canvas or not, but she was sure enjoying the challenge of trying.

Dean looked over at her. "It's terrific, Marcie. You've really captured the essence of the place—and how it looked that first day we saw it."

He gave her a smile and surprised her by reaching out and taking hold of her hand.

"Do you remember what it was like when we walked through the place the first time? And how you sat on the front stoop and looked out across the meadow and talked about how it must have felt to have lived there?"

Marcie looked down at their intertwined hands and then back up into his green eyes, staring so intently into hers. She nodded. Of course, she remembered.

"Yes," her voice not much more than a whisper.

"Marcie, you have such a gift. With a few strokes of a paintbrush, you've been able to take me back to that day and everything that happened. Thank you."

He smiled and gave her hand a gentle squeeze, then turned back to look at the painting again.

"Once it's finished, I want to purchase this painting. May I buy it from you?"

She stared at him a moment before his words sunk in.

"You want to buy it?" She shook her head. "No. I'll give it to you, Dean."

"No." He firmly shook his head and the hold he had on her hand tightened. "No. Your work is worth it, Marcie. And I want to actually own it. I want to have something you've created with your own hands. It would mean a lot to me."

"Okay, then. Sure." Marcie nodded, feeling shocked at the intensity she saw in his eyes. "Sure. I'll let you know when I have it finished."

"Good."

And the smile on his face as he gazed at her went straight to her heart.

DEAN slid his bishop a few spaces across the chessboard and leaned back in his chair to await his opponent's next move. He and Ethan Carter had played dozens of games of chess, and it was always a challenge to Dean. He'd beat the man before, but the quiet, reserved pastor seemed to have a real head for the strategy and logic of the game and was usually two moves ahead of Dean. As he stared at the chessboard, trying to decide what his next move should be, Dean waited for Ethan to play and allowed his mind to drift in the direction it often seemed to these days.

Marcie.

Even though he'd tried his best to remain on a 'friends only' basis with Marcie, his heart wasn't cooperating anymore. Dean was fairly certain that somewhere along the way he'd fallen totally and completely in love with her. The big question was, did Marcie return the feeling? So far, they'd walked and talked and held hands, but that was as far as their relationship had gone—other than that long ago kiss on his mom's back steps. Dean had never tried to kiss her again. Although he'd wanted to—almost daily. But the question was, was she ready for him to take it to the next level? Was he? The possibility of her rejection scared him to death.

"Pretty quiet over there, Dean. Everything all right?"

Dean watched the older man's large hand move one of his castles forward and take out another one of Dean's pawns. The man was on the move, and it was time for Dean to get his mind back on the game, or it was gonna be a short one.

"Everything's jist fine, Ethan. Why do you ask?"

The older man's quiet chuckle reached across the table to Dean.

"Can't say as I can remember you ever being so quiet during one of our matches before. Afraid you're gonna lose again?"

Dean released a nervous laugh. "Maybe."

Then he sighed. Could he talk to Ethan about his worries? Was it even right to discuss his growing feelings for Marcie with her stepfather? But who else could he talk to? Certainly not his mother! And it didn't seem proper to discuss Marcie and his feelings with the three guys that worked for him.

Ethan must have seen his lips turn down at that thought as the older man sat back in his chair and crossed his arms, his eyes still resting on Dean's face.

"Spill it, Dean. What's goin' on?"

Dean raised his eyes from the chessboard and sighed again.

"I don't know if I should talk with you about this or not, Ethan. I appreciate your friendship, but I'm not sure how you'll react."

The older man chuckled again. "Afraid I'll punch your lights out, huh?" Another chuckle. "I'm guessing this has to do with your growing feelings for my stepdaughter."

Dean glanced up quickly to see Ethan's eyes twinkling back at him.

"Am I that obvious?"

Ethan grinned. "Just a little. Lois asked me the other day if you'd asked Marcie to marry you yet."

Flinching at those words, Dean couldn't hold back a little groan. *Marriage.* Was he ready for that huge step? He'd done the marriage route once before and had ended up getting burned.

"You *do* love her, don't you?"

Again, Dean raised his eyes to look across the chessboard at the older man. This time Ethan wore a serious look on his face and the twinkle in his eyes had been replaced by steely blue. It appeared the man was all done teasing.

"Yeah, I do. So much, sometimes I can't breathe."

A little nod was the only response Dean got.

"So, what are y'all gonna do about it?"

Dean sighed again, wondering for a second if he would hyperventilate if he sighed too much.

"I don't know. I mean, I'm not sure how Marcie feels about me. And I don't want to rush things, you know?"

It was quiet between the two of them for a moment or two as Ethan reached out and moved another piece on the board. Dean frowned as he realized that while he'd been thinking about his feelings for Marcie, Ethan Carter had put him in check. Again.

Obviously, Dean's mind wasn't on the game.

"Marriage is a lifetime commitment, Dean. Not something that should be taken lightly, so I'm glad you're puttin' some serious thought into it and not doing anything rash.

"As it says in the book of Matthew, husbands should love their wives as much as they love themselves—even more. They should love them like Christ loves the church."

Ethan gave a little chuckle. "Plum scares a body to think we're supposed to love our woman like Christ loves us. I mean, who are we to think we have the capability of that kind of love?" He nodded. "But you get the gist of what I'm sayin', right?"

Dean nodded, feeling more than a little uncomfortable at the man's choice of topic. He did care about Marcie in that way. But he also wasn't about to go into another marriage lightly. If and when he married again, it would be forever.

"'For this cause shall a man leave father and mother, and shall cleave to his wife: and they twain shall be one flesh...'" Ethan gave a firm nod. "The Holy Book spells it out pretty clear, don't ya think?"

Again, Dean gave a little nod, not knowing what to say at this point in the conversation.

He watched as Ethan moved another piece on the chessboard. The game was going to be over in just a few more moves, and once again, Dean wasn't going to be the winner.

Ethan leaned back in his chair, and Dean groaned inwardly, wondering what the older man was going to say next. He was almost sorry he'd started down this road with Marcie's stepfather. So Dean was surprised by the little laugh coming from the other side of the chessboard.

"Did you know Marcie's got Cherokee blood in her?"

Dean brought his head up and stared at the other man, shocked by the sudden change in the topic. Rubbing his hand across his chin, Dean wondered where Ethan's conversation was going next. The man was brilliant—even though he tended to speak like one of the locals—probably thinking that as long as he sounded like them, he wouldn't scare them off.

"Her momma mentioned it to me one time. That would be Marcie's great-grandad, right? Wasn't his name Jack?"

"Yup. He was a full-blooded Cherokee."

Dean thought about that for a little while. There had been Cherokees in the Smoky Mountains for generations, and Marcie certainly had the jet black hair and dark eyes of the other Cherokees he'd known from the area.

She sure was a beautiful woman. He could spend the rest of his life looking at her and never get enough.

Ethan's deep voice brought him back from his musings.

"One thing I found interesting in my studies was the customs of the Cherokee Nation—especially when it comes to marriage and women's rights in the marriage."

Ah, here it comes.

"In the Cherokee society, the women were the ones who owned the home and any children born to the marriage. Of course, the wife was required to get the husband's input on any decisions made about the raising of the children and such, but nonetheless, they saw man and wife as a team. Just like it talks about in the Bible. I believe with all my heart, that's the way God intends for a marriage to work."

Dean politely nodded his head, wondering where Ethan was going with this story. He knew sooner or later, Ethan would get around to telling him the real reason for his tale. It usually took some time, but there was always a purpose for Ethan's words whether he was behind the pulpit of his church or not.

"I also found out some other interestin' information I'll pass along—for what it's worth. In the Cherokee culture, when a man found a woman he wanted to marry, he would kill a deer and bring it to her home. If she chose to marry him, she would cook the meat and offer it to him. If she rejected the deer meat, it was considered to be a denial of his offer of marriage."

It was quiet in the room a few seconds before Ethan asked, "So, tell me, Dean McRae, do you hunt?"

Dean raised his eyes to the older man, trying and failing to hold back his smile.

"As a matter of fact, Reverend, I do."

28

D ean pulled his pickup into the yard and parked, glancing around long enough to note that Marcie's SUV wasn't anywhere. It was a Friday, so he assumed she'd made her weekly trip to the bank. He was disappointed he wouldn't get to see her, but that hadn't been the primary purpose for him coming back to the house. He'd driven back to pick up the paperwork he'd forgotten to take with him for the job that morning. Seeing Marcie would have been a pleasant side note, but he guessed he'd have to wait until his Sunday afternoon visit.

Just the thought of how far away Sunday was left him feeling deflated. Ever since his talk with Ethan Carter, Dean had done nothing but think about Marcie and how much he wanted to get serious in their relationship.

Unlocking The Barn's outer door, Dean took the stairs two at a time to get to the upper level where his office was located. When he entered his office these days, it always brought a smile to his face. No more were ledgers and papers spread over his desk in chaotic disarray. Since Marcie's arrival at *McRae's*, his office was now a place of organization and contentment.

Pulling out his desk chair, Dean took a seat, breathing in the aroma of Marcie's light floral scent that still wafted around the area. The office even smelled like her. It was just too bad he wouldn't get a chance to see her before he headed back to the work site. A quick glimpse of her smiling face would have made his day.

Digging in the bottom right-hand desk drawer, Dean quickly found the file folder he was looking for—a file that had documentation and permits for their current job. He shoved the drawer closed and stood from his chair, only then turning around. That was when Dean noticed the flashing light on the answering machine on top of the credenza behind the desk. His first inclination was to leave the machine for Marcie to deal with, then decided he should at least listen to the message since it could possibly have something to do with their current job. Pushing the button to 'play,' Dean sat back down in the chair and grabbed a pen and notepad so he could take notes.

This message is for Marcie Starr. My name is Bill Moran, and I'm calling from the D.C. Architectural Digest. I called your parents' house, Ms. Starr, and your mother informed me I should be able to reach you at this number. If you would give me a call as soon as possible, I would greatly appreciate it. I've talked to your former employer, and we believe you'd be a good fit for our magazine, so I'd like to talk to you about a position we have open. Please call me back at 555-175-3298 as soon as you can. Thank you.

The machine finished the message and beeped, and Dean sat frozen in his chair, feeling as if he'd just taken a sucker punch to his stomach.

All this time…all this time he'd thought Marcie was staying. He had believed her when she'd told him she was going to make her home here, and he'd even started to believe they could have a future life together.

What a joke.

Evidently, she was still looking for employment back in the city. Why else would this magazine call her if she hadn't submitted a resume?

She's going to leave. Just like you thought she would. Why did you ever let yourself fall for her?

Dean raised his head and took a deep breath and slowly released it as he attempted to get his emotions under control.

Evidently, he'd been wrong—wrong about a lot of things when it came to Marcie Starr. The pain that went through his chest made it almost impossible to breathe. How could he have opened himself to be hurt again? What a fool he'd been.

Leaving the message on the machine for her to find when she returned from town, Dean stomped out of his office and back down the stairway and out the door to his waiting truck. He didn't have time to deal with this right now. He had a business to run. And if Marcie Starr wanted to take the fancy job at a magazine back in D.C., then they were welcome to her.

He'd been an idiot to think she'd ever stay here in the mountains anyway.

An absolute idiot.

MARCIE left the bank with a smile on her face. She'd made the weekly deposit for *McRae's*, and had even done a little banking for herself by depositing two checks she'd received for sales of her paintings. She was still in awe that people would actually pay good money for something she'd created with some paint and a brush.

Once she was in the car, she automatically dug in her purse to look for her cell phone to check for any messages and then groaned when she remembered she didn't have it with her. There had been no reason to bring it with her today as the battery on it had gone dead—and the phone charger hadn't worked to charge it overnight. Once she'd made the discovery, she'd immediately gotten on her laptop and ordered another charger which would hopefully arrive in a few days. But in the meantime, she was without her cell.

She made the short drive back to Dean's place, and once there immediately went to work on the computer recording the deposit. Then she started processing the week's payroll. It was hard to believe it was Friday again and she'd been working for Dean for several months.

Marcie took a few moments to stare across the room where the afternoon sunshine was pouring through the tall stained glass windows installed at that end of the barn. She loved the light in the office this time of day. When Dean had designed the room, he had done a great thing putting those windows in on this side of the building.

While she sat there and watched the muted and colored sunlight filter through the tall stained glass windows onto the desk, Marcie felt something she hadn't felt in all her years at the magazine, something she'd never felt back in Washington, D.C.

It was contentment.

Back when she was working in the rat-race of the city, Marcie never would have believed she'd be happy working a part-time job doing accounting and painting pictures to sell. There was no way she could have ever seen a day when she'd be speaking to her mother again, let alone living with her and a step-father Marcie had never even known existed. And she certainly wouldn't have believed that after being dumped by her old boyfriend, that she would actually be falling hard for her current boss—because Marcie knew now that was what was happening to her. She'd tried to ignore her feelings for several weeks, but no matter how much she tried to deny them, the attraction to Dean just kept getting stronger.

So, here she was.

And the truth was, she was incredibly happy doing what she was doing where she was doing it. Marcie had re-discovered her love for the mountains, for the people of her hometown and her old church, and of course, her mother. She and Marcie had made peace with the past and had developed a new friendship and relationship for the future. God had truly known what He'd been doing when the magazine had sent her here.

And then, of course, there was Dean.

Marcie enjoyed her friendship with Dean McRae—much more than she'd ever experienced in a friendship in the past—man or woman. But the past few months of getting to know him had made something very clear to her. She didn't want to be just friends with him anymore. She wanted something more serious and much more permanent. He was so shy, though, when it came to making any sort of advances toward her. It was as if he were afraid of her or something.

Well, perhaps he was. He had gone through a painful and heart-wrenching divorce, after all. Maybe he was afraid of being hurt again. Or maybe he was fearful of hurting her. She couldn't fault him for that.

So maybe she'd have to be the one to take the first step toward a different kind of relationship with him or would that scare him away even further?

Turning in the desk chair, Marcie's eyes fell on the blinking light of the answering machine, and she reached out with her right hand and punched the play button. A man's voice immediately started talking, and Marcie gasped when she realized the message was for her.

"This message is for Marcie Starr..."

Marcie listened to the entire message, then hit the replay button and listened to it again. Sitting in Dean's office, she allowed the meaning of the message to sweep over her. She could go back. She could go after this new job and regain the life she'd had before in D.C.

It was an opportunity she'd never expected.

But was that what she wanted—and even more importantly, was it what God wanted her to do?

FOR the first time since he'd begun to visit her mother's house, that week Dean didn't show up for supper Sunday night. Marcie didn't know why as he'd called and talked briefly to Ethan that morning before they'd left for church. All Ethan said was that Dean had told him something had come up, and he wasn't going to make it.

Even when her mind should have been on Ethan's message during the church service, all Marcie could do was worry and wonder what had caused Dean to cancel. He had never done so before. And if he couldn't come, why hadn't he called and talked to her personally? She'd thought they were closer than that. She'd thought she should rate more than a cryptic message passed through a third party.

True, her cell phone wasn't working right then, but still. Fortunately, her new charger should arrive the next day. Marcie couldn't believe how much she'd come to depend on the stupid piece of technology, and it was a real inconvenience to not have it working.

After church, Marcie helped her mother prepare the noon meal and then clean up the leftovers and the dirty dishes. Once she finished those small jobs, Marcie felt unsure what to do for the rest of the day. Every other Sunday afternoon, Dean had arrived only an hour or so after their noon meal, but today there was no knock on the door nor the sight of his cheery smile and twinkling green eyes.

She missed him. A lot.

For a time, Marcie tried to read a book but couldn't seem to get her mind to concentrate. The more she thought about the situation with Dean, the more confident she was something was wrong. She could just feel it.

Dean hadn't said he was ill when he left the phone message earlier with Ethan though. He'd simply stated something had come up, and he wasn't going to make it to their house, so maybe she was worried about nothing. But it didn't feel that way to her.

She puttered around the house the rest of the afternoon and evening, totally at a loss for what to do with herself. She missed Dean. And she was concerned. Marcie had a feeling deep in her gut that something elusive had changed and she didn't know what to do about it—even though part of her kept thinking she was being overdramatic.

Surely there was nothing wrong, and she would see Dean again in just a few days.

At least, that's what she prayed for.

MARCIE sighed as she stared at the computer screen in front of her. What felt like one of the longest weeks she could remember was almost over. Friday had finally arrived, and she had a multitude of things she had to accomplish before she left for the day. It was time to focus and do the job she'd been hired to do.

She knew she was acting like a love-sick teenager, sitting in Dean's office and day-dreaming about things that would never happen. By his not contacting her the past Sunday to let her know what had happened, and then not hearing from him for the past week other than brief snippets of a phone message, it was apparent she had read something into their relationship that hadn't been there.

Dean McRae was a friend; that was all. He'd been hurt in the past by a woman. What made Marcie think he had any desire to have another relationship—even with her?

But she could wish. Her heart couldn't help but hope for what it longed for.

The slam of the outer door downstairs brought Marcie back to reality, and she immediately sat up straighter in her chair as she silently prayed that it was Dean and not one of the other guys. In only moments, the man she'd been daydreaming about strode through the office door, with his unruly dark red hair sticking up in every direction as if he'd just run his hand through it. He gave her a quick glance, but the usual warmth wasn't in his eyes.

And he looked as if he hadn't slept in a week.

"Hey."

"Hey, yourself fella."

Her eyes sought out his. When he didn't drop his eyes from hers, she struggled to read what she saw in his green eyes. There was something different, but she wasn't sure what.

He still looked the same. Just as he always did—even though he was tired and dirty after working all day—Marcie thought Dean McRae was the most handsome man she'd ever known. He might be exhausted, but it was because he'd accomplished a good day's work. If felt good to Marcie to know she now knew what that felt like. It had been a lot of years since she'd felt happy with the work she was doing.

Now, if she could only figure out how to make that happiness come about in her personal life.

Dean dropped into the chair across the desk from her with a weary sigh.

"The payroll's finished, and the checks are ready for you to sign." She pushed a stack of paper toward Dean, hoping he'd talk to her—about what he'd been doing—about how the job had gone today. About something.

Without even giving her a glance, Dean pulled a pen out of his shirt pocket and leaned over the desk and went to work signing them. When he finished, he left them on the desk and then sat back in his chair again and stared at the floor.

Why won't he look at me? What's happened between us?

"Thanks. I'm sure the boys will thank you too."

His deep voice sounded gruffer than usual, and much wearier to Marcie, and again she worried that he was working too hard. She knew *McRae's* had tons of work lined up. She fielded most of the phone calls anymore and had seen their schedule. It almost seemed as if Dean McRae was on a mission to see how much he could personally accomplish before dropping over dead from exhaustion.

"So, you guys are done early. Did you finish the job already?"

He shook his head.

"The job isn't totally finished, but I decided to cut everyone loose early so we could get in a little bow hunting before dark."

Marcie's eyebrows went up. She knew the deer bow season had started the previous Saturday as several guys had been talking to Ethan about it at church on Sunday.

"You're a hunter?"

Dean finally raised his eyes to lock on hers with the ghost of a smile on his face. Her heart-rate immediately picked up, and it was difficult to not run around the desk and pull him out of the chair and try to find out what was going on in his head. That was the first time he'd looked at her since he'd come through the door. And even though the smile seemed forced, it picked up her spirits to see it.

"Ms. Starr, you know darn well you can't be raised in these here hills and not know how to hunt."

His intense green eyes gazed at her a moment as if trying to find the answer to a question he hadn't asked her yet. Marcie nervously chewed on her lower lip and refused to drop her eyes from his, hoping and praying that he'd read her concern for him in her eyes.

After days of no personal interaction with the man, she was having trouble concentrating now that he was right there in front of her.

"Do y'all like venison?"

Marcie struggled to get her mind wrapped around the question Dean had just asked her as she continued to stare at him. Venison. That was what they were discussing. When was the last time she'd eaten deer meat? Maybe in her freshman year in high school? Her dad had still been alive back then, and he and one of his buddies had gone out deer hunting. She could remember how proud he'd been to bring home a big buck. Marcie had watched him dress out the deer, thinking how fascinating it had been in one way, and how sickening it had been in another. But once her mom had simmered the meat until it was tasty and tender, Marcie had forgotten all about the sickening part. And she'd reminded herself that after all, back in the pioneer days, hunting was the only way they had to provide meat for their families. There were no grocery stores with meat counters back then.

"I do, although it's been a lot of years since I've had any."

He gave her a little nod, and Marcie wondered why he suddenly looked out of sorts. She was tempted to ask him what was going on but was afraid she wouldn't like the answer, so hesitated. Then the moment was lost as he stood and scooped up the stack of checks.

"Well, best get these passed out to the fellas so they can leave and start their weekend."

When Dean reached the door, he turned back and gave her a half smile, his eyes sparkling with a touch of the mischief she was used to seeing there.

"You gonna wish me luck, sweetheart?"

Marcie's heart jumped at hearing that unexpected endearment from the man, and her smile soon matched his.

"Of course, I will. Good luck, Mr. McRae." Then she winked at him. "But something tells me hunting is more about skill than luck, so I figure you'll get your deer no problem."

The sound of his quiet chuckle followed him out the door and down the stairs, and Marcie couldn't help but grin at the sound as she leaned back in the desk chair. She listened for the door closing downstairs to know for sure he was gone and then finally released the breath she'd been holding.

Perhaps she'd been worrying about Dean for nothing. It did seem as if he acted a little differently toward her, but then he was exhausted from working so hard. The poor man needed to slow down before he killed himself. Maybe some time out in the woods hunting would help lift his spirits.

That sure was an odd conversation, though.

But then, in the short time she'd come to know Dean McRae, she'd discovered he was a man of many layers. Some of them, she was reasonably certain she would never uncover.

That was okay, though. She still liked him. A lot.

The next day was Saturday, and Marcie spent most of it catching up on the week's laundry and cleaning the house. Her mom was doing so much better now she was able to help with a great many things, but the heavy cleaning still fell on Marcie's shoulders.

That afternoon, however, she was free to spend on the porch with her paint and brushes. Now that autumn had arrived, the days had grown cooler, and Marcie knew she didn't have too many more days she'd be able to work out there. Fortunately, today bright sunshine was pouring through the glass windows and had warmed up the room nicely.

She had three more pieces finished and ready to frame and then she'd take them over to the gift shop in Gatlinburg to sell. Her mom had also crocheted about a dozen doilies, and Marcie was going to take those along too. It had taken a while for her mother to get full use of her left hand back, but the crocheting seemed to help with her manual dexterity, and she'd improved dramatically in the past month. Marcie hoped the doilies would sell quickly as that would boost her mom's confidence in her abilities even more.

Marcie had finally finished "The Potter Cabin" painting, and it was framed and wrapped with brown butcher paper so she could give it to Dean—if he ever showed up at the house again. She felt funny taking it to work with her, but she supposed that might be the only way she could get it to him.

She'd just finished putting the last few strokes of paint on her latest canvas when the door to the porch opened, and her step-father stepped onto the porch to join her. Marcie felt him come to a stop directly behind her and knew he was studying the painting.

"I really like this one, Marcie girl. You have a real gift of being able to make the mountains look real when you paint them."

She stepped away from the easel and watched Ethan's face as he stared at her painting, tipping his head a little. "Maybe it's the way you use the light in the painting." Then he gave her an embarrassed look and shook his head. "What do I know? I'm not an artist."

She smiled at him and reached out and patted his arm.

"Thank you, Ethan. As long as people like my paintings and keep buying them, I'm happy. And I sure do enjoy painting them. I can't believe I didn't take up painting with oils before. Thank you so much for suggesting it."

Cleaning her brush, she scraped the paint off the palette, her mind suddenly wondering what her dad would think about her paintings. He'd also told her she had talent. And when she had a paintbrush in her hand, it felt as if it were an extension of herself—a way to let all her hopes and dreams flow down her arm through her fingers and onto the canvas.

"My Daddy always used to call the mountains around here 'Marcie's Mountains.'" She tried to smile past the lump in her throat. "I spent so much time sketching them and drawing them when I was little; it was like I couldn't find a way to make them look alive enough on the paper."

Marcie released a little sigh and turned her head when she felt Ethan put his large hand on her shoulder to give it a brief squeeze. Marcie was surprised at the emotion that swept through her at that small gesture of affection. He wasn't her father, but that didn't mean he hadn't come to mean a great deal to her.

He released her shoulder, and it was quiet between the two of them for a moment as Ethan leaned up against a table along the outside wall. Marcie felt his eyes resting on her as she went about the mundane tasks of cleaning up her painting supplies and covering her latest canvas. She would work on framing them another day, then take them into Gatlinburg next week.

"So, how's Dean doing?"

Her head came up as Ethan's question hung in the air.

"He's doing all right, I guess." She frowned and looked back down at the brushes in her hand. "Haven't seen him much other than last night when he stopped in the office. He and the guys quit work early yesterday so they could go deer hunting."

Ethan's chuckle echoed around the small room. "Is that so?"

Marcie lifted her lips in a small smile but kept her head down, hoping Ethan couldn't see her face. After a week of not seeing or talking to Dean, it had been like a breath of fresh air to speak with him the previous afternoon. She continued to pray with all of her being that whatever had come between them could be worked out. Marcie didn't want to lose the friendship they'd had before. It was too precious.

"Is Dean planning to come for our chess game tomorrow night, do you know? I missed him last week."

Marcie didn't look up at him but shook her head.

"Don't know. He didn't mention it."

As she listened to the sound of Ethan's footsteps walking back into the main part of the house, Marcie raised her head and stared out the window as she struggled to come up with answers for Dean's attitude lately.

Was he angry with her about something she'd done or said? Half of the previous night when she should have been sleeping Marcie had sat in a chair near the open window, struggling to come up with some reason for the change in Dean's behavior. No matter how much she thought about it, she kept coming up empty.

What's going on, Lord? I really thought Dean cared about me. Was I wrong? Am I wasting my time thinking there can ever be anything more between us than friendship?

29

nother Sunday afternoon came, and as usual, Marcie cleaned up the kitchen following their after-church meal. It had been an excellent church service. Ethan's sermon had been from the book of Romans and had been an uplifting, encouraging message, and the worship music had touched Marcie's heart. She hummed a part of one of the praise songs they'd sung as she put the last dish into the dishwasher and pushed the buttons to start it running, then left the room in search of her mother. She found her in the family room sitting on the sofa, looking through old photo albums.

"Come sit next to me, dear so we can look through these together."

Marcie sat next to her mother, marveling at the vast improvement in her mother's health. Oh, there were still a few remnants of the stroke that had almost killed her—an occasional lapse in memory when searching for a word, and she still had a tendency to drag her left leg a little when she was tired. All in all, though, Lois Carter was doing much better than the doctor had thought she'd ever do.

The photo album her mother was looking through was an old one from when Marcie was a baby. There were pictures of her and her father—a happy smile on his face as he held his baby daughter in his arms. While Marcie gazed at the old photos, she waited for the pain that always accompanied memories of her dad, but for some reason, this time there was only a quiet peace in her heart. Along with that peace, was a tremendous thankfulness that she had been able to have him as her father as long as she had. Some children weren't as fortunate.

The two of them had been looking through the old photo albums for about an hour when the doorbell rang. Marcie got up from her seat to answer it but heard Ethan's heavy footsteps heading down the hallway and knew he'd get there before she did, so sat back down. When she heard Dean's deep voice from down the hall, a thrill shot through her. She'd hoped and prayed that he'd show up today, but after the chilly reception he'd given her in the office on Friday, she'd been unsure what to expect.

In a few minutes, Dean walked into the room. Marcie stood while he came over and greeted Marcie's mom with a quick hug and kiss on the cheek. Then he turned toward Marcie, and she noticed he was carrying a large paper sack in his arms. It didn't look like he'd brought her mother flowers today. So what was in the mysterious sack? She reached out to take the bag from him, but he gave a shake of his head, his eyes twinkling.

"It's kinda heavy, and it needs to go into the freezer right away."

Wondering what in the world 'it' was, Marcie pulled the top of the sack toward her enough so she could peek inside. What she saw confused her even more—individual packages wrapped in what looked like white butcher paper. She raised her eyes to find Dean's green eyes twinkling at her over the open sack, and there was a noticeable red flush running up his neck and pinking the ends of his ears.

"I went huntin' yesterday morning and got myself a buck."

Marcie returned his grin. "Told you it was all about skill, McRae."

Ethan and her mother both congratulated him, and then she and Dean headed toward the kitchen to put the meat in the freezer. Marcie waited until they were out of the front room before she turned and gave him a smile and a little punch in his arm.

"Well congratulations, oh great hunter."

Her comment just brought a nervous laugh from Dean, and his face turned an even darker shade of red.

"Thanks. He was a big one, so I gave Momma some of the meat and put a little in my freezer. Then I remembered you said it had been a long time since you'd had any venison, so I thought you might like to have some too."

"Thank you, Dean. That's nice of you."

And it *was* nice. Marcie was surprised at the feelings rushing through her at Dean's appearance at their front door with a sack filled with venison. It wasn't something she would have thought anyone would do for her, but it was certainly appreciated. She and her mother and Ethan would be able to enjoy the fruit of Dean's hunting trip, and it was generous of him to think of them. Once again, Marcie was reminded of how good and decent Dean McRae was.

She led the way to the storage room off the kitchen where the large chest freezer was located. With no conversation between them, Marcie helped him take the packages out of the larger sack, noting they were marked on the outside with the different cuts of meat included; ribs, steak, several packages of ground venison, and stew meat. Before Dean put the last packet of stew meat in the freezer, Marcie reached out and took it from him.

"Might not want to freeze all of it, McRae."

Again, Dean's ear tips turned pink. Why was he so embarrassed with everything she said today? But at least he was talking to her again and had lost that cold, detached mood he had with her the previous week. So things were finally looking up.

Once the meat was safely stored in the freezer, and the packet of stew meat tucked into the refrigerator, the two of them joined Ethan and Marcie's mother in the family room, Ethan immediately stood and came over to shake Dean's hand—as if it had been ages since he'd seen him. She knew Ethan had missed having Dean around the previous Sunday afternoon. Somehow or another, the two men had become good friends. She didn't know everything they talked about but had heard their deep voices speaking for hours over the chess board as they played game after game.

"Thank you for the meat, Dean. I haven't had venison in ages." Marcie's mother said quietly from where she sat on the sofa with a big smile on her face.

Marcie noted Ethan's eyes land on Dean who gave the older man a little nod and a nervous smile. It was as if a silent message passed between the two men.

What was that all about?

Then Marcie remembered what she wanted to ask her mother.

"Speaking of which. Momma, do you have that recipe for your slow cooker venison stew someplace?"

Her mother gave her a little nod and stood, motioning for Marcie to follow her. "I do. Not sure where, but we'll find it."

After her mother found the recipe in an old cookbook stuffed in the back of a kitchen drawer, Marcie chopped onions, celery, carrots, and parsley while her mother browned the cubed up meat. With the two of them working, it wasn't long, and they had the mixture in the slow cooker. After they cleaned up the kitchen, her mother motioned for Marcie to sit down at the kitchen table where she was nursing a cup of hot tea.

"It was very nice of Dean to bring us the meat."

Taking a sip of the iced tea she'd poured for herself just a moment earlier, Marcie nodded.

"Yes, it was."

"But then, your Dean McRae is a good man."

Marcie raised her eyes to find her mother's blue eyes studying her face. There was something more behind her words than what her mother had just said.

"Dean *is* a good man, Momma. It didn't take me long to realize that when I initially became acquainted with him through the magazine assignment." Marcie sighed as she allowed her mind to drift back to the first time she'd seen the man, standing in his doorway, dark red hair shining like bronze in the late afternoon light, barefoot and wild, and looking like some sort of Celtic warrior.

"He's loyal and kind to everyone he comes in contact with. And gentle, and sweet," she smiled as she remembered the teasing light that often came into those green eyes of his. "And he has a wonderful sense of humor. He and the fellas he has working for him tease each other back and forth constantly—but they're more like brothers than co-workers. They'd do anything for each other."

It was quiet between the two of them for a while, then Marcie was surprised when her mother reached over and firmly took hold of her hand.

"Your daddy was that kind of man, Marcella. There aren't a great many men like that left in this ol' world, so if you have feelings for Dean, don't be afraid to let him know about them. Sometimes menfolk need a little encouragement when it comes to matters of the heart."

Marcie felt a moment of shock rush through her. How had her mother known how much Dean had come to mean to her? Her heart ached as she thought about how disappointed she'd been when she hadn't talked to him all week. Then there had been the way Dean had distanced himself from her on Friday when she finally had seen him, and again she remembered how much her heart had hurt at his rejection.

There was no doubt that she had much deeper feelings for the man than just friendship.

The sound of Dean's and Ethan's laughter drifted down the hallway from the family room where they were waging another war on the chess board, and Marcie turned her head in that direction. Just the sound of Dean's deep laughter sent goosebumps up her arms.

Goodness. She was surely smitten with the man.

Her momma's gentle chuckle made her turn her eyes to the woman across the table.

"Didn't you know you were falling in love with him, darlin'?"

Marcie felt her eyes fill with tears, not only at the newest revelation of her feelings for Dean but also at hearing that endearment from her mother. She shook her head.

"I knew I cared about him as a friend, but I figured that would be all we'd ever be. Really good friends, but just friends. I mean, I'm not sure he wants to be more than that."

"Oh, sweetheart. Anyone with two eyes in their head can see that man is head over heels in love with you. Every time he looks at you…well, let's just say those green eyes of his can't see anything or anybody else in the room. But you."

30

Dean looked up from the chessboard toward the door leading to the kitchen. He'd been catching a whiff of something good cooking for the last couple of hours, and his stomach growled in response. The man sitting across the chessboard from him chuckled at the sound coming from the direction of Dean's middle.

"Must be you're gettin' as hungry as I am, young man. Wonder what they're gonna feed us tonight?"

Taking another deep breath through his nose, Dean couldn't hold back the smile.

"Smells like venison."

A warm sense of well-being surged through Dean, and for the first time in over a week, he started to think that maybe— just maybe—everything would be okay. He almost hadn't come to visit the Carters and Marcie today, and whenever he thought about that cryptic message that had been left on his business answering machine, he couldn't help but wonder if he was setting himself up for another heartache. But then again, Marcie had never mentioned one word about receiving that message to Dean, which left him wondering why she hadn't.

Sitting back in his chair, Dean rubbed his hands down the legs of jeans—hands that had suddenly become sweaty. The more he thought about what he wanted to confront Marcie with after dinner, the more nervous he became.

As if reading Dean's mind, Ethan spoke up. "How 'bout right after supper, Lois and I'll leave you two kids alone in the kitchen to clean everything up. That'll give you and Marcie some time to talk. How's that sound, Dean?"

Dean nodded. "Thank you, sir." He swallowed hard. "And could you please pray for me too?"

"Consider it done."

EVEN though the stew was best he'd ever eaten, and the biscuits Marcie had baked to go with it were light and fluffy, Dean's appetite wasn't as good as it usually was. He was already thinking about what he was going to say to Marcie when the two of them were finally alone. He'd barely slept the night before, thinking about what he should or shouldn't say to her, and praying fervently that things would go the way he hoped they would.

After listening to that annoying answering machine message, Dean had spent most of the previous week trying to figure out what to do about it. If Marcie was leaving Tennessee, then he needed to protect his heart from getting broken again. But if she truly were staying, then Dean didn't want to wait any longer to stake his claim on her. He was crazy about Marcie and wanted to spend the rest of his life with her. If she'd let him.

While he tried to do justice to the delicious food she'd prepared, Dean watched Marcie's willowy form as she stood up from where she'd been sitting across the table from him and went to the kitchen. When he turned his eyes back to the table from watching her walk away, it was to discover two sets of eyes watching him. Both Ethan and Marcie's mother wore identical smiles. Dean swallowed hard and dropped his eyes back to his plate.

Is it so obvious that I've fallen in love with her?

By the matching looks on the older folks' faces, it apparently was.

Marcie returned a few moments later with two plates each covered with a large slice of apple pie, topped off with a scoop of vanilla ice cream. As she placed his plate in front of him, her dark eyes sparkled, and she gave him a gentle smile. Oh, he could read so much in those eyes. He just hoped and prayed he wasn't reading them wrong. She gave the second plate to her step-father, then returned with two more plates of pie—one for her mother and one for her.

After they'd finished their dessert, Ethan pushed back from the table and patted his lean stomach.

"Well, dear hearts, thank you for preparing another fabulous meal for us. That was tasty."

Dean hoped when he was Ethan's age, he could still eat the way the older man did and look that good. He was reasonably sure there wasn't an ounce of fat on Marcie's stepfather. He watched as Ethan stood and walked over to Lois's side, gently taking her arm and helping her from her chair.

"We'll just mosey on into the family room and set a spell and let you young 'uns clean up the mess if that's okay?"

Marcie smiled at her step-father. "Good idea, Ethan. You two go relax. I'm glad you enjoyed it."

Lois turned and gave Dean a pointed look. "Jist so you know, young man. I may a helped a little bit, but Marcie made most of it."

Dean smiled as the tall man looked down on his much shorter wife with a look of love. "Well, darlin', it was delicious. You both did good."

The two older folks left the room, and Dean stood and immediately started grabbing dishes and bowls and followed Marcie to the kitchen with his load. The two of them worked quietly together, the only conversation between them a question from him every now and then about what to do with something.

Fifteen minutes later, the leftovers were all put away, the dirty dishes were in the dishwasher, and the kitchen was once again spotless. Dean watched Marcie hang the hand towel back on the towel rack, and as soon as her hands were free, Dean reached out to take hold of her arm and turned her around.

"Will you go for a walk with me, Mars?"

He glanced out the window, noting it wasn't dark yet, but it wouldn't be long, and the sun would go down. Her eyes were deep dark pools as she looked at him, and once again, Dean prayed he wasn't about to make the biggest mistake of his life.

"Sure."

She followed him to the rear door where they each grabbed a jacket off the coat rack and made their way down the back steps. Dean automatically reached over and took hold of her hand as they walked, praying silently with each step he took.

Lord, I could use a little help right now. I'm not sure what I should say to her next. I don't want to make her mad, and I sure don't want to scare her away.

They wandered across the backyard, past the gardens, and toward the bench near the river where they usually went on their walks. Tonight Marcie was unusually quiet, and Dean wondered what she was thinking. She took a seat on the bench, and he sat next to her, her hand still firmly clasped in his.

Dean released a sigh and tried to slow his heartbeat as he listened to the usual noises of the earth, getting ready to sleep around them. The birds had quit singing an hour or so earlier, and the night insects were starting their songs. He could hear the crickets from the edge of the yard and the gurgle of the water from the riverbank drifting up the slope toward them. Other than that, the night was silent.

"I'm so glad I came back home," Marcie's quiet voice finally broke the silence.

Dean's flinched on hearing her words, and it felt like his heart stopped for a second. Did she mean she was staying—or was this the beginning of her saying goodbye? There was only one way to find out. He took a deep breath for courage and decided to come right out and ask. That was the only way he was ever going to have any peace.

"That almost sounds like you're jist here for a visit and plan to leave soon. So, does that mean you've decided to accept that job offer back in D.C.?"

Marcie's head instantly swung toward him, her eyes wide.

"How did you know about that?" Her eyes narrowed, and then she chewed on her lower lip like he noticed she did whenever she was nervous or upset. He knew precisely when she figured it out.

"You listened to the message on the machine before I did."

Dean nodded, struggling to control the lump in his throat. Just thinking about Marcie leaving made him feel physically ill.

"Yeah. I stopped at the office that afternoon to get some paperwork I'd forgotten and saw the light blinking on the machine."

He sighed. "Since you've never mentioned the message, I wasn't sure what that meant—if you were leaving again and going back to the city, or if you'd decided to stay. I didn't know what to think—or how to feel. And just the thought that you might be leaving again is shredding my heart into pieces."

Marcie's black hair hung down like a sheet, almost hiding her face from him. He finally reached out and gently took hold of the silken strands and pushed them behind her ear and over her shoulder. He needed to see her, needed to be able to read the truth in her eyes, and know what was going on in her head. Dean wasn't going to allow her to close him out. Not this time.

For a moment or two, he saw her jaw clench as if in anger, then she released a sigh.

"You could have just asked me, Dean." There was a certain amount of frustration in her voice, and Dean flinched a little at the sound. Then she turned to look directly at him, and the disappointment on her face was evident. She didn't look happy with him. At all.

"So, that's why you've been acting so cold toward me. You listened to the message and just assumed I'd take the job. Really, Dean? Why didn't you just ask me?"

She shook her head. Dean didn't know what to say, so he decided silence might be his best answer. It was easy to tell Marcie was still angry, and her next words solidified that notion.

"Well, for your information, Mr. McRae, I called Mr. Moran back that same afternoon and told him I wasn't interested."

Then Marcie turned her dark eyes on him. Dean's heart melted at her next words, her voice soft and gentle.

"Dean, I'm *not* leaving. I told him I'd found what I wanted right here in the mountains of Tennessee, and God willing, I was never leaving again unless God told me differently."

Dean's breath caught in his chest as her words finally sunk in.

She's staying.

Finally, giving her hand a little squeeze, he let go of it, then reached over to take her face in both his hands, forcing her to look directly at him.

"Sweetheart, when I opened my front door that day and found you standing on the porch, my whole world changed. It was like the earth shifted somehow. I don't know what you found here in Tennessee, but I know what I've found."

With those words, Dean stood and pulled Marcie up into his arms, then pulled back enough that he could look down at her upturned face. Her dark eyes were pools of emotion. He had a moment's hesitation while he worried that maybe neither of them were ready for things to be so serious between them.

Then Marcie reached up with her right hand and placed her warm palm on his cheek, and Dean had to close his eyes again at the feeling of her touching him. The love that engulfed him made the rest of the world around them disappear. He only knew he wanted to stand there with her in his arms and her hand on his cheek forever. He wanted to spend the rest of his life gazing into those beautiful eyes.

When Dean felt her hand drop from his face, he opened his eyes, afraid she'd left him. But she was still there, staring up at him with such a look of love on her face, he had to struggle to remember to breathe. Finally surrendering to his emotions, Dean gave her a small smile before he lowered his face to hers, his lips lightly touching her soft ones. At first, the kiss they shared was just a gentle one as if they were both afraid. Then Dean pulled her into his arms, and the kiss deepened, and when they finally pulled apart, Dean felt as if his heart was about to beat out of his chest.

She is the most beautiful woman I've ever seen.

Dean swallowed hard. It was time—before it got any darker and they weren't able to see each other's faces at all. Positive that she could hear his pounding heart, Dean reached his right hand into his pants pocket and pulled out an item, then dropped to one knee. Marcie's eyes never left his face, but Dean's heart soared at the sight of the smile on her face.

"You know, Ethan told me one day that you're part Cherokee. He told me that if a Cherokee brave gave a woman in the tribe deer meet and she cooks it for him, that meant she'd accept him as her husband. Well, you and me—we did that part—although I'm not sure you are aware that was *why* I gave you the deer meat.

"So, I'm gonna ask you straight out, Marcie Elaine Starr, will you have me as your husband? Because I love you more than I can ever put into words, and I can't imagine going through life without you at my side. Will you marry me, Mars?"

There was a second or two of silence—that to Dean seemed as if it lasted at least a week. Then Marcie gave a little nod and a grin, and reached down with her hands and pulled him to his feet.

"Seriously, Dean. Deer meat?"

"I'm desperate, Mars. I was willing to try anything to get you to stay."

She laughed then. "I love you too, you crazy man. Yes, of course, I'll marry you! I thought you'd never ask!"

31

M arcie took the last wet towel from the wicker basket sitting in the grass next to her feet and hung in on the clothesline in front of her. Then she stood tall and stretched out her back muscles. Thankfully, that was the last load of freshly washed clothes. Now they just needed to dry and be folded and put away, and the laundry was caught up. At least for a day or two. She couldn't decide if she and Dean were extremely clean people or terribly dirty people, but they sure did seem to create a lot of laundry.

Shading her eyes with her right hand, Marcie turned her head and looked toward the driveway, hoping to see a little dust rising in the air which would mean the men were home from their latest job—this one located the other side of Gatlinburg. Their business had been thriving, which was a good thing as the McRae family was close to growing by the presence of one little person.

Picking up the now empty laundry basket, Marcie waddled over and took a seat on the next to the bottom step of the front porch of Dean's house—her house too now, although it was taking her time to get used to the idea. It had been almost a year since the two of them had stood up in front of the church and God and said their vows with Ethan officiating the ceremony. She still woke up most mornings in awe of the gift

God had given her in the form of the wonderful man lying in bed next to her. God had truly blessed her the day He'd sent her back to the mountains.

My mountains.

She loved to sit on the front porch during the day and listen to the sounds of the mountains around her. She was still in awe that God had brought her back to her mountains—and to Dean.

This afternoon, though, Marcie was tired. In addition to doing all the laundry, she'd spent the morning over in the office, catching up on all the bookkeeping. And she'd cleaned the house. The sudden burst of energy she'd felt when she'd gotten up this morning, had now vanished.

Releasing a weary sigh, Marcie heaved her heavy body up. She was just turning to head into the house when the familiar sound of engine motors came down the lane leading from the main road.

She felt a deep ache tighten across her lower back and rubbed at it to try and relieve the muscles. As she went up the last two steps and reached the porch, the ache turned into a sharp pain that raged along her back with a vengeance, bending her almost double. Seconds later, moisture gushed between her legs to the porch floor. She stared at the moisture on the porch floor in confusion before what had happened finally registered in her brain. Her water had broken.

The baby's comin'.

Marcie felt a moment of panic, then she remembered Dean was home. She turned around at the sound of a vehicle door slamming and took a deep breath to calm her nerves.

"Hey, gorgeous."

His tall, muscular frame bounded up the steps, and he quickly pulled her into his arms as close as possible considering her large front and gave her a firm kiss on the mouth.

As another pain hit her, Dean pulled back from her, his eyes narrowed.

"What's wrong? Is it the baby?"

She gave him what she was sure looked like a weak smile.

"I know y'all just got home, sweetheart, but I think our baby is comin'. Would you please get my bag and take me to the hospital? Now." The last word was ground out around another pain.

Dean flew into action and ran into the house to grab her bag—already packed for almost two months—then came back and gently led her to his truck. He did take the time to holler at Mac and Dutch and fill them in on what was happening. He also asked them to phone his mother and Marcie's folks, just to let them know they were on their way to the hospital to have a baby.

Marcie was positive she wouldn't be able to remember much about the drive to the hospital. She was concentrating on breathing through the pains and struggling to assure Dean she was fine. The white, pinched look of worry on his face was almost comical. She knew what she was going through was completely normal. But by the look of horror on Dean's face, Marcie was sure he hadn't thought about the actual pain she'd have to go through to have a baby.

Four hours later, however, the suffering was all worth it is as Marcie gave birth to their first child—a healthy boy with strong lungs and a shock of red hair just like his daddy. As Dean stood by her bedside while she held the little bundle in her arms, he reached out his large hand and gently stroked the forehead of their new son.

"Oh, Mars—he's absolutely perfect. Thank you, sweetheart."

Dean leaned over and gave her a kiss, then gazed back down at their baby. Like Marcie, Dean couldn't seem to stop looking at their new little man.

"So, which name do you think fits him the best? You said you wanted to wait until he arrived to name the little guy. So, what do ya think?"

Marcie smiled. She'd known from the moment she found out she was pregnant that the baby was a boy. She couldn't explain those feelings to anyone else; it was just something she'd been sure of. So, the name that came to her mind was one she and Dean had talked about most often. They had come up with two names if it were a boy and two for if it was a girl.

But only one name seemed to fit this little guy.

"Matthew Dean McRae, meet your Daddy—the most wonderful man in the world."

Dean leaned over and gave Marcie a soft kiss before turning to look at his son.

"Matthew. A fitting name for him. He is *truly* a gift from God."

Marcie relaxed back against the pillow and snuggled the little guy closer to her. She couldn't agree more. God had blessed them in so many ways the past year, but the birth of their little Matthew had to be the biggest blessing yet.

Thank you, God. Thank you for making me come back to the mountains and facing my past and for giving me the strength to forgive my mother. Thank you for giving me this wonderful man at my side, and thank you for Matthew.

A scripture from Ethan's most recent sermon came to Marcie, and it fit her emotions perfectly.

Delight thyself also in the LORD; and he shall give thee the desires of thine heart.

Even though Marcie hadn't known what she wanted or needed, the Lord had—and even then, He had given her so much more.

MARCIE'S BUTTERMILK PANCAKES

Ingredients:
- 1 cup all-purpose flour
- 2 tablespoons cornmeal
- 1 tablespoon sugar
- 1 teaspoon baking powder
- 1 teaspoon baking soda
- 1 teaspoon cinnamon
- 1 large egg – beaten
- 1 cup buttermilk or sour milk**
- 1 tablespoons cooking oil

Optional: You can add mini-chocolate chips, cut up bananas, walnuts, or blueberries to add even more flavor

In a medium bowl, mix together the flour, cornmeal, sugar, baking powder, baking soda, and cinnamon. Make a well in the middle of the mixture and then set it aside.

In another medium-sized bowl, stir together the egg, buttermilk (or sour milk), and oil. Add this mixture (all at once) to the dry mixture. Stir just until moistened. The batter will be lumpy. If desired, add optional items.

For each pancake, pour about ¼ cup batter onto a hot, lightly greased griddle or heavy skillet. Cook about two minutes over medium heat on each side, or until pancakes are golden brown. Turn to the second side when the pancake has a bubbly surface, and the edges are slightly dry. Serve warm.

Makes 8-10 pancakes.

**Sour Milk (substitute for buttermilk)
To make a cup of sour milk, place 1 teaspoon lemon juice or vinegar in a glass measuring cup. Add enough milk to make 1 cup total liquid and stir. Let the mixture stand for about five minutes before using it in the recipe.

Made in the USA
Las Vegas, NV
15 January 2022

41469764R00194